Careful WHAT YOU Wish for

JOANNE TRACEY

First published in Australia in 2020

by Joanne Tracey

https://joannetracey.com

Print ISBN 978-0-6484533-8-3

Kindle ISBN 978-0-6484533-5-2

Epub ISBN 978-0-6484533-6-9

Cover design by Lana Pecherczyk of Book Coverology

A catalogue record for this book is available from the National Library of Australia

For Grant and Sarah...

Always

CHAPTER ONE

'Okay, thanks, everyone, let's wrap it up there.' As I took my headset off I made a face at my computer screen and thanked the office gods for the umpteenth time that our IT department hadn't yet made video conferencing easier. Not that I needed to see my colleagues to know which of them had spent the last hour of that teleconference on their social media or catching up on emails rather than concentrating on what was being said.

Out the corner of my eye I noticed my colleague Drew jigging around on the spot, playing that game between trying not to look impatient but also needing me to notice that he *was* impatient.

'Do you need me?' I asked.

'Only if you've finished,' he said.

I sighed heavily. 'Okay, Drew, what does she need?'

'How do you know it's about Ainsley?'

I shrugged and smiled sweetly. 'Just a lucky guess.' It was always about Ainsley.

Our boss, Ainsley St James, was a smiling assassin

in designer clothes – one of those women who'll smile to your face and then stab you in the back. Although she wasn't usually so obvious as to inflict the injury herself. Oh no, that could mean damaging a nail or putting a hair in her sleek up-do out of place, which would absolutely not do. Instead Ainsley got other people to do her dirty work for her: conscripted minions like Drew. Ainsley was the sort of woman who did more to damage the sisterhood than support it. She had trodden on a lot of toes and kicked plenty of people off the ladder in her climb to the top, and would allow nothing and no one to take that position away from her. Another thing about Ainsley: she didn't believe there was room up there for anyone else. As a consequence she spent more time keeping an eye on who was doing what on the ladder below her rather than actually managing her business in the way it needed to be managed.

She'd previously been in human resources in our Sydney office, and had been parachuted in above me late last year as general manager of a new change and projects team. To say that we didn't get along would be an understatement. It wasn't just the fact that she saw me as a threat that needed to be nullified, I'd so far resisted every one of Ainsley's attempts to shake me off – and was absolutely determined to continue to do so.

Drew looked at his feet, then at a spot somewhere on the wall behind me. 'Ainsley wanted me to let you know that she needs to halve your travel budget.'

'For next year? It's a little early to be talking budgets, isn't it?'

He coloured and looked at his shoes again. 'No, sorry, Tiff. She means for the rest of this year. She needs to pull some costs back.'

I widened my eyes and nodded slowly. 'I see. No problem. I'll simply manage the Hong Kong clients from here.' I shrugged one shoulder to let him know how little it mattered to me.

'I'm sorry, Tiff,' he said again, doing his best to avoid meeting my eyes. I cursed Ainsley for putting him in this position. 'Ainsley said to remind you that all existing schedules are to be maintained. She suggested you could travel economy instead of business class and maybe find somewhere less expensive to stay.'

'I'm sure she did.' He obviously had more to say, but I decided to put the poor man out of his misery. 'It's okay, Drew. I'll go talk to her.'

He reddened. 'I don't think that's a good idea. She's in the middle of reviewing budgets.'

'Don't worry, I'll make sure she knows you passed on the entire message. Now tell me, how's that baby of yours?'

His face lit up. 'She's gorgeous — and growing every day. I'd love to spend more time with her, but it's a busy time for reporting, you know. And in my last appraisal Ainsley commented on how other people had mentioned that they'd felt I'd had too much time off work when Skye was pregnant.'

I'd worked with Drew for a long time and knew that the road to parenthood had been a tough one for him and his wife Skye. Ainsley knew it too. She probably even knew the size of Drew's mortgage down to the last cent and had used that to threaten him with performance management. Now that he and Skye had the baby they had dreamed of for so long, Drew was rarely home to see her.

Sometimes I thought that working for Chartered Pacific was a bit like being on one of those reality shows where the producers keep the contestants in a constant state of exhaustion with just the right amount of insecurity so they lose the will to think logically and either turn on each other or follow orders blindly. The end prize for this particular survival of the fittest wasn't a huge sum of cash, but rather the chance to keep your job.

Unfortunately for Ainsley, rather than being brought to heel by her power plays I was energised by the challenge of being the one to topple her from her perch. I could do my job – overseeing change management for the Asia-Pacific region – blindfolded and had decided that my next move was into Ainsley's role. That was if I could last the distance without cracking under her brand of pressure, which meant out-bitching the bitch.

I didn't bother knocking on Ainsley's office door before walking in.

As always she was immaculate: her silvery blonde

hair tightly secured in an elaborate topknot; her faultless body encased in a sleeveless white shift dress, the matching jacket hanging from a coat stand in the corner of her office. I knew that if I looked under her desk I'd see a pair of red-soled nude-coloured heels on her feet, and a matching designer-label tote bag.

'Tiffany.' She greeted me with a slight smile that didn't reach her eyes. 'Now isn't convenient. Can you come back later?' She pushed one of the spreadsheets in front of her with a red-tipped acrylic fingernail to make her point.

'No, I can't, I have a full afternoon,' I replied, ignoring her raised eyebrows. 'I need to talk to you about your latest budget cuts. I think it's a risk to meet with some of our most important clients immediately after flying economy. Particularly when they're clients who have their doubts about the relocation and who are making noise about moving their business elsewhere as a result. I need to be fresh and properly rested, not crumpled and under-slept.'

'No one said you can't get your work done while in economy.'

I resisted the temptation to plant my hands on my hips. 'When was the last time you attempted to open a laptop the whole way in an economy seat? And that's if the person in the seat in front decides to sit upright the whole way. Plus, I usually work while I'm in the lounge and in the air, so all of that time will be lost.'

Ainsley gave a little shrug of her bony shoulders. 'Travel on the weekend then.'

'You'd prefer me to give up my weekend and incur additional accommodation costs?'

'It's cheaper than a business-class airfare, and if you can't manage your workload and need to work weekends, well … Anyway, now really isn't the time to talk about this. I thought Drew would have explained it to you more clearly than it appears he has.' She shook her head in an it's-hard-to-get-good-help-these-days way.

'Drew told me what you wanted him to say. He was crystal clear.'

She sighed. 'But obviously not clear enough. Did he tell you you're to maintain your existing schedule of relationship visits? I know you're overseeing the change management for the relocation of both sites in Hong Kong, but I also want you to oversee the communication piece for the branch closures we've got happening in the domestic market over the next few months.'

'Isn't that Scott Rose's project?'

'Yes.' If Ainsley's forehead had been able to move, I thought she would have frowned. 'He's on extended leave. Some people can't manage a little healthy pressure.'

I read between the lines – Scott must be on stress leave. Last time I'd caught up for coffee with him he'd wondered aloud how long he'd cope with the escalating demands that went along with keeping Ainsley even remotely happy.

'And to be absolutely clear, this is on top of your existing objectives – as is your new budget objective,' she went on, smiling as tightly as the muscles around her mouth allowed. 'I think you know what will happen if you fail to meet your objectives, or if I read anything about these branch closures in the press. It's not just the Masters conference you'll be kissing goodbye to.' She patted at her hair and touched her earlobes, presumably to ensure that the diamond studs she usually wore were both still there and that I'd noticed them. 'Speaking of which, I wouldn't advise packing for Masters just yet. I very much doubt I'll be sharing my position by the pool with you.' She dropped her eyes back to the spreadsheets in front of her. As a dismissal it was an effective one.

So, it was like that, was it? Masters, the all-expenses-paid conference that Chartered Pacific rewarded its top performers with each year, was being held on a resort in Fiji that I'd always wanted to visit. Up until today I'd been so on top of my targets that I could have sat around doing very little for the next few months and still achieved them. Now, though, I was even more determined to be on that particular business-class flight – and I didn't care how many hours I had to work to get there. Nothing was going to stop me, and if I could wipe the tight little smile off Ainsley's face? Well, that would be the icing on the cake.

My friend Alice called as I was walking back to the partition I shared with three of the guys from the credit team after Ainsley had moved me out of my office two weeks before. Apparently a more inclusive team atmosphere was required, as were more meeting rooms. Whatever. At the time I'd smiled serenely and packed up my desk, not that I had much in the way of personal items to pack.

'Hey Tiff,' Alice said, 'just wanted to see if you're okay for a catch-up next Friday night? I've just checked in with Callie and she's keen.'

The three of us – Alice Delaney, Callie Jones and myself – had been best friends since primary school in Brisbane. Inseparable growing up, we'd drifted away for university and work, but had somehow all ended up down here in Melbourne.

'Sure,' I said. 'I was worried you were going to suggest this week – I have to go to Hong Kong on Saturday.'

'Saturday? It's not like you to travel on a weekend.'

'Tell me about it. Ainsley's decided to halve my travel budget. It's part of her tactics to keep me away from both Masters and her job.'

'Which means you're out to beat her at both,' Alice said.

'Naturally.'

'You do of course know that if you manage to halve your budget and still deliver, she'll look even better? You'll have done the work and she'll get the accolades. I can't see how it's worth it myself.'

'Maybe, but I'm determined to get to Masters this year.'

'Okay, well, let's think about the bright side to this situation.' If I was the ambitious one of our group and Callie was the romantic one, Alice was definitely the bright-sider – she could find a silver-lining in most situations. 'Plenty of people would be thrilled to spend a weekend in Hong Kong. Why don't you book yourself on a tour? You might as well see something of the city you spend so much time in.'

'What would I want to do that for? I've lost count of the number of times I've been up there for work. Besides, I'm not the tour type.'

The last thing I wanted to do with my limited free time was to be herded on and off a bus with other tourists.

'But have you actually seen much outside the office?' Alice said. 'Except the shopping malls and those bars my brother takes you to?'

Alice's older brother, Matt, had been based in the Hong Kong office of a sleek international bank for the past two years. We caught up fairly regularly when I was in town, although the only sight I was likely to see with Matt was the inside of his bedroom. Not that Alice knew about that; or if she did, she certainly hadn't said anything. It had been a couple of months since Matt and I last hooked up; I made a mental note to call him this afternoon and see if he'd be in town.

'I see plenty of the city,' I argued.

'I'm not taking no for an answer,' she argued back. 'If you're flying in on Saturday evening, I'll book something for you for Sunday morning. Where are you staying?'

'The usual. Although I'm going to need to find somewhere cheaper in future.'

'That won't hurt you,' Alice said. 'It's a ridiculous waste of money anyway. I hate to think how much gets wasted on travel every year. It's no wonder customer fees are as high as they are.'

'How quickly your tune has changed! It's not that long ago that you were doing the same.' Up until last year Alice also worked for Chartered Pacific, but in the Sydney office.

'Yes, well, I now know better. No arguments, Tiff. You'll be hopping on a bus on Sunday morning with other tourists and pretending to be happy about it.'

I pouted into the phone. 'I'll have nothing in common with any of them. What if they're wearing matching raincoats, and we have to follow around someone with an umbrella?'

Alice's grin was almost audible. 'You'll play nicely with the other children on the bus, Tiffany Samuels.'

'Yes, Mum,' I grumbled.

'Trust me,' she said. 'You'll thank me for this.'

Somehow, I didn't think so.

•

True to her word Alice booked me on a tour. She called while I was waiting for my flight – which had been delayed by three hours.

'Isn't it lucky you'd paid for your lounge membership before Ainsley's cutbacks took effect,' she said. 'Otherwise you'd have been sitting at the gate for all that time.'

'Not helpful,' I grumbled.

'And you've got a lovely adventure to look forward to tomorrow morning.'

'Now there's a bright side.'

'Don't think I can't hear your sarcasm,' said Alice. 'Get ready to be amazed and astounded.'

'By what?'

'A bridge, a beach and a buddha.'

'Do we at least stop somewhere decent for lunch?' I asked. 'Or will it be one of those all-you-can-eat buffets with unrecognisable meats?'

'There's no point in me telling you anything else, Tiff. You'd only complain about it or find reasons not to go. Besides, what else are you going to do on a Sunday in Hong Kong – aside from plotting your revenge and Ainsley's downfall, that is?'

I laughed. 'Are you implying that revenge fantasies aren't useful employment? Aside from that, what else would any woman do in Hong Kong other than shop?'

Or spend the afternoon doing unspeakable and lovely things with your brother, I thought. Unfortunately, Matt wasn't around on the weekend. He'd told me he was flying out to Singapore for a few days, but we'd arranged to catch up for a drink on Wednesday night when he got back. He'd emphasised the word 'drink' so I didn't think anything else was on offer and hadn't yet decided how I felt about that.

'You have enough clothes and shoes and bags,' said Alice. 'Go on the tour, be amazed and astounded, and make new friends.'

CHAPTER TWO

Because of the flight delay, by the time I arrived and checked in to my hotel it was close to two in the morning. The tour pick-up was at eight, so I emerged into the lobby two minutes before and, bleary-eyed and unenthusiastic, took the last available seat on the bus, put my sunglasses on and closed my eyes. As a result, I paid no attention to my seating companion until we arrived at our first stop – the bridge.

I could feel my eyes glazing over as the tour guide ran through the technical details, so I wandered away to look out across the water. Okay, the bridge was actually pretty impressive. As I was contemplating this and wondering how long it would be before I could get back on the bus and close my eyes again, I felt a tap on my shoulder. I turned around to face a man I vaguely recognised as being my neighbour on the bus.

'It's massive, isn't it?' he said.

I nodded. He was about my age, early thirties, maybe a little older, and, judging from the accent, a fellow Australian. As for looks, he was average height, average build, wearing average dude-type casual clothes. A cap with a motor racing slogan on it hid his hair, so I couldn't tell whether he had any or not. Not that it mattered. If he did have hair it was sure to be average as well.

'Did you know there are sheltered carriageways on it for when typhoons hit?' he added.

I shrugged to show that I didn't much care. 'No, but I probably would if I'd been bothered to listen.'

'Do you mind taking my photo?' he asked. 'With the bridge behind me,' he added, indicating some other tourists who were completely ignoring the bridge and posing against some flowering shrubs or the bus itself. He held out a camera that looked as though it had the technical ability to make a perfect espresso – which, now I came to think about it, I needed desperately.

'With that?' I said.

I must have looked horrified because he laughed; and when he did it was as if the sun had come out from behind a cloud – his blue eyes twinkling, his teeth white against his tanned face.

'Sure,' he said. 'I've got it all set up. All you need to do is look through here, move it about a bit until you see me in the arrangement you like, and then click the button. Too easy.'

As he passed the camera across, his hand brushed mine and I felt a tingle of awareness. Really? He was *so* not my type. My type was Matt Delaney, or someone just like him – tall, lean, well-dressed, professional, expensive, powerful. This guy was absolutely none of those things. He even had stubble, for god's sake. But when he smiled … I looked into his eyes and, for just a heartbeat too long, had difficulty wrenching my eyes away. That sort of thing – getting lost in a guy's eyes, the tummy-flipping – didn't happen to me. Ever. Oh man, this one was trouble.

I clicked the shutter and handed the camera back before I could think too hard about what had happened when he smiled at me, or the arrangement that I'd really like to see him in.

'Thanks,' he said. 'Do you want a photo too?'

I shook my head.

'Go on,' he urged. 'Otherwise how are you going to prove you were here?'

'Do I need to prove it to anyone? It's just a bridge. An impressively long one, I grant you, with very thick steel cables, but a bridge nevertheless.'

'It's not just about the bridge; it's about how you felt when you saw it – about staying in the mood of the moment. The whole point of these technological wonders isn't what they've built or how they've built it – it's how you *feel* about what they've built.'

I raised my eyebrows. Okay, he was one of those guys. The realisation should have sent a message to my hormones to calm down already, but they didn't seem to be listening.

'Also, how are you going to show our kids where we met?'

What the fuck? I looked across and saw him grinning. Oh, very good.

'Well, seeing as how you put it like that.' I smiled and handed over my phone. 'Where do you want me?'

He grinned and I knew he'd felt that sizzle too. Unfamiliar heat rose to my cheeks and I moved to lean against the fence, the bridge spanned behind me.

After he'd taken the shot and handed back my phone, I held out my other hand to him. 'Seeing as how we'll be telling our kids about this one day, we should introduce ourselves. Tiff Samuels.'

He shook it. 'Pleased to meet you, Tiff. I'm Jake Stewart. Is Tiff short for Tiffany?'

'It is.'

'I like it.'

'I'm so pleased you approve.'

He laughed, and I did too. Back on the coach, I asked him why he had such a sophisticated camera.

'Do you actually know what to do with all those buttons and dials, or are they just for show and you really run it on auto the whole time?'

'They sure are necessary; I need it for work.'

'Are you a photographer?' I asked. Bloody hell, a creative. Absolutely not my type. 'Not exactly. I'm a travel writer, so a camera is one of the tools of my trade. When I sell a story, it helps if I also have the images.'

Crap. A writer. Even worse. Writers came down towards the bottom of my list of suitable careers – a list that, if asked, I'd deny I had – on a par with footballers. I would never consider dating either. In the case of the former, it was about the erratic, possibly non-existent nature of their income. In the case of the latter, it was about ego. I was no man's accessory.

'I thought travel writer was just a made-up job,' I said. 'An urban myth. Do you really go to places and write about them for a living?'

'I sure do.' He smiled again, and I wished he wouldn't. It made me forget he'd failed the job test and probably didn't meet any of the other criteria on the checklist I absolutely didn't have.

'Doesn't that make for a lot of … instability?' I tried to stop my nose from screwing up, but like the rest of my body it wasn't listening to instructions.

'It does, but I'd be bored by the routine of a corporate role. And this way I get to see some fabulous places and meet some interesting people – all in a day's work. What do you do?'

'I'm in banking.'

He was silent for a minute, then said with that distracting twinkle, 'Oh, banking – with a "b". For a minute there I thought you had a made-up job too.'

'Oh, ha ha.' I tried to keep a straight face but couldn't. 'To be honest, there are similarities.'

'I know, I've met a few.'

'Bankers?'

'Yes, those too.'

This time I didn't even attempt to hide my laugh.

The next stop was a fishing village, where we strolled through markets selling all types of fish and fishy products. Some were still wriggling in buckets of seawater; some were lined up on tables, their silvery backs shining in the sun; and some were hanging in rows from the stalls to dry in the wind.

Jake left the group briefly to chat to a stall holder. When he returned he was carrying a paper bag. 'Try one,' he offered.

I looked at the contents suspiciously: a bamboo skewer with three balls threaded onto it.

'Go on,' he urged, sliding one of the balls off the skewer and popping it into his mouth. 'They're good.'

'What are they?' I took one and gingerly nibbled its edge. It smelled okay, and tasted good.

'Fish balls.'

'From what sort of fish?'

'A big one.' He said it with a straight face, and I choked as I giggled.

Jake took my arm as we walked past a narrow red-framed doorway. 'Let's go in,' he said.

He seemed unaware of the tingles his touch started in me. Tingles that, for now, I'd given up trying to control.

Once inside, the space opened up into a temple.

Hanging from the ceiling were massive coils of incense, and dust motes danced on the shards of light that beamed in from the open door.

'How did you know this was here?' I asked, looking around.

He shrugged. 'You get to recognise them. I love these unexpected temples more than the grander ones on the tourist circuit.'

I watched as he dropped a coin into a box and picked up three sticks of incense, lighting them from sticks already burning in the large urn. He raised them into the air before placing each very carefully into the urn.

'Are you Buddhist?' I asked when he turned back to me.

He shook his head. 'No. It's just something I feel drawn to do when I'm here. I have no idea if I'm doing it properly, but it feels right to me. Besides, temples in Hong Kong are more likely to be Taoist than Buddhist.'

'Is there a difference?'

'Uh huh. But it's not about the religion for me.'

'Are you making a wish on the incense?'

If his answer was yes, that would be another cross beside his name on the list – for all the tingles his touch gave me. I was experienced enough to know that wishful thinking got you nowhere.

'No. It's more a gesture of respect and gratitude, I suppose. It's a moment to stop, show my respect to the temple and the faith, and feel gratitude for being allowed to share it.'

'Oh.' I didn't know what else to say, but couldn't deny that it felt as though my stress levels were falling by the second just by being in this space.

'It's quite meditative, isn't it?' he said, watching me.

I nodded. 'It is. I do yoga most days, but this …'

'I know exactly what you mean.' He smiled and took my arm again. 'We should get back to the bus.'

Our next stop was the beach, where I posed obligingly against a rock for a photo, and laughed when Jake insisted on adopting the same pose. I snapped a quick photo of him on my phone and swore to myself I'd delete it later.

As Jake lined up shots to go with his article, I stood ankle deep in the water, my sandals dangling from one hand. Without thinking I used the index finger and thumb of my right hand to form a viewfinder. Jake noticed and handed the camera to me.

'It's set up,' he said when I raised my brows in silent question.

I dropped my sandals on the beach, took the camera from him, and snapped a few frames, enjoying the satisfying click of the shutter, imagining the image frozen in time. Then I pulled my phone out and took a few photos of the same scene.

Using Jake's camera again, I focused on the silhouette of a fisherman casting his line into the ocean, the waves rolling in at his feet. I was embarrassed to admit to myself that although I knew Hong Kong was an island, the idea that there'd be beaches and fishermen hadn't occurred to me. The city was all I'd known, and I hadn't opened my mind to the possibility of there being anything else.

Over a vegetarian lunch, Jake flicked through the photos I'd taken. 'You've got a good eye,' he said, pausing at the photo of the fisherman. 'You've managed to capture this perfectly.'

I'd automatically taken a meter reading from the diamonds of light on the ocean, so the man was shown in dark silhouette. I'd smiled wryly when I found myself doing it – muscle memory perhaps. For all the bells and whistles Jake's camera had, the basic principles of photography hadn't changed – it was still all about light.

'Thanks,' I said. 'I used to do some photography – a long time ago.'

'Why did you stop?'

'Oh, you know.' I shrugged a shoulder. 'Life, study, work, all of the above. When life got serious, I grew out of it.'

He watched my face, waiting for me to say more. 'You should take it up again,' he finally said when it became obvious that I wasn't going to elaborate.

'Maybe.'

After lunch we wandered around the village under the gaze of a giant buddha that even I had to concede was mighty impressive, then sat in the shade of a tree and watched the stream of people making their way down the steps from the buddha. I ate an ice-block while Jake wrote in a notebook he'd pulled from his backpack.

'I find it easier to get my impressions down as I experience them,' he said.

I nodded, happy to watch him, happy to watch the tourists crowding around the entrance to the cable car that would take us back to the bus, happy that there was nowhere else I needed to be or anything else I needed to be doing that Sunday afternoon. As much as I'd protested when Alice suggested this tour, I couldn't remember a time when I'd relaxed or laughed so much.

CHAPTER THREE

On the bus on the way back to the city, my lack of sleep caught up with me and I dozed off. I woke up with my head on his shoulder, and an embarrassing patch of drool making its way down the sleeve of his T-shirt.

'I'm so sorry,' I said, rubbing at the moisture.

'Don't worry about it,' he reassured me. 'Your snoring didn't bother me at all.'

'I don't –' I started, then saw the grin in his eyes. 'Very funny.'

'Now that you've had that power nap, do you feel like having a drink with me?'

His look told me that if I was interested there was more than a drink on offer. The parts of my body that had refused to listen to me earlier all jumped back to attention.

I thought about it for a few seconds. He wasn't my type. In fact, there was nothing about him that ticked any of my boxes. But there was that twinkle in his eyes, and the tingle when my hand brushed his. I was here for work, he was obviously just passing through, this was just a hormonal reaction, and we need never see each other again, so why not?

'Sure,' I said. 'Your hotel or mine?'

'It'll have to be yours – we just passed mine. You looked so beautiful with your mouth open and the dribble running down your chin that I didn't want to wake you.'

Once inside the lobby, I made a final, feeble effort to save myself. 'Do you want to get that drink in the bar?'

'No.'

'You don't really want a drink, do you?' I asked.

'No. Do you?'

Unable to speak, unable to drag my eyes from his, I slowly shook my head.

He stepped forward until there was scarcely a breath between us and leaned in to kiss me, taking my lower lip between his so gently that I closed my eyes and sighed. When I opened them, he was smiling and again I couldn't look away.

'Let's take this upstairs,' he said.

I nodded and led him towards the lift.

We rode to my floor in silence, each in our own corner of the lift. I touched my mouth where Jake had kissed me and looked across and smiled at him as the doors opened and people got out.

At my room, he waited as I fumbled with the card to unlock the door. When it bleeped red for the third time, he gently pushed me back against the wall and, with both hands holding my face, kissed me properly, his tongue moving against mine, his body hardening. Pulling back he smiled at me, a smile that curled my toes and had me aching to pull his mouth back to mine.

He took the card from my hand, opened the door and stood aside to let me enter first. I was undressing him before the door was closed, grabbing at his shirt to pull it over his head. As he reached for my T-shirt I fumbled at the fastening of his shorts. I toed off my sandals and he did the same with his trainers, our lips still joined. By the time we reached the bed there was a trail of shoes and clothes on the way.

As he paused to fumble in his wallet for a condom, I stopped him and said, 'This is just a one-nighter – you know that, right?'

'Sure,' he panted, no doubt prepared to agree with anything I said at that point in time. 'I'm not in the market for anything more either.'

And then he was inside me and I was unable to think about very much at all.

When I woke it was to the unfamiliar presence of someone in my bed. I screwed my eyes tightly shut as I let my brain wake up and decide where I was – and who was there with me. Opening my eyes, I checked on my surroundings. Dark wallpaper, slightly oriental in nature; a writing desk in the corner with a lamp on it. On a fold-out stand in the corner rested my hard-sided steel-grey suitcase. Good, that at least meant it was my hotel room I'd woken up in. Dark curtains with a sliver of light coming through where they weren't closed properly – or, as I was beginning to remember, had been closed in rather a hurry.

Jake. It was all coming back to me now, but what was he still doing here? If I lay still and pretended to be asleep maybe he'd leave. What time was it anyway? Oh god. If he didn't stir soon, I'd have no choice but to wake him and that would mean a conversation and …

I shivered as a series of feather-light kisses trailed down my spine and his hand found its way to my breast. Okay, so maybe he was awake. I turned in his arms and gave myself up to his kiss.

Afterwards he said, 'I know we agreed that this was only a one-night thing, but I'm only here for two more nights, so what do you say? Can I see you again tonight?'

What could I say? Although Alice would argue to the contrary, the rules of engagement for one-night stands were, by their very nature, loose. Besides, last night had been good and this felt like something I needed to get out of my system. Another night should do it. But there was no way I was allowing him to spend the night next time; that was a mistake I never usually made.

'Sure, I'll be back here from work by seven.'

'Cool, I'll wait for you downstairs. There's this place I've been meaning to try.'

As I was about to protest that it sounded too much like a date, he stopped me. 'Don't worry, it's not a date – I need to write something about dumplings. I'll use your hands in the photos.'

'Dumplings? I don't eat dumplings.'

'And you call yourself a Melbourne girl?' He nuzzled down my throat, his stubble rasping across my soft skin. A shiver ran through me as I remembered how that stubble had felt between my thighs last night – or was it the early hours of this morning? 'Of course you eat dumplings – you just don't know it yet. Besides,' he added, lifting his lips from my nipple, his fingers continuing to trace a delicious line around first one breast and then another, 'these are very special dumplings. Well worth making an exception for.'

Then he made love to me again. For a brief moment I thought about reminding him that I'd be late for work, that I still needed to straighten my hair, do my morning yoga, but then all rational thought left me.

For the first time in years, I went to work with wavy hair. If anyone asked, I'd blame the humidity.

Midway through the day I changed my mind about seeing Jake again. What was I thinking? It had been enough of a mistake allowing him to stay the night; I wasn't going to compound that by seeing him again. I resolved to ring him and tell him I couldn't meet him – then I remembered that he hadn't given me his number.

Okay, so I just wouldn't show up. He'd wait for a bit, realise that I wasn't coming, shrug and chalk it up to a no-show. We'd agreed that it was just a one-night stand; no one was in love, no one would get hurt. But what a night. At the memory of it I almost groaned aloud – but thankfully remembered in time that I was sitting at a boardroom table surrounded by colleagues waiting for me to make a decision on a proposed date for the relocation of our back-up site.

At no point did it occur to me that I might turn up to meet him and he'd be the one who didn't. I knew he'd absolutely be there. Sure, it had all happened quickly, but last night was an experience worth repeating. Then I remembered that we'd arranged to meet in my hotel, so unless I intended staying away until late in the evening I might as well turn up as arranged.

Then the day went downhill, and I was so busy putting out fires that I almost forgot about meeting Jake – until I looked at my watch and realised it was half past six. When I clattered into the hotel lobby just before seven and saw him there waiting, I couldn't speak. It must have been the heat that took my breath away. Or the humidity. In fact, it felt as though there was a storm brewing – or was that only inside of me?

'I wasn't sure if you'd show,' he said, his smile sending my tummy into a spin.

'I nearly didn't,' I admitted.

'But you did.'

I nodded, lost in his eyes again, deep in ridiculous cliché territory.

He looked me up and down, taking in my sleeveless black linen dress and black heels.

'You look different in your work clothes,' he commented. 'Do you need those glasses?'

'You look the same,' I said, ignoring his question about the glasses.

In fact, he looked wonderful, in a pair of khaki shorts that reached just above his knee, the same trainers as yesterday, and a T-shirt in a soft grey that brought out the blue in his eyes. I wanted to rip his clothes off and bury myself in him. Right now.

He smiled. 'This *is* my work suit. With you, it's as if you're a different person.'

'I'll change,' I said. 'Do you want to come up?'

He shook his head. 'I don't think that's a good idea.' His eyes held mine, offering a promise that made the goosebumps rush to my chest again.

I looked away to break the spell. 'Perhaps not. I'll hurry.'

When I emerged from the lift, he was sitting in the bar, a half-finished beer in front of him, a glass of white wine waiting for me.

'That's much better,' he said, eyeing my outfit. 'You look like you again.'

I'd changed into a denim skirt, T-shirt and sandals, put my hair up into a ponytail and washed off my make-up. The black-rimmed glasses that I didn't really need but which lent my face a useful seriousness were gone. I smiled but ignored his comment. The way he looked at me when he said it tempted me to suggest we skip dinner.

The waiter arrived with some spring rolls.

'I thought we were going out for dumplings,' I said reaching for one, suddenly hungry.

'We are, but there could be a queue – okay, there will be a queue – and I don't know yet whether you're one of those women who gets bad-tempered when she's hungry. I'm not taking any chances.'

I grinned and crunched into the crispy spring roll. 'My friend Alice is like that. She hates queuing for food, especially when she's hungry – and she's hungry a lot. I'm one of those women who don't usually queue for anything.'

'I thought you might be. But as I said this morning, these are very special dumplings – Michelin-starred, in fact – and well worth queuing for.' He smiled into my eyes and every nerve in my body tingled in response. 'Besides, some things in life are worth waiting for.'

I knew he was talking about dumplings, but it felt like his real meaning was very different.

'Michelin stars? I wish you'd told me,' I said quickly. 'I wouldn't have worn this, and would have kept my make-up on. It's just that Hong Kong in June and make-up don't go together unless there's air-conditioning involved.'

'You look perfect.'

He smiled at me again and I found it difficult to swallow. Yes, the sooner Jake Stewart was shagged out of my system, the better.

'The cheapest Michelin-star feed in the world,' Jake quipped a few hours later as I closed my eyes to savour the awesomeness of a steamed pork dumpling that had exploded fragrant juices into my mouth.

'Maybe so, but I don't usually eat carbs between Sunday evening and Friday lunch,' I admitted, reaching for a crab dumpling.

'Isn't there some convention that being in a different city means the carbs don't behave in the usual way, so it's okay to eat them whenever you want?' I didn't think he was only talking about carbs or dumplings. 'Besides, dumplings aren't ordinary carbs,' he went on. 'They're a food group of their own.'

'So I can have another one?'

'You can have as many as you want.'

There was absolutely nothing about this place – other than amazing food – to indicate we were eating somewhere world-class. I said so. 'Where are the waiters, the white tablecloths? Where's the pretension?'

'There is no pretension. Good food doesn't need to be expensive or have unnecessary stuff done to it to be good. The best thing about food like this is you don't have to be anyone special to eat here – which is why we queue. It's also why I'm going to share it with the world – or at least the small portion of the world who read my articles. Places like this really are all about the food. The rest is just surface drama – nice every so often, but boring when you've seen it all before. Give me great street food any day as an experience over a five-hundred-dollar dinner. You can't tell me that you won't remember this experience for longer than you did your last posh meal?'

My mouth was too full to argue with him, but to prove him wrong I tried in vain to remember what I'd eaten the last time I went out in Melbourne.

Later, over fluffy buns filled with char siu pork I asked, 'How many stories will you sell from these couple of days?'

He frowned as he thought. 'I'm doing a review for the hotel – that pays for the accommodation –'

'Have you actually made use of the accommodation yet?' I wondered aloud.

'Maybe we should road-test my room tonight,' he suggested.

I felt my face warm and dipped my head so he couldn't see. 'Tell me more about these articles,' I encouraged.

'I have a piece to do on yesterday's tour that was pre-commissioned, and I'll get at least another two ideas out of that. I'm playing around with a few in my head now. Maybe something about giant buddhas, or the ten most annoying things people do on tour. This,' he indicated the dumplings, 'is part of a "Ten places you must go to in Hong Kong" piece. The cable car from yesterday will go into that one as well, and I'll get the dumplings to do double duty in something about the foods you must try before leaving Hong Kong. I might even write a piece about how to eat xiao long bao – those soupy dumplings we just had – without burning your mouth or destroying your clothes. I'm gathering material for a book, so it's all useful.'

Great. A book. I reminded myself that this was just a drive-by and it didn't matter what he did for living.

That night we made good use of Jake's luxury hotel. I declared the bathrobes and the pillow menu to be suitably decadent, although his suggestion regarding potential uses for the showerhead – however pleasurable they turned out to be – probably wouldn't make it to the weekend travel lift-out. The next morning when he asked if we could catch up again that night, it didn't occur to me to say no. The things he was doing to me at the time didn't allow me to think. When I moaned my acceptance, he grinned up at me before resuming operations.

Afterwards he walked me to my hotel and kissed me goodbye. I could taste myself on his lips. For the second day in a row I didn't straighten my hair but put it up in a tight bun instead to try and contain the frizz.

On Tuesday night we caught the tram up to the top of Mount Victoria. There was a breeze where we stood, but far below the lights from the city appeared to swim through the heat haze.

Jake handed his camera to me. 'Go on,' he urged. 'Just shoot – whatever feels right.'

I looked at the camera in my hands for a couple of seconds, and then at him.

'Go on,' he said again.

So I did – framing my shots and loving the whirr of the shutter each time I squeezed it. After a few minutes I settled in and fiddled around with the controls before starting again. It was all coming back to me, and although his camera was more sophisticated than the film version I'd worked with all those years ago I quickly found the settings I wanted.

'You look at home behind the lens,' he said.

I allowed myself a brief smile before returning my attention to the viewfinder. 'It feels good to hold a camera again.'

Sometime later Jake came up behind me and wrapped his arms around my waist, pulling me back into him, and kissed his way down my throat.

'Thank you,' I said. 'Tonight has been good.'

'You're very welcome.' He turned me in his arms and kissed me.

As I kissed him back, I reminded myself that this was just for tonight. Tomorrow he'd be gone and my life would be back to business as usual – hair straightened, mind focused on work. Then I closed my eyes and gave myself up to the pure sensation that was Jake.

Before Jake left for Macau on Wednesday morning, he asked me for my number – just in case he ever found himself in Melbourne, he said.

I shook my head. 'This was just an interlude,' I told him. I was sitting up in bed, a sheet pulled over my nakedness. It seemed important to be covered for the conversation. 'It can't ever happen again. We agreed that right from the start.'

He grinned. 'I thought you'd say that, but I've left my number on the desk – just in case you're ever in Sydney and you feel like calling me. It's entirely up to you.' He leaned over and kissed me, then reached down to kiss the top of my breast. 'Whatever happens next – *if* anything happens next – is entirely up to you.'

Although I had no intention of using it, I saved his number to my phone.

CHAPTER FOUR

On Wednesday my thoughts drifted to Jake more often than they should have. Every time I pushed them away, they'd sneak back in. A dim sum lunch with the Hong Kong project team took me back to the dumplings we'd shared on Monday night, so I sipped at my tea and firmly steered the conversation to where it needed to be. Those few nights with Jake had been a break from reality – like eating carbs on a weekend – and now everything was back to business as usual, with the emphasis on business.

Maybe that was what was upsetting my brain chemistry – all those carbs. I shook my head when offered har gow – a steamed prawn dumpling – and reached across the table for more vegetables instead.

In the taxi on the way to meet Matt I wondered why, despite the difficult meeting I'd just sat through, I was still thinking about Jake – and decided that the root cause of my distraction was that he'd stayed the night. I never let anyone stay the night. While I occasionally liked to feel the unfamiliar closeness of a warm body when I went to sleep, I certainly didn't want anyone there when I woke up. Nor was I usually interested in a repeat performance. That just complicated matters. Men tended to be, in my experience, too needy. They got attached and ended up getting hurt; and if that happened I'd be distracted – like I was now. Jake, though, had slipped under my guard. He'd worn me out so satisfactorily that it was too easy to fall asleep in his arms. And when I did wake and would normally have nudged him out of bed he had somehow known, and soon the idea of him leaving my bed no longer seemed quite as important.

That's why things had always worked so well with Matt – he played by the same rules as I did. Both of us had our eyes on our careers; anything else was purely recreational. It wouldn't occur to either of us to spend the night. No strings, no mess, no relationship.

Matt was in the bar when I arrived, a glass of white wine for me already on the table in front of him. He stood as I walked towards him and pulled me in for a light hug. I turned my head so the kiss he'd aimed at my cheek landed close to my lips. I squeezed my eyes shut and forced myself to concentrate on remembering the way I used to react to his touch, but this time there wasn't even a tingle.

He shifted away and raised his eyebrows but said nothing and sat back down. 'It's been a while, Tiff.' He was smiling, but there was something more in his voice.

I wondered if he was surprised by my attempt to resurrect something we both knew was finished; or if he was upset that we hadn't managed to get together for the last few months. Surely not the latter. I'd never kidded myself that Matt was any more interested in a relationship than I'd ever been. We'd always had an understanding about that – friends with the occasional no-strings and no-hard-feelings benefits. But even that had finished a few months ago. These days I thought he was probably a friend without the benefits; something that came with its own set of complications. I hadn't really had a male friend before and wasn't sure what the protocol was.

This week certainly was turning into a week of firsts – bus tours, sleepovers, midweek carbs, unstraightened hair and a male friend.

I shrugged. 'A few months, I suppose. I've been busy, you've been busy.'

'Things to do, places to be,' he said lightly.

'Let's face it,' I finished. 'We're both so terribly important.'

I managed to hold a straight face for less than a second before laughing at myself, and then he laughed with me, and just like that we were back to normal.

We spent the next hour or so talking about work, his travels, my travels; the subjects that usually kept us occupied until we could go to bed. Tonight, though, sex was off the agenda, which was perhaps why the conversation strayed into deeper territory than it ever had before.

'Have you seen much of my sister lately?' Matt asked.

'A little. We're due to catch up on Friday night. The three of us have been so busy of late that finding time when we're all free has been a challenge.'

'The three of you?'

'Yes, Callie, Alice and me.'

His smile surprised me with its tenderness. 'Little Calliope Jones?' When I nodded, he added, 'There's a name I haven't heard in a long time. How is she?'

'She's great. Except for mooning over this guy she broke up with earlier in the year. He was a real dick, treated her badly, yet she's still hung up on him. I think if I gave her one wish right now she'd use it to bring him back into her life so he can treat her badly all over again.' I shook my head slowly. 'I just don't get it. She's a smart woman, yet ... Your sister's just as bad. It's been how long since she turned up in Melbourne after being cheated on by Luke?'

'You can hardly call it cheated on,' said Matt. 'As I remember it, both of them were in relationships, it's just that Alice broke hers off so she could be with Luke, and Luke changed his mind and stayed in his.'

I waved away his clarification. 'However it happened, it wasn't fair that Alice was the one who lost her job.'

Matt shrugged. 'No one said it was fair, but you know the rules, Tiff – you don't shit where you sleep, or in this case shag where you work.'

'I'm not sure it even got that far, which makes the price she paid even higher.'

'Perhaps, but you know Alice – she's never been one for thinking through the consequences of her actions. She jumps, and then halfway down questions whether anyone remembered to pack the parachute. In this case it was the no fraternisation policy she'd forgotten about.'

I laughed. That was a perfect description of Alice. She had been steadily climbing the Chartered Pacific corporate ladder when she became involved with Luke, a colleague, and had broken off her engagement to be with him. When Luke changed his mind and instead reconciled with and then very quickly married his never-quite-ex- girlfriend, Alice was devastated. To make an already bad situation worse, word had somehow spread to management with the result that Alice lost her job. Luke, however, was promoted. It would have all been so laughably typical if Alice hadn't been the one it happened to.

'No one ever abides by those fraternisation rules,' I said, 'least of all management. It's completely hypocritical. In any case, Alice says she's put some rules in place to make sure that kind of thing never happens again.'

Matt's snort of disbelief interrupted me. 'My sister

with rules? Now that I have to see.'

I grinned. 'She has rules for everything these days. But I know that if someone like Luke came along again, she'd be right back where she was last year. And Callie's the same. If Jamie turned up at her door, she'd welcome him in. The problem is,' I mused, 'neither of them venture far enough outside of their own boundaries. If you keep doing the same thing in the same way, of course you're going to fall for the same men.'

'And you don't?' he asked, a knowing grin on his face.

'No, I don't. For a start, I know exactly who I need in my life – not that I need anyone right now. But when I decide that I do, I know exactly who it will be. Until then I'm happy keeping things purely recreational.'

A picture of Jake came into my head and I pushed it away. I caught the eye of a waiter and held up two fingers to indicate that we needed more drinks.

'No distractions,' said Matt. What did that grin mean? It was almost as if he was laughing at me.

'Exactly. The problem is that Callie and Alice have no idea what they need.'

'And you think you do?'

I nodded. 'I know better than they do. I just need to work out how I can get them to know it too.'

'Do you really think you should be interfering in their lives like that?'

'I'm not interfering,' I said, smiling at the waiter as

he placed fresh drinks in front of us. 'I'm just trying to guide them in a different direction. I don't want to see either of them hurt again by men who don't deserve their tears.'

'You can't control everything, Tiff,' Matt said softly.

'Maybe not, but they're my best friends and if I can look out for them I should.'

'And what about you? Who's going to look out for you?' The grin had left his face.

'I'm fine,' I said. 'I can look after myself perfectly well. Besides, I don't believe in love, therefore I can't get hurt.'

'If you say so.'

'I do. You and I are the same, Matt. That's why this thing between us has worked for as long as it has.'

'But we're done with that now, aren't we?'

'Absolutely. And with no fuss.'

'We're not the same though,' he said quietly. 'You might say that you don't believe in love, but I do.'

His gaze was so intense that my tummy flipped. Surely he didn't mean that he'd fallen for me?

'Don't worry,' he said, laughing at the look of horror on my face. 'I'm not talking about us – that was always going to be only for as long as it was convenient. But I do believe there's someone out there who will turn my life upside down.'

'Only if you let it happen.'

'Tiff, sweetheart, I'll not only allow it, I'll welcome it.'

'Even if it's at the cost of your lifestyle and career?'

'Uh huh. For the right woman I'd give it all up.'

I peered at him across the table. He wasn't smiling. 'You're serious, aren't you?'

'I am. Don't worry though,' he said, the grin back on his face, 'I can't see that happening for quite a while yet. Who knows, it could even happen to you.'

'Not a chance,' I said. 'My eyes are firmly focused on the prize.'

'And that prize is?'

'Getting a spot on Masters this year, wiping the smirk of Ainsley's face, and then having the pleasure of taking her job. When I finally choose someone to commit to, and I suppose I will have to at some point, I'll be making that particular decision with my head and not my heart.'

'What if you meet someone who sweeps you away?'

'Not going to happen, my friend,' I said firmly.

And when Jake's face appeared again in my mind, I chased it away with the rest of my drink and proceeded to order another.

CHAPTER FIVE

Twenty-four hours later, I was squeezed into a middle seat in economy class between a husband and wife, my knees at a weird angle because the husband sat with his legs spread wide, his knee pushing into mine.

'We always book the window and the aisle,' the wife said when I offered to move so they could sit together.

'I like the window and she likes the aisle,' the husband added.

'Because he's tall and takes over my space,' she said.

'And it's a travel hack because often it means we don't have anyone sitting in the middle seat.'

'I'm happy to move,' I said again.

'No, no need,' said the wife. 'But thanks for offering.'

They then proceeded to talk across me.

'I'm having the chicken, so tell them I don't want the fish.'

'Can you order me another beer?'

'Are you awake?'

When the husband finally went to sleep and began snoring, his leg still splayed into my few centimetres of personal space, I sighed and put my earplugs in and my eye mask on. Which was, of course, when the person in front of me decided to recline their seat.

I gave up on any hope of sleep and turned my thoughts to my friends. I was looking forward to seeing them both on Friday night. Matt's words from last night floated through my mind. What had he said? Something about interference? But it wasn't interference if you were doing it because you cared, was it? Callie and Alice were my best friends and I hated seeing them hurt. I'd do whatever it took to prevent that from happening again. I only wished that someone had been able to protect me when it had mattered.

Callie had broken up with Jamie – supposedly for the last time – months ago, yet she still loved him and harboured a hope that someday they'd get back together. If Jamie did come back, I knew he'd be all over her at first, professing his undying love – until he knew he had her where he wanted her and then the hurtful remarks and absences would start up again. It would be just like last time: Cal would stop doing the things she loved to wait at home for him – only for him not to show.

Jamie wasn't the first to treat her like that. Cal had a romantic past full of Jamies. The first was the man she'd followed down here to Melbourne – I couldn't even remember his name now. She'd dropped out of uni for him, saying he was the love of her life, but the relationship was over within a month of them arriving in Melbourne. It wasn't that Cal wasn't smart – far from it, she was the human resources manager in a large call centre – it was just that she didn't use those smarts when it came to men. She had a soft and trusting heart that was too easily exploited. Cal needed a man who was confident enough in himself to encourage her to follow her own interests and not be completely wound up in him.

Alice, as Matt had said last night, had a pattern of jumping into situations with the wrong men. She'd get into trouble, declare she'd never be tempted again, and choose as her next partner someone stable and pliable, eventually becoming so bored that she was tempted by trouble again. She'd been engaged to Hayden when Luke strayed across her path, but although Hayden was a lovely guy, he wasn't right for Alice. He was far too agreeable, and Alice needed someone to challenge her. She'd said as much to me only a few days before they announced their engagement. But when Hayden proposed, Alice said yes. 'It was nice of him to ask, wasn't it?' she'd said. 'He'll be good for me, keep my feet on the ground.' Then Luke came along.

The problem, as I saw it, wasn't so much that Callie and Alice didn't know what they wanted, it was that they didn't know what they needed. And even if they did work that out, unless they tried something different they'd continue to fall for the same completely-wrong-for-them men. Didn't someone once say that the definition of insanity was doing the same thing over and over again and expecting a different result? This whole business of love, I decided, needed to be approached from a different angle. If I could find a way to coax them both out of their comfort zones and try something new, they might begin to think differently.

The problem with that idea was Callie's habit of over-thinking everything for so long that the only safe option was to say no. Alice said it was because Callie's a Cancer and Cancers don't like to stray too far from their shell. She'd also said something about how they know the tide's going to come and wash them away but by then I'd stopped listening. Whatever explanation Alice put on it, I knew that once Callie attached to something – whether it be a habit or a person – she stayed attached. The key to getting Callie on board was convincing her to say yes to something new without thinking about it and without looking back. Then she might be able to see her relationship with Jamie as it really was.

Alice presented a different challenge entirely. Alice needed someone who was tempting, but also challenged her. Someone who rocked her boat, but could also keep her above water. I knew that she'd embrace the challenge of something new – knowing Alice she'd jump in feet-first. What Alice didn't realise, but thankfully I did, was that deep down what she really wanted was to control the outcome of a situation. It was why she'd put all those rules in place.

What was required for this project was a project manager's brain. We needed to decide what was in and out of scope, what qualities were critical, and then approach the solution dispassionately. That's how I would do it if I was in the market for a relationship.

My mind shifted to Jake again. Waking up without him this morning had felt strange; almost as strange as waking up with him had felt. And I hadn't been able to stop thoughts of him intruding into my work day. Why? Matt was perfect for me in every way and yet I usually only thought about him when I was with him or planning to be with him. Jake ticked none of my boxes, but for some reason I couldn't stop thinking about him.

If I was Callie or Alice, I knew that by now I'd be deluding myself that this meant I was in love with him. I managed to stop myself from snorting out loud at the thought. Thank goodness I wasn't Callie or Alice, and thank goodness I knew what – and who – was good for me.

I'd always considered myself an expert on avoiding jet lag. I was that person who could disembark a plane looking as fresh and as fabulous as when I'd boarded it. I'd always boasted that I could sleep from take-off right through to descent and arrive ready to do business. But that was before I had to sit up all night in economy class, in clothes that I'd been wearing all day. Trust me, in the middle of a humid Hong Kong summer that was never a great idea. To make matters worse the flight was late to land and Ainsley had (deliberately) booked a meeting to talk budgets so I had to go straight into the office from the airport.

If I hadn't felt so tired and flight-worn I would have laughed when Ainsley looked at me with her eyebrows raised as much as her frozen forehead would allow and wrinkled her nose. A couple of times during the flight I'd attempted a surreptitious sniff of my armpits and hadn't liked what I smelled either.

Refusing to show my discomfort I smiled sweetly. 'Sorry, I flew all night. I'm off home after this for a shower. I'll be back online in an hour or so.'

Cal called late in the afternoon to convene an emergency teleconference to let us know that she was standing us up for a last-minute date with Andy Campbell, a colleague she'd been crushing on for marginally less time than she'd been heartbroken about Jamie for. Normally we had a rule – well, it was Alice's rule – that we never cancelled a date with each other in order to see a man, but this was the first time that Cal had been out with anyone since she broke up with Jamie. According to Alice that made it an acceptable exception to the rule, and I didn't have the energy to argue with her or point out that Andy Campbell, from what Cal had told us, was almost a carbon copy of Jamie and would therefore treat her in exactly the same way.

My mood wasn't improved by the thirty-minute wait to get to the front of the line of the restaurant we'd chosen, only to be told that a table was still about an hour away. Poor Alice looked as though she was about to collapse from hunger, so I left my number with the maître d' and we ducked down the lane to the bar for a drink and smaller versions of what we hoped to eventually be eating upstairs.

'It's a smart business move,' I said, stifling a yawn as Alice poured large glasses of wine.

'What is?' she asked, reaching for the snacks menu.

'This. The nightly queues make one of the city's hottest restaurants even hotter, especially when you throw in a few stories – true or otherwise – about celebrities being turned away. Then, to stop people going somewhere else for drinks while they wait for a table – and possibly staying there – you invest in more space downstairs, and offer cocktails and snacks with the same vibe as the food upstairs. It keeps the punters on the premises so there's less likelihood of them bailing during the wait, and in the process they spend more money. Win-win.' It really was a clever strategy.

'I wonder how Cal's going,' said Alice. 'I might check in.'

I put my hand over my mouth to hide another yawn while I waited for Alice to finish texting Callie.

'How was Hong Kong?' she asked me. 'Was the tour any good?'

It must have been exhaustion that caused images of Jake to flood into my mind at Alice's mention of the tour. Jake pulling me back into him with all of Hong Kong spread out below us, Jake laughing at the way I gingerly bit into my soupy dumplings, Jake rising above me as he thrust deeply inside …

I swallowed a large mouthful of wine. 'Actually, it was surprisingly good and took my mind off this branch closure Ainsley's decided I need to manage, so thanks for organising it.'

Alice pulled a face. 'Ugh, Ainsley. Even I can't come up with anything nice to say about her – and that's saying something!'

I laughed. We'd always joked that Alice could find something good in every situation and every person. And if she couldn't find something to like, she could find something to feel sorry about. But not when it came to Ainsley. It had been Ainsley who'd officially terminated Alice's employment at Chartered Pacific. She'd wrapped it all up in nice words and called it a redundancy, but Alice knew it for what it was – and we both knew that Ainsley had been more than just the messenger.

'How's your work going?' I asked, keen to change the subject before Alice realised that I'd diverted her attention from the tour.

'I'm getting some business filtering through from

the radio show, and I've just landed another monthly horoscope column with one of the women's magazines.'

When Alice lost her job and left Sydney behind, she'd set herself up as an astrologer – much to the surprise of Callie and me, as well as probably everyone else who knew her. Not, she was quick to point out, the woo-woo new-age type who sat under a pyramid with crystals, but the type who looked for potentials and possibilities and helped her clients to make the most of what they had and work through challenges and excuses. There was very little that Alice liked more than a fresh possibility. As well as client work she also did some freelance writing – mostly horoscopes – and a few months ago had landed a twice-weekly slot on The Toast Team, the highest-rating breakfast radio program in Melbourne.

'That's really good to hear,' I said. 'It's coming together then?'

'It sure is. I'm even making a profit now. I've set up a Facebook business page and an Instagram page too – you should follow me.'

I screwed my nose up. 'You know how I am about social media. I don't need the world knowing my business, or people who couldn't be bothered to talk to me at school reaching out as though we should be best friends now.'

Alice laughed at the look on my face. 'That's because you're a Scorpio and you're paranoid.'

'It's got nothing to do with my star sign,' I said,

'and everything to do with the fact that I don't want the world knowing my business.'

Alice's phone screen lit up. 'Text from Cal,' she said. 'Turns out it wasn't just the two of them out for a drink but knock-off drinks for the whole team. I suggested she join us.'

'As soon as she said they were going to the Mitre I was afraid it was something like that,' I said. The Mitre Tavern was one of the oldest bars in Melbourne and known as the Friday night favourite for anyone working at the financial end of town. It definitely wouldn't have been my choice for a get-to-know-you drink.

'Yeah, me too,' Alice said. 'I was hoping they might have started there and ended up somewhere else. Cal sounded so excited this afternoon – I really wanted this to turn into something for her.'

'So did I.'

Alice grinned. 'I think the outcomes we were each hoping for were very different though.'

I giggled. 'You're probably right. It's been months since she broke up with Jamie – what she needs now is a rebound shag.'

'Perhaps, but Cal isn't the rebound-shag type. She's way too sentimental for that.' Alice frowned as I tried to hide another yawn. 'That's the second time I've caught you yawning tonight. A hard week?'

A shiver ran through me as the main reason why I was low on sleep flashed across my brain. 'Yes. A lot of tough meetings. Plus, last night's flight was late – we sat on the tarmac for ages. If the time on the ticket is nine thirty, that's the time they should be putting that plane into reverse and getting the show on the road. I'd been wearing the same clothes all day – never a good idea in Hong Kong in June – and sitting up all night unable to sleep didn't help matters.'

Callie had arrived as I was talking and gave us both a kiss hello. 'I thought you usually rode up front,' she said.

'Yes, normally, but Ainsley decided to exert her authority and save some money by making us all fly economy. She even called a budget meeting for this morning so I wouldn't have time to get showered and changed. Bitch. It's why I had to fly out on Saturday afternoon last week, because even with the extra night's accommodation it's marginally cheaper.'

'And why I booked you on that tour,' Alice added, 'so you could see more of the city than the bars my brother takes you to. How was it? You didn't say.'

I shrugged and tried my best to look nonchalant. 'It was okay. A bridge, a village, a beach, a buddha and a cable car.' I turned to Cal. 'Anyway, let's not talk about that now – I want to find out what happened tonight.'

Cal was only too happy to tell us the sorry details of the way her evening had unfolded. Towards the end of her tale the food arrived – an assortment of Asian-style bar snacks – and Alice's sigh of relief was audible.

I grinned and shook my head. 'You do know there's a fine line between hungry and horny? Why else do people put on weight when they're not having sex?' I didn't wait for her to answer. 'Because we mistake being horny with being hungry – that's why.'

Alice giggled. 'Can't it just mean that I'm hungry?' She dipped a spring roll into sauce and held her hand under it to catch the drips as she guided it to her mouth.

'Perhaps, but you're hungry an awful lot.' I frowned at her. 'How long has it been?'

Alice deliberately misunderstood. 'Since I last ate?'

'Since you got laid.'

'Nearly a year, I suppose. How good do those satay sticks look?' She signalled to a waiter, pointing towards the satay sticks being delivered to the next table. 'How long has it been for you?' she asked, turning back to me. 'Or are you still having random sex with my brother every time you're in Hong Kong?'

'You know about that?' I'd been congratulating myself that Matt and I had been so careful.

'Of course I do. I know what my brother's like, and I know what you're like, and I know that when you're in town you often catch up for drinks. You don't need to be Einstein to figure out what comes next.'

'Fair enough. But no, not this time – Matt was in Singapore.' I figured our drinks together didn't count. 'This was some guy I met on that tour you booked me on. We sat next to each other on the bus, and because

I'd had about two minutes' sleep the previous night,
I fell asleep on his shoulder. He missed his drop-off
because he didn't want to wake me, so when he asked
me for a drink, I couldn't very well say no. Anyway,'
I shrugged in a way that I hoped looked casual, 'one
thing led to another. You know how it is.'

'No,' said Alice. 'I don't know how it is – not any
more. I have the three-date rule now, remember?'

The three-date rule was to make sure she never
succumbed to temptation again. If she hadn't been
dating though, her resistance to temptation hadn't been
tested.

'Oh, that's romantic. Are you going to see him
again?' Callie's eyes were full of the hope of a happy
ending.

I smiled at her. 'I shouldn't think so. It was a one-
night stand that we doubled up – okay, tripled up – on,
but he's not my type. A travel writer for god's sake, but
a lovely distraction.'

'What's his name?' Alice was addicted to the travel
pages. She was always dreaming about where she'd go if
she decided to be irresponsible and act on impulse again.

'Jake Stewart.'

'I know his stuff. He writes for the weekend lift-
outs. I follow him on Instagram too. Hang on, I saw
some shots he posted last week from Hong Kong.
Maybe from when you met him?' Alice flicked through
her phone, then passed it over to us. 'Here.'

The photo was of Jake posed in front of a bridge. He was grinning into the camera lens in a way that made me feel as though he was grinning into my eyes. Just looking at it reminded me how I'd tingled all over when he smiled at me. Like the sun was coming out from behind a cloud. And that stubble. Under the table I rubbed my legs together at the memory. Oh, for god's sake, get a grip, Tiff!

'Yeah, that's him,' I said. 'I took this photo – and he hasn't even given me a credit. I've perfectly exposed that bridge. After all these years, I haven't lost my touch.'

'He's cute,' Alice said.

'Absolutely,' Cal agreed. 'He's got that thrown-together look that writers, surfers and artists do so well.'

I felt Cal's eyes on me, but couldn't stop looking at the photo of Jake.

'How old is he?' asked Alice.

'Probably our age, maybe a little older. Mid to late thirties? I wasn't really interested in finding out.'

'So not your type,' Alice said.

'And absolutely so her type,' Callie added.

I handed the phone back. 'I think I know better than you two what my type is – and it isn't Jake Stewart.' I pretended not to notice how they grinned at each other.

'Oh good, here are our satay sticks,' Alice said.

'Save some room for dinner,' I warned. 'Anyway, that tour helped me realise that we're going about this man thing all wrong. We haven't been thinking logically about it. We need to tackle the problem the same way we'd look at any other project. Decide on the outcome, set the scope, and determine our CTQs.'

'CTQs?' Callie asked.

'Critical to quality requirements,' Alice explained. At Cal's questioning look she shrugged. 'What can I say? I haven't been out of corporate for that long. Besides, no matter how hard you try there are some things you can't forget.'

'We're talking about those requirements that are absolute deal-breakers,' I continued. 'Anything else falls into the nice-to-have category.'

'It all sounds too hard and unemotional,' Callie complained. Next thing she'd be telling us that the only man who met all her criteria was Jamie.

'Perhaps,' I conceded, 'but I know exactly what I want in a man. I don't believe you two do.'

Callie opened her mouth to interrupt, but Alice stopped her with a warning glance.

'What about you, Ally?' I said. 'You've allowed yourself to stay frozen since Luke. Don't you think it's time?'

'Maybe,' she allowed. 'It's just that no one interesting has asked me out.'

'What about Mac?' Cal asked. 'You talk about him a lot.'

Alice had met Mac soon after she moved to Melbourne: they'd bonded over their dogs, and had been coffee and walking buddies ever since. Cal was right: Alice did speak a lot about Mac – they always seemed to be off having breakfast or coffee somewhere or other. Although she hadn't said anything, I'd assumed they were doing the friends-with-benefits thing – like Matt and I had been. That's why it had surprised me when Alice said there'd been no one since Luke.

Alice wiped the last of the satay sauce off the plate with her finger and grinned cheekily when I frowned at her. 'No, he's a friend so that's a no-go area. Besides, Mac isn't what I want. He's trouble – and trouble is the last thing I'm looking for. After Luke, I'm staying away from colleagues and friends – and especially colleagues who are friends who tell you they're single when they're obviously not. My next man will be someone completely unconnected to me and absolutely not trouble. I'm not leaving anything up to chance any more.'

As much as Alice tried to impose rules on her actions, I knew that temptation only needed to crook its little finger and Alice would jump again. The funny thing was that she knew it as well.

'That's why I'm going along with whatever it is that Tiff's come up with,' she told Cal. 'It can't possibly be any worse than leaving me to my own devices.'

'I'm glad you feel that way,' I said, 'because I've decided that from now until the end of winter you girls are going to say yes. We're all going to say yes.'

'Yes to what?' Cal asked.

'Yes to everything. To every invitation that comes our way. None of this staying at home because you don't know anyone, or because it's cold outside. If you're invited, you say yes. It's that easy. By the end of winter, you'll know what you want. I guarantee it.'

Callie didn't appear convinced.

'But what has that got to do with a bus tour in Hong Kong?' Alice said, looking puzzled.

'It was something I wouldn't normally do,' I explained. 'I only agreed to shut you up. But look what came out of it – a couple of nights of great sex and the realisation that we all need to push our boundaries a little and see what happens.'

My plan would do them both good, I knew it. Just as I knew that I needed to force my interlude with Jake to the back of my mind and concentrate all my energy on work for the next few months. Getting to Masters was my only goal and if that annoyed Ainsley, well, that would be a bonus.

Alice smiled. 'That sounds like something I'd say.'

When Callie attempted to create an excuse, I firmly closed it down. 'It's never going to be the perfect time,' I told her. 'It can only be the right time. I figure the first challenge this week is general maintenance – tidy up the split ends, buy clothes that fit, and deal with any hair where it shouldn't be. For the rest of the winter we're going to work out what it is we really want and do something about going after it. No distractions, no excuses.'

Alice and Cal looked at each other. If Alice was in, I knew that I had Cal too.

Alice nodded slowly. 'Sure, why not. What have we got to lose?'

'Cal?'

She squirmed in her seat, before finally declaring, 'I guess I'm in too.'

I topped up our glasses and raised mine in a toast. 'In that case, Project Yes starts now. Here's to us getting what we want.' I saw Alice's attention wander towards the waiter. 'And no, Alice, that doesn't start with pork sliders.'

CHAPTER SIX

Despite being exhausted when I got home that night, I slept badly. Overtired, I supposed. After tossing and turning for most of the night I gave up at six and dragged myself out of bed and into my yoga gear. Whatever it was upsetting my equilibrium – mid-week carbs, too much alcohol, Jake, or a combination of all those things – an early morning Bikram hot yoga session would flush it out of my system.

I was back home by eight, showered, made a coffee, smashed some avocado onto sourdough that I'd picked up on my way home from yoga – my weekend treat – gathered the travel pages from the weekend paper and took it all back to bed.

Jake's column was something about how people take chances on holiday that they'd never take in their normal lives. Even though I knew there was a lead time to his stories, I was still disappointed to not read something about Hong Kong. What he'd written was right though. In Melbourne, I would never have brought somebody I'd just met back to my place for the night. And even if I did know him, I wouldn't have let him stay the night. Everything that I'd done with Jake was completely out of character. It was no wonder I felt out of balance.

Folding the newspaper away, I took my breakfast dishes to the kitchen and stacked them in the dishwasher, and wiped down the board where I'd cut my sourdough. I'd take the newspaper down to the recycling bin in the basement when I next went out.

From where I stood in the middle of my sleek white kitchen with the stainless-steel appliances that I rarely used, the fridge that held little other than wine and this morning's avocado, I took in the rest of my space. Because I'd been away for a week nothing was out of place; even my cushions were as plump as they were last Saturday morning. Other than the splash of colour from my father's artwork on the wall, everything was tastefully neutral. The floors were a warm wood; the round table with its white top, blond-wood legs and matching white chairs, and the coordinating television stand and soft cream lounge, did nothing to distract the eye. Even the cushions were in textures of cream and sand. Normally the Nordic simplicity of the room filled me with a quiet satisfaction, but this morning it seemed … stark. Cold, even. Perhaps it was because outside it was grey; or maybe it was because I'd come from Hong Kong and after the colour of its streets everything else seemed so ordinary.

My eyes were drawn to Dad's paintings. I was so used to them hanging there, but this morning they brought to mind the vibrancy of the reds and golds in the temple that I'd captured using Jake's camera.

I went through to the guest room and pulled a suitcase out from under the spare bed. Inside was my old Nikon camera, a set of lenses and a variety of filters. After I'd commandeered Dad's old manual Leica camera, my parents had bought the Nikon for me for my sixteenth birthday. It seemed so sophisticated back then, but all of this kit dated back to before digital cameras so none of it was any good any more. I didn't even know if it was still possible to buy film these days, let alone have it developed and printed.

Back then I used to spend most of my pocket money on the best slow film I could afford. It was slide film, because that had the best resolution – and I used to keep it in the cheese compartment in the fridge door. It annoyed Mum no end, which was possibly why I continued to do it. Knowing Dad, I'd probably find some still in there today.

Meeting Jake had tempted me to pick up a camera again – something I thought I'd never do. I was sure that I'd put those days and those dreams behind me that summer after high school, when everything fell apart at home and Mum moved to Perth, leaving Dad and me behind in Brisbane. I hadn't realised just how much I'd missed the pleasure of looking through the viewfinder, hearing that click that only the shutter on an excellent camera can make, and seeing the image frozen in time.

I hadn't been back to my childhood home in years. Dad lived there with Mary now – a fellow artist, his partner of many years and wife of just a few months. They were on an extended honeymoon somewhere or other – it had been weeks since I'd heard from them.

I placed the camera back into the suitcase, shut the lid and pushed it back under the bed. I had no use for any of that now.

Wandering into my bedroom I straightened the bed, plumping the pillows and placing the cushions back where they belonged. I'd gone for cool and calming in here too, with white bed linen and cushions in soft grey and sage. It was simple, tasteful and clean. Again, the only colour in the room was from two of Dad's paintings. The first was a still life of a vase of wildflowers – daisies, mostly. The flowers tumbled all over themselves in a riot of colour against a background of bold slashes in every possible shade of pink and purple with flashes of green. It was as if Dad had run his brush through the palette, picking up bits of colour as he went. The second was a garden in full spring colour. He'd painted it a number of years ago when he and Mary spent some time in Scotland, where Mary was originally from. The flowers in this one were foxgloves, irises and hyacinths. Again, rectangular strokes of bold colour formed the background, while the flowers themselves reached into the sky with an almost folk-arty simplicity.

Dad's art had always been technically good, but since he met Mary, a year or so after my mother left, it had changed. He used to paint a lot of portraits, the colours muted and shaded, the features almost photographic in their accuracy. Now he painted nature – landscapes, seascapes and gardens mostly. These days his work was full of colour and confidence. His skies were bluer than Scottish skies would normally be; his lochs and oceans were more aqua; and his forests contained more shades of green than you'd ever normally notice. All painted with an exuberance which I could now acknowledge had been missing from his work when my parents had been together. Yet when my mother first left, Dad hadn't been able to pick up a paintbrush for months.

I shook my head. I hadn't thought about any of that in years, although I supposed it stood to reason that my mind would go in that direction after I'd allowed myself to look inside the suitcase. I was so used to these pictures that I couldn't remember the last time I'd really looked at them. Now, I wanted to escape into that garden, feel the flowers brushing against my bare legs and the scent surrounding me.

I scratched idly at my wrist. This was all Matt's fault. If he'd been in Hong Kong last weekend, I would have spent at least part of Sunday in bed with him instead of on that blasted bus tour meeting Jake and taking photos.

I forced my thoughts in a different direction – to Callie and Alice and Project Yes. Alice tended to meet Mac most Saturday mornings for a dog walk and breakfast, but Callie would probably be at a loose end and feeling sorry for herself. A new haircut and some freshening up of her wardrobe would be just the thing to help her feel a bit better about herself and enough to lift me out of my mood, which felt the same as the weather outside looked – cold, damp and grey.

I picked up the phone to arrange an appointment with my hairdresser. I wouldn't bother calling Cal, I'd just show up. After all, she couldn't say no.

Ever since Friday night Alice had been following Jake's movements through social media, texting me information like:

Macau looks interesting. He posted this photo of a tile.

The pic with your hand and the dumpling is on Instagram.

You really need to get onto social media – it's the best way of stalking people.

On Tuesday morning I gave in and set up an Instagram account – and then spent the entire time that I was in the airport lounge waiting for my flight to Sydney flicking through Jake's photos instead of tackling my overflowing inbox. The last time he'd posted was a couple of days ago from Hong Kong – did that mean he was still there, or was he back in Sydney? Not that it mattered, I had no intention of calling him. None at all.

Even if I hadn't arranged dinner with Pen, a colleague in the Sydney office, I wouldn't have called him.

I flicked through his feed some more. His pictures weren't bad – although if I was being really critical, I'd say that the composition could have been better in some and the exposure better in others. If I ever saw him again I'd tell him that. Not that I had any intention of seeing him again. He probably wasn't even in town.

Once at the office I was able to put all thoughts of Jake from my brain as I ran from meeting to meeting. It was just after six when I closed my laptop, gathered my coat and umbrella and went to find Pen. She was in one of the meeting rooms at the far end of the floor, her eyes on her phone, her fingers tapping out a text, a frown on her face. Also at the table was Luke, Alice's ex. Great.

'Are you right to go, Pen?' I asked. 'Oh hello, Luke, I didn't notice you there.'

His grin told me he hadn't believed my lie. Arrogant bastard – and way too good-looking. I could see exactly why Alice had been taken in by him. Alice and temptation were never a great mix, and I had to admit that Luke was tempting – if you liked the Italian stallion look he had going on, which I didn't.

'I'm sorry, Tiff,' said Pen. 'That was my husband on the phone. He's been called into work – the doctor on call has come down with something that sounds disgusting – so I need to get home for the kids.'

I nodded my understanding. 'That's okay. Maybe next time?'

'Absolutely. I'd better run, so I'll see you tomorrow?'

'Yes. I'm here until late afternoon.'

'Great.'

Once she'd gone, I was left in the meeting room with Luke. I smiled thinly at him and turned to leave.

'How's Alice?' he said.

I paused before swivelling to face him. 'Why do you care?' Although I'd seen Luke occasionally when I'd been in Sydney on business, up until now I'd managed to avoid having to talk to him – and vice versa.

'Of course I care. Alice and I had some good times together.'

'Until you got married and she lost her job, you mean?'

'It wasn't quite like that.'

For the first time in the conversation he looked uncomfortable and concentrated on closing his laptop and piling up the papers he and Pen had obviously been discussing. A wave of indignation swept through me as I remembered how upset Alice had been when she and her dog Stella had arrived at my apartment on that September afternoon. Luke hadn't deserved her love and was nowhere near good enough for her tears.

'What was it like then? Actually, no,' I shook my head, 'I'm not interested in anything you have to say. Alice is much better off without you.'

'I heard that she's in Melbourne, but what's she doing?' He stood, the pile of papers balanced on his laptop.

I turned to walk away. 'Whatever she wants.'

'Don't you mean whatever you want her to do? You never did approve of her relationship with me.'

I faced him once more. 'No, I didn't. And look how it turned out. As for the idea that I have any sort of control over Alice, that's ridiculous. You managed to ruin her life all on your own. I was just there to pick up the pieces and make sure she never makes that sort of mistake again.'

Even as I said the words, I thought of all the rules and boundaries Alice had put in place for herself. I didn't for a second believe that they'd hold if Luke – or someone like him – ever reappeared in her life.

'Is she dating anyone?' he asked.

'That,' I glared at him, 'is none of your business.'

As I walked away, he called, 'Say hi to her from me.'

'Hardly,' I muttered.

It was cold walking from the office back to my hotel in Darling Harbour. I wound my scarf around my neck and pulled my coat more tightly around me. Without the planned meal with Pen my evening was suddenly empty. I could, I supposed, use it to catch up on some emails. Or I could take myself out to dinner – although the idea of going out into the cold to eat alone didn't excite me.

Waiting at the traffic lights I noticed the way the cars' headlights and the lights from the buildings blended together to make a watery sea of colour in the puddles left from the rain earlier. Pulling my phone from my bag I snapped a quick photo. Then I took another of the city skyline against the black night sky. Perhaps I should post them to my new Instagram account – after all, no one would know it was me. I could stay anonymous. Not that it mattered if anyone knew it was me; it was just a few photos, my privacy was still protected. Of course, what I really wondered was whether Jake would know it was me – although he probably hadn't given me a thought since we'd parted last week and certainly wouldn't be logging into Instagram every day wondering if I'd suddenly opened an account.

When the pedestrian beside me gave me a strange look I realised I'd been frowning. Maybe I should call Jake. He probably wasn't even in town, but it would be rude to be here and not say hello. Wouldn't it?

The lights changed to 'walk' and I determinedly put the idea out of my head.

CHAPTER SEVEN

Back in the hotel I toed my shoes off, put my hair up and changed out of my work suit, hanging it in the wardrobe. I'd get something from room service and do some work. Perhaps I'd go down to the bar and have a glass of wine. That would relax me.

This time last week I'd been in Hong Kong and coming back from work to meet up with Jake. Last Tuesday we'd eaten Chinese barbecue and roast pork in a little shopfront in Kowloon. The barbecue was stickily sweet and the roast was fatty and crunchy. We'd washed it down with beer that we drank from the bottle, and then crossed back to Hong Kong Island on the ferry before heading up to Victoria Peak. If I closed my eyes I could still feel his arms around me and his kisses down the side of my neck.

Maybe it wouldn't hurt to text Jake. After all, he'd said that if I was in town and he was in town … And if I texted it wouldn't be the same as if I called. There was no way anyone could construe a text as being a booty call. I was just saying hello and letting him know I was in town. That's all. That way if he called back it would be as if he was making the booty call – not me. Besides, he might not even be in town.

Hi Jake, it's Tiff – from last week in Hong Kong.

I went back and deleted the part about Hong Kong. How many other Tiffs would he be likely to know?

I find myself in Sydney at a loose end tonight – I don't suppose you're around and would like to catch up for a drink? I'm in Darling Harbour.

I didn't need to wait long for the response.

Sure, I'm just finishing a story – can be there by 8. Jx

What did the 'x' mean? One kiss?

Text me when you're close. I'll meet you in the lobby.

As I sent through the hotel details, I reminded myself that I was absolutely not going to sleep with him tonight. We'd have a drink in the bar downstairs, and I'd look into his eyes and realise that whatever it was we'd had in Hong Kong had been shagged out of our systems and left over there.

I was so sure of not sleeping with him that after I'd showered, I dressed in a pair of soft yoga pants and a loose long-sleeved T-shirt. I only shaved my legs again because they needed it, and I only changed into my favourite bra and undies because they were comfortable. Okay, not because they were comfortable but because they made me feel good. I had no excuse for why I'd packed them in the first place. After all, I hadn't intended to call him, and I certainly wasn't going to sleep with him.

I might have stuck to my guns if when he grinned and kissed my cheek, I hadn't looked into his eyes.

Instead I said, 'The bar looks crowded.'

'We won't be able to talk properly,' he agreed.

His eyes crinkled at the edges, and the stubble on his jaw reminded me of exactly how it felt on my much softer skin. I shivered as a line of goosebumps marched up my arm, across my chest and down the other arm.

'Maybe we'd be better talking in my room and opening a bottle of wine from the minibar,' I suggested. 'Unless you want to go out and try somewhere else that isn't so crowded?'

He shook his head, his gaze holding mine, those damned twinkles making my tummy do somersaults. 'It's cold out there,' he said. 'And I think it might rain again.' He took my hand in his. 'I really don't want to get wet.'

His thumb was drawing circles on my wrist, a trail of sensation heading south. My bra suddenly felt too tight and I knew that if I looked down at my T-shirt I'd see my nipples standing to attention under the soft fabric. 'Don't you?' His eyes flicked down my body and his slow and sexy smile was my absolute undoing. One more night wouldn't hurt.

Jake waited only until the lift doors had shut before gently pushing me back against the wall and kissing me. I felt the same urgency between us as there had been that first night in Hong Kong. Inside my room, we barely made it to the bed, somehow undressing ourselves and each other with our lips still connected. It had only been a week, but we devoured each other as if we'd been apart for much longer than that.

Afterwards I rolled off him with a satisfied sigh. Oh, that was good. Possibly even better than it had been in Hong Kong.

As if he'd read my mind Jake stretched his arms high over his head before bringing them down to pull me close and said, 'Man, we're good together.'

I burrowed into him. Just a few minutes wouldn't hurt, then I'd send him on his way. He smelled of the wool jumper he'd had on before I pulled it off him. It was nice – both the smell and the chunky jumper.

'Don't you think?' he asked.

'Uh huh,' I agreed.

'Is this classed as a one-night stand when it's the fourth time we've done it?'

'If we're actually counting, it's probably more than that,' I said. I didn't know how many times we'd made love over those few nights in Hong Kong. 'We haven't had sex before in Sydney – or in this hotel – so that's sort of like doing it for the first time.'

'So we could have sex in another hotel and if we haven't been there before it would count as a first time?'

'Or a one-nighter.'

I felt his fingers idly tracing patterns on my back.

'I like that idea. We can have a series of one-nighters.'

'We could.' That back-tracing thing he was doing was making it difficult to think logically. 'Just while we shag each other out of our systems. Nothing else.'

'That means we can hook up again in Melbourne if we want and it'll be classed as a one-night stand too?'

'Absolutely.' I shivered as his hand moved from my back to my hip. 'Why, are you going to be down there soon?'

'Uh huh, I was only ever planning to be in Sydney for a few months.' He kissed the top of my head. 'They wanted me working out of the Sydney office for a bit while one of my colleagues was on maternity leave, so I rented my place out in Melbourne and subleased up here from a mate who was doing some work in KL. I'll be in Melbourne next weekend for a story, but I'll be moving back permanently soon.'

A rush of something that felt suspiciously like excitement ran through me at his words. To quell it, I pushed him onto his back and straddled him, trailing my fingers and lips down his body.

'Mmmm,' he breathed. 'So if you want, we could see each other more often. Just until we get whatever this is out of our systems. There aren't any restrictions on how many times we have sex on each night, right?'

'None at all. It's the number of occasions and where we do it that matters.' The Law According to Alice. 'We can't double up anywhere because that would change the one-night-stand status.'

I licked at his nipple, flicking it with my tongue. He moaned and I felt the sound rumble through his body.

'What about Hong Kong?' he said. 'We met twice in your hotel. Does that change it from a one-night stand to a potential relationship?'

I moved up his body to suck at his lower lip. 'Hong Kong didn't count – that was a business trip. The same rules don't apply.' Alice would be proud of my ability to manipulate the rules to my own satisfaction. I reached between us to hold him in my hand, squeezing him gently and watching his eyes darken. 'Do you really want to talk about it now?'

He swallowed hard and shook his head as I slid back down, my nipples grazing his chest.

Just before I took him in my mouth, I said, 'You know this doesn't change the fact that this isn't going anywhere.'

'Sure,' he groaned. 'It changes nothing.'

I fell asleep in his arms and when I woke sometime later, he looked so peaceful that it would have been cruel to send him away. And this time when he asked if he could call me, I agreed. Given he was still inside me at the time, it would have been rude not to.

He texted me just as I was settling into my first meeting: *I can still taste you.*

I allowed myself a smile but didn't reply.

•

When Jake called on Friday morning to ask if we could spend the day together on Saturday, I said yes. After all, if the girls were committing to Project Yes, it would be hypocritical if I didn't.

To make sure there were no misunderstandings though, I reminded him that we didn't do dates.

'Oh, this isn't a date,' he said. 'What gave you that idea?' I could feel his grin through the phone. 'While I don't mind eating alone, when I'm reviewing it's better if I have someone else with me. Otherwise the other patrons watch me ordering all the food I need to try to write a decent review and then make judgments about wastage when I send half of it back. This way they can make a judgment about how much my girlfriend – they don't need to know we're just sleeping together – eats. Plus, you can help me out with the images – my editor really liked some of those shots you took in Hong Kong. So really, this isn't anything like a date.'

'Okay, but don't go getting any ideas about how the day will end.'

'Absolutely not. I don't care what you think, but I am not sleeping with you tomorrow night. Is that clear?'

I couldn't help the giggle that escaped me – earning me a puzzled glance from Jude in the credit team. Heavens, from the look he gave me, anyone would think I never smiled in the office, let alone laughed.

CHAPTER EIGHT

Despite Jake saying that we would absolutely not end up in bed tomorrow night, that was all I could think about during Friday night drinks with Callie and Alice. Ridiculous. I couldn't remember the last time a man had gotten under my skin to the extent Jake had. Which was all the more reason to enjoy the day tomorrow and then nip this in the bud before he got too attached. I'd spend Saturday with him, we'd both realise that we really had nothing in common outside of sex, and we'd go our separate ways. Job done.

As if he somehow knew I was thinking about him my phone pinged to herald an incoming text.

I'll pick you up at 11 tomorrow morning. Wear comfy shoes and loose pants. And remember, don't try anything – I'm absolutely not sleeping with you tomorrow.

I turned my head so Cal and Ally couldn't see the smile I couldn't stop. I texted back: *I'm absolutely not sleeping with you either.*

Although I really had no intention of sleeping with him, it would be fun to see how long he could hold out. I chewed at my bottom lip as I contemplated that thought. Fun and more than a little exciting.

'Are you listening, Tiff?' Callie's question brought me back to the bar and my two friends. 'I just said that Ally and I tried belly dancing during the week. Kerry, a friend from work, asked me and I couldn't say no because of Project Yes, so I figured I'd ask Alice who also couldn't say no. As it turned out it was really fun.'

'That's fabulous!' I said. 'It's exactly the sort of thing I was hoping would come out of this project.'

Even to my ears it sounded as though I was gushing – and gushing was something I didn't do. When I caught Alice and Cal sneaking raised-eyebrow looks at each other I knew they'd noticed as well. Inwardly I gave myself a good shake and reminded myself to focus on what my friends were saying. After all, I'd invented Project Yes to help them – the least I could do was listen to them.

It appeared that while I'd been saying yes to Jake, they'd also been stepping outside of their comfort zones. Alice had managed, in the space of just a few days, to have two dates with the IT guy from the radio station she worked at.

'Our first date was for lunch, so I've already had the daylight date. Then we went for dinner last night.'

'You didn't waste any time,' I commented. I hadn't mentioned my chat with Luke to her and still hadn't decided whether I would say anything. If she was starting to see someone else there didn't seem to be a lot of point. But if she ever found out I'd kept it from her ...

'I couldn't see the point,' she went on. 'And Tommy – that's his name – was a sensible choice to say yes to. My fear was that I'd need to say yes to a non-sensible but possibly more short-term exciting choice and that would put me right back where I started – in trouble. I'm not about to fall in love with Tommy, but I really like him.'

'I don't believe in falling in love,' I said. 'I think you find someone who ticks the boxes and it grows from there. The falling in love thing is really only about sex – and even then, only at the beginning.'

That's all this thing with Jake and me was, and thankfully we both knew it.

'I still believe in love at first sight,' Alice said, 'even after Luke – and that should have been enough to turn me off forever. That feeling, that rush – it reminds you you're human. That's how I know Tommy's an in-between option, just someone to get me back on the horse. I'm holding out for love at first sight again.'

'That's the hormones speaking,' I pointed out. 'Like me with Jake the other week. It was nothing to do with love – just two people who needed to shag each other out of their systems.'

Alice gave me the look that meant she thought I was either protesting too much or trying to convince myself of something. Neither was the case, so I stared right back at her.

Cal hadn't noticed and was back on her favourite subject: Jamie and how they were unfinished business and would now never get the chance to see whether they could have made it. Alice soothed and smoothed and empathised, as she always did when Cal talked about Jamie.

Normally I'd at least try to bite my tongue, but tonight I downed the rest of my wine in one swallow and said, 'You and Jamie had five years together – that's plenty of time to work out he's a cheating fuckwit who doesn't deserve you mooning about him months after it's over. The thing is – and Alice, you can put this in your rule book – you never end up with the one who got away. That's not how it works. *Sex And The City* was right: the bad boys – the Mr Bigs – are only there so we can see and appreciate the real thing – Aiden – when he comes along. That's why you have to have at least one Mr Big before you settle. They cause too much trouble if you fall for them afterwards. Or worse,' I looked directly at Cal, 'if you keep going back to them.'

'But Carrie ended up with Mr Big,' Cal argued.

I poured more wine. 'An exception to the rule that's caused way too much angst for women around the world who now think there's a slim possibility their Mr Big could become their Aiden. The *Sex And The City* writers have a lot to answer for with that.'

I was beginning to suspect that Jake was my Mr Big – sent by the universe (now I was starting to think like Alice) to help me get something reckless out of my system before I found an Aiden and settled down. However, unlike Carrie in *Sex And The City* – who, in my opinion, remained hung up on Mr Big for far too many seasons of the show – I was aware of that and would let Jake go if he got too close or, unlikely as it seemed, I got too desperate. At the moment Jake felt like a drug coursing through my blood, but I was confident I could stop anytime I wanted.

'What about you, Tiff? What do you want?' Alice asked, before the conversation could get out of hand.

I took a big swallow of my wine. 'Ideally, someone exactly like your brother. Matt's as close to my perfect man as it's possible to be. Tall, professional, great taste in clothes, and earning good money. Any man I end up with needs to be confident in his own career, and not interfere with me wanting to further my ambitions. I'd prefer it if I didn't meet him through work, but that would be too much to ask, I guess. And someone who doesn't expect me to pop out a heap of kids.'

'Doesn't Matt want children?' asked Callie.

I shook my head. 'He likes Laura's children and all that, but he's like me – career comes first.' Laura was Matt and Alice's sister. She and her husband Mick and a large number of children – all boys – lived on the Sunshine Coast in south-east Queensland.

Alice was looking sceptical. 'It sounds to me like you've described a male version of yourself.'

'What's wrong with that?'

She shrugged. 'Nothing, I guess, but don't you want someone you can share new experiences with? Someone who can make you laugh? Someone whose differences will keep you interested.'

Cal nodded. 'I agree. You need someone to have fun with.'

'That's what I've got you girls for,' I told them.

'Similarities are fine, but you need someone to challenge you in order to grow.' Alice pulled a face. 'Man, I'm talking like a new-age therapist or life coach. Soon I'll start telling you about closure or journeys or opening doors and putting one foot in front of the other!'

I laughed, but I wasn't really amused. I wasn't about to settle with someone just because they made me laugh. When I eventually decided to commit to one man it would be someone who took me and my needs as seriously as I did, and that meant someone who satisfied my checklist.

'I think I know better than you what I want,' I said.

'Okay, so you want someone professional, earning mega dollars and wearing designer suits. You may as well settle for my brother.'

I shrugged. That might have been a good idea except it was apparent from our last conversation that Matt was as susceptible to the follow-your-heart thing as Callie and Alice were.

'When I talk to a client about relationships,' Alice began.

'And you're such a good example,' I said, smiling so she knew I was making fun of her.

Alice acknowledged the smile and continued. 'As I was saying, when I talk to a client about relationships, we concentrate first on what they need, what gets them motivated, and what type of relationship style they prefer.' She stopped for a mouthful of wine. 'Let's face it, ending up with the wrong person is ridiculously easy. I'm extremely good at it, and I should know better. We all know I've never been good at walking my talk.'

Cal and I laughed, as we knew we were supposed to.

'So how does this theory of yours work?' I asked.

'Well, the first step is to know yourself. I already said that, right? In my case, I know I'm a contradiction. I need someone who's relatively stable, yet I want someone who appears not to be. I need someone I can be friends with, but I go after the guy who makes my heart thump but has no follow-through.'

'But how do you know when you've found the right person? The one you can be happy with forever and ever?' Of course, that question came from Cal.

Alice and I looked at each other and grinned.

'Are you going to say it, or will I?' Alice asked.

'I will,' I said. 'Is there really such a thing as happily

ever after? Why do you think romance novels end when they do? No one's interested in what comes next because it tends to be pretty disappointing. You think that once you're in a relationship all your problems will miraculously go away, but they don't. Once that first rush of lust dies down you begin to realise you still have whatever it was that made you stressed and miserable when you were single, but now you have someone to share it with. Plus, you're sharing whatever it was that made him stressed and miserable when he was single. So, when you think about it, being in a relationship is like being single – but with regular sex. Believing it's all going to be rainbows and unicorns is a short cut to heartbreak.'

I knew that one first-hand. My parents got married because Mum was pregnant with me and once they emerged from the lust bubble, they spent the next sixteen or so years trying to destroy each other. For a time, I think they succeeded.

'That's why one of my deal-breakers is I have to be friends with the guy, so that when the lust dies down there's something to build on,' said Alice. 'But given that one of my rules is I don't date guys I'm already friends with, I'm basically screwed.'

'That's why great sex is one of my deal-breakers,' I said. 'I have you guys for friends.'

'Okay,' said Alice, 'if we're being scientific about this, let's talk deal-breakers.'

'And grooming in your case,' I pointed out.

'Okay, and grooming. For me, aside from what I said before, the guy has to be able to deal with my contradictions and hypocrisy, talk about my job without laughing or mentioning his uranus, and be able to fix things. It would be extra nice if he could fix my website. Oh, and he has to love dogs. Stella and I come as a package, and I often have Kevin at my place too.'

Kevin was Mac's dog. Mac travelled quite a bit for work and had gotten into the habit of leaving Kevin with Alice and Stella.

'As for grooming,' I said, 'if your eyebrows are joined, I hate to think what's happening down there.' I raised my eyebrows to indicate which part of Alice I felt needed a little landscaping. 'I thought you were going to deal with that last week.'

Alice tilted her glass in my direction. 'Okay, it's a trip to the waxers for me before tomorrow night's date with Tommy. Cal – your turn.'

'I don't think I'm ready to be with anyone else yet,' Cal said. 'I know that sounds pathetic, but part of me feels I need to close things off with Jamie.'

There it was again. Jamie.

'Actually, yes, it does sound pathetic,' I said. I'd had enough wine that I didn't attempt to temper my words. 'I love you, sweetie, but you took him back once before – that was your opportunity for "closure".' I used my fingers to mime quotation marks.

'That was different,' she protested. 'Yes, he did what he did, but it was my fault he left this time. I'd like the chance to put it right.'

Jamie deserved nothing more from Callie. She'd already given him too much of herself. Before I could say as much, Alice had frowned a warning at me.

'I know how to make you feel better,' she told Cal. 'You can make up the numbers for our table at trivia tomorrow night. It's for Tommy's soccer club – it'll be fun. You can come too, Tiff – you can't say no, remember.'

'Yep, a trivia night with a table full of computer geeks. That's bound to make her feel better,' I said, and Alice scowled at me again. 'Anyway, I've already got a date tomorrow night.'

'Who with?' Alice said. 'Anyone we know?'

I looked around the room in an attempt to attract a waiter's attention. 'Do you think we should order some food? I'm getting hungry.'

'That's my line,' Alice said. 'Who's your date with?'

I gave in. 'Jake.'

'The Jake who just a few minutes ago you said you'd shagged out of your system?'

'He called and said he'd be in town and could we catch up.' I shrugged as if it meant nothing but even saying his name sent a secret thrill of sensation running through me. 'I can't tell you girls to say yes to everything if I'm not prepared to do the same, can I?'

I grimaced inwardly at my high-pitched laugh. If I was Alice or Callie, I wouldn't be convinced for even half a second.

'Does he make you laugh? Does he make you feel relaxed? Are you able to talk to him?' Alice looked like she had a list of more questions like that.

I stopped her before she could go any further. 'Yes, he does. But that doesn't make him right for me. We've had a series of one-nighters that mean nothing – and that's the way it should be. Besides, I'm concentrating on getting to Masters this year. I won't be letting any man get in the way of that.'

If I told myself that often enough I might even start to believe it.

CHAPTER NINE

Alice called me early on Saturday morning. 'Don't you think you were just a bit hard on Callie last night?'

'Where are you?' I asked. 'It's very noisy.'

'In the park with the dogs. Mac's away so I have Kevin this weekend.'

'Again? He travels almost as much as I do. What is it that he does again?'

'Oh, I don't know. Something in IT, I think, we never really talk about it. And if it's IT I'd probably be bored if we did. Now, don't change the subject – I think you were tough on Cal.'

Sometimes I thought that Alice was the conscience of our little group – well, mine at least. Callie was too soft-hearted to need one.

'Maybe,' I acknowledged. 'It just frustrates me how she is about Jamie.'

'And you don't want to see her hurt again,' Alice said softly. 'You know, Tiff, you can't control that. Cal is always going to love whole-heartedly – she wouldn't be who she is if she didn't.'

'But Jamie? He doesn't deserve her.'

'No, he doesn't, and Luke didn't deserve me, but you can't control how your heart feels.'

'Yes, you can,' I muttered.

'I heard that,' said Alice. 'Anyway, Cal will get over Jamie in her own way, and if she's hurt again we'll be there again – just as you both were for me.' As I was about to interrupt she added, 'Who knows, it might even happen to you one day. Speaking of which, where are you going with Jake tonight?'

'Actually, we're spending the day together.' I said the words quickly as if that might stop Alice reading anything into it.

'A daylight date? Really?'

'Don't go thinking that,' I warned. 'It means nothing. He's in town to do some reviews and I'm tagging along, that's all.'

'Of course it is.' She said it in a way that told me she didn't believe me. 'Where are you meeting?'

I hesitated for just a beat too long.

'Oh. My. God. He's picking you up? At your apartment?'

'Yes, but –'

'But nothing. I can't recall you ever bringing anyone home to your place – so that tells me that either this guy's really special, or you think that him seeing what you have will reinforce the differences between you, to remind him – and yourself – that this can't go anywhere.'

'That's ridiculous,' I dismissed.

'Is it?' Before I could answer she said, 'Anyway, I have to get these dogs home so I can go and do the deforestation thing – I've decided that Tommy will get lucky tonight. Have a great day. I want to hear all about it tomorrow.'

Jake must have been channelling Alice because when he walked into my home after kissing my cheek – an action that left me both surprised and disappointed – he looked around and said, 'Is this your way of showing me what your very important banking with a "B" job gives you?'

'No, of course not. I just thought you might like to see where I live.'

He grinned at me, which had its usual impact on my hormones. 'Okay,' he acknowledged, 'then I'd say that showing me your home is an interesting move from someone who's repeatedly told me we're not dating but just hooking up. I wasn't even allowed to have your phone number until a few days ago, and now you're inviting me into your home. Are you sure this isn't moving too quickly?'

'If you don't want to be here, just say so.' I felt my chin push out and my shoulders square.

'Calm down, I was just making an observation. I'm glad you've shown me your place. It tells me a lot about you.'

'Like what?'

He gripped his chin between his thumb and index finger and looked around. 'Firstly, that you're a contradiction. Take this art for instance. This has been painted by someone with a love for colour, yet everything else in this room is neutral and classic. It's an interesting choice of art by someone who otherwise lives in a very tasteful display home.'

'It's not a display home,' I objected. 'It's Scandi and it's very now.'

He smiled. 'Settle down, I didn't say I didn't like it, just that it could be anyone's home – but these pictures tell a different story.'

He stepped closer to examine the first painting. It was of summer wildflowers against a madly turquoise bay, with white croft-style cottages on the banks of the bay and rugged mountains rising behind them to a blue sky.

'Hmmm, it's a John Samuels,' he observed, and moved onto the next one – a path leading through a bluebell wood, the trees all blending into countless shades of dappled green light, the forest floor a riot of blue and purple. 'I know his work – always so much exuberance. I love how he layers the colour with huge brushstrokes. I don't recognise these works though.' He turned his attention back to me. 'Any relation?'

'Yes, my father.' He raised his eyebrows. 'These were painted in Britain a few years ago, from a series I don't think he'll ever sell.' I walked across to stand beside him. 'This is from Arran, one of the Scottish islands. And the bluebell wood is somewhere out of Edinburgh, in the Trossachs, I think. Mary, his new wife, is Scottish.'

'New wife?' He asked the question quietly, his eyes not leaving my face.

'Very new – they're on their honeymoon at the moment. To be honest I have no idea where they are right now. One of the Channel Islands, I think.'

'And your mother?'

'She's in Perth.' I turned away, keen to change the subject.

'Is she a creative too?'

I laughed shortly. 'Hardly. Mum's the CEO of a recruitment company that supplies resources to the mines.'

'I see.' His eyes stayed on mine, as if what he was seeing was the very deepest, most private part of me. Then he grinned and turned away. 'Let's see what the rest of this apartment says about you.' He paused at my bedroom door. 'What will I find in here? A boudoir with a four-poster bed draped in swathes of fabric perhaps?' He tilted his head slightly, his eyes twinkling madly. 'Or will it tell me something else about you?'

He wandered into my bedroom and opened the wardrobe doors. My eyebrows raised at the breach of privacy but if he noticed he ignored it.

'Like you're the type of person who likes to keep

order in their life. I bet you have a schedule for your dry-cleaning and hang it up the minute you get home. I also bet you're the type who makes her bed as soon as she gets out of it.'

'What's wrong with that? Don't you?'

'No, I pull the covers up and straighten it before I get in each night. See, we're already finding out things about each other that we wouldn't know if we'd stuck to meeting in hotels.'

'Don't go thinking that we're having sex here,' I warned.

'I wouldn't dream of thinking that. Why do you think I didn't kiss you properly when I first arrived? I know what you're like – you wouldn't be able to help yourself. And as I told you, I'm absolutely not having sex with you today.' He tilted his head to the side and smiled again. 'Is that why you brought me here first? So you could have your wicked way with me? Shame on you, Tiffany Samuels.'

I shook my head in exasperation. 'If you're quite finished going through my cupboards, questioning my motives and criticising the way I like things, we'd better go to wherever it is you have planned.'

'No, I'm not finished yet. Aside from your secret desire for colour in your life,' he ignored my snort of disbelief, 'I think I've discovered your dirty little secret.' He held up this morning's travel lift-out, folded to where his story was. I groaned inwardly. 'You bring me to bed with you on a weekend morning, don't you? I bet you have a little tray that you put your breakfast on, and you pile your pillows up just like this.' He organised the pillows in the same way I usually did. 'And you sip your coffee, eat your toast and think of me.' He slapped his hand against his forehead. 'Don't tell me that our chance meeting on that bus tour wasn't a happy coincidence! Have you been sitting in bed reading my articles for months and somehow contrived to get yourself on the same tour? Next you'll be telling me you have an Instagram account just so you can keep up with where I am.'

I felt my face grow warm and lowered my eyes.

'Oh. My. God. You have, haven't you?' I didn't need to see his face to hear the grin in his voice.

'For the record, I'd never heard about you until I met you,' I said, 'but now I do read your articles. And yes, I read them in bed. What of it? Also, I signed up to Instagram so I can post the occasional picture from my phone. It seems to be what everyone else does. I'm not even following you. So there.' I groaned inwardly at the "so there" comment, which even to my ears sounded immature.

His smile grew wider as he walked slowly towards me. 'Now, that's not really the truth, is it, Tiff?'

'I don't know what you're talking about.' As he moved closer, I took a step back, my progress halted by the wall.

'What I'm talking about is how one of my new

followers has the name "sammytii". That wouldn't happen to be you, would it?'

He was so close now that there were just centimetres of space between us. I felt my breath coming faster and bit at my bottom lip in an effort to stop my body doing what it wanted to do – push forward to meet his. His eyes had darkened and his pulse beat faster in his jaw. I knew that if I took even half a step towards him, I'd find more evidence of what we both wanted.

'Is it, Tiff? Are you sammytii?'

I nodded and closed my eyes in preparation for the kiss I knew was coming. Instead, I felt him move away from me.

'If that's the case, we'd better get out there and take some Insta-worthy images for you to post.' He paused. 'Hold on, what's this? A guest room? Is that why you brought me here – so I can see if this space will work as my office when we move in together? And what do we have in here?'

I shut my eyes again – this time in mortification rather than anticipated pleasure.

'You've been holding out on me, Ms Samuels.' Jake had picked up my old camera. I'd had the suitcase out again this morning and hadn't put it away. 'That's quite a bit of kit for someone who said she gave up photography years ago? What's the story?'

I snatched the camera body out of his hands, and put it and the lenses and filters I'd been looking at back in the suitcase and slid it under the bed where it belonged.

'No story. I've just not got around to getting rid of it, that's all.'

'Well, I don't think I believe that explanation, Tiff. I'd lay good money on there being nothing else in this apartment that isn't used, which has to make me wonder why it is you've kept this?'

I turned away from the question in his eyes. 'It's a long story and one for another time.'

Even though I'd walked out of the room I could feel his eyes burning into my back. He followed me, and watched as I picked up my handbag and headed towards the door.

'One last question,' he said.

'Would it make a difference if I said I don't want to talk about this?'

'No, not really. Have you still got any of your work lying about that I can look at? And,' he warned, 'I'll know if you're not telling me the truth.'

I rubbed the side of my wrist against my jeans. 'No. I don't. Are we going to hang around here all day or do you have somewhere for us to be?'

I forced a smile to lighten my words, but I knew he wasn't fooled. The slight twist to his mouth told me that he knew I'd just lied to him.

'Yes, we do have somewhere to be,' he said. 'So if you've decided you're not going to seduce me, we may as well get going.'

I relaxed. If the banter was back, he'd got my message to drop the subject – for now at least.

Jake's article involved seeking out some of the best Vietnamese-style street eats in Melbourne, and he warned me that we'd be doing plenty of walking in between if we wanted to survive the day with waistbands intact.

'This is why I need you,' he said as we walked up Chapel Street towards Richmond. 'Not just for your sparkling company, but also because there's no way I can eat that much food in one day.'

'You could always split them across both days of the weekend.'

'True, but what if a better offer came up?' At the 'not likely' look on my face he laughed. 'Seriously though, the first rule of freelancing is to never put off until tomorrow what you can eat or experience today. If there's a problem the next day and I can't get there, my whole story is blown. This way, if I do happen to visit somewhere else tomorrow it's a bonus. The biggest mistake you can make in this industry is keeping your options narrow.'

We turned left into High Street. 'Okay, here we are. Our first stop.' When we were seated with menus he asked, 'Do you eat much Vietnamese food?'

I shook my head. 'Not at all. One of my favourite restaurants in Flinders Lane does Vietnamese-style food – or is it Thai? – but I'm not familiar with much on this menu other than spring rolls.'

'Right, well, you're in for a real treat. Are you okay if I order for us?'

I waved my assent and settled back in my seat. 'Have you been to Vietnam?' I asked.

'Yes, a couple of times. I'm going again in August and it's the food I'm most looking forward to.' He paused and leaned forward. 'Hey, you should come with me. It's a fabulous place – lovely people, great food, and you could even get more of those work suits of yours made. They'd be able to do them in black, grey and beige – or is it camel? Who knows, you might decide to splash out on navy?'

'I don't think so,' I said, refusing to acknowledge the fission of an idea that had lodged in my brain at the thought of exploring somewhere new with Jake. Not that we'd be together still by then – although, I reminded myself, we weren't in a relationship now.

'You've got some time to think about it.'

I was saved from answering by the arrival of plates of spring rolls and assorted rice paper rolls.

'If you were styling these, how would you do it?' Jake asked.

I looked at the plates in front of us and thought for a few seconds. 'I think we need some beers, and then I'd take the shot from above so it looks more feast-like, but I'd first turn the fresh rolls over so we can see through the rice paper – it is rice paper, isn't it?' He nodded. 'I'd turn them over so we can see the prawns inside, and cut a couple in half and pile them on top so we can see all the filling. As for the deep-fried ones, I'd have the platter in soft focus and a hand dipping a roll into the chilli sauce – but capture it on the way out with the sauce dripping.'

'Okay then,' he handed me his camera, 'you do it. Those ideas sound better than what I was going to do.' He signalled to the waiter for a couple of beers.

I took the camera hesitantly. 'Are you sure? I'd hate to stuff up the pictures for you.' Even as I said it, my fingers were itching to arrange the plates and click the shutter.

'It's fine. If the images aren't what I need we can come back tomorrow and do it all again.'

We set the food up as I wanted and I quickly took the shot. I even took a couple with my phone to post on my Instagram page. Now that Jake knew I was following him there was no point in hiding away.

'You really do have a good eye for composition,' he said as he looked through the images. 'These are much better than I could have done.'

'I doubt that very much.' I reached for another spring roll, delighting in the crunch of the flaky pastry and the sweet spice of the chilli sauce. Thank goodness we were doing a lot of walking today.

'I'm serious, Tiff. I have enough technical knowledge that I can churn out photos that keep my

editor happy, but your talent seems to come naturally.'
I felt my cheeks grow warm at the compliment. 'Why
did you put your gear away and give it up?'

'As I said to you before – life got serious and I got
sensible.'

Before he could ask more questions, our next
dish arrived – plates of little meat patties, vermicelli
noodles, herbs and dipping sauces. I leaned over the
table so I could inhale their fragrance, looking up only
when I heard the click of a shutter.

'You'd better not be using that,' I warned.

'Nope,' said Jake. 'This one's for my private
collection.'

'Hmmm. I'm not sure I like the sound of that
either.'

But I did like the idea of Jake looking at a photo
of me very much. Maybe even … no, Tiff, get that
picture out of your mind! When I snuck a glance at him
his smile told me that he knew exactly what I'd been
thinking and he liked the idea just as much as I did.

To bring us back on to safer ground, I asked about
the food. 'Tell me about this dish.'

'This is bun cha. Essentially, it's chargrilled pork
patties with a sweet and sour dipping broth. You put
some noodles into the bowl with the pork, add the
herbs and pour the broth over the top.'

'Yum. Is the food really like this in Vietnam?'

'The street food we get here is pretty similar,

although we don't have access to some of the herbs they use and we don't have an appetite for some of the more, shall we say, exotic ingredients. Take this dish for example. In Hanoi it's served on a plate and the dipping sauce is exactly that. In Hoi An, though, in Central Vietnam, it's served this way – in a bowl with a broth. Same same but different.' He grinned. 'You hear that saying a lot over there – same same but different.'

I'd taken a picture of the dish as it was presented to us, but as Jake was talking he was also putting together his bun cha. I snapped away, capturing his hand dropping herbs into the bowl and the broth being poured over.

As we ate, we chatted about the places Jake had been and the different foods he'd tried.

'Don't you ever get sick of it?' I asked.

He was silent for a few seconds as he pondered my question. 'I don't know. I've been scammed over the years; I've been pickpocketed in Paris, and again in Rome when I fell for exactly the same move. I've been delayed in places I didn't want to be delayed in, and there've been times when I've eaten things I didn't want to be eating. Let me tell you, it is not at all fun to be in a backpacker hostel in Kuta with a bad dose of Bali belly.'

I laughed. 'I can imagine. Actually, I don't want to imagine.'

'Trust me, that's a picture you're much better off not having in your head. There are times when the queuing and the delays and the waiting at airports or for connections to somewhere or other get me down, but do I ever get tired of it?' He shook his head. 'I can't say that I do. The getting there doesn't worry me – I'm that person who doesn't complain about plane food, can stand in a queue without whining, and can curl up in an economy seat and sleep for the whole trip. I still feel the same excitement every time I step out to explore a new city as I did when I took my first trip overseas back when I was nineteen. It was during the long uni break in July and I took off for Europe with a backpack and not nearly enough money. And I meet so many interesting people along the way – present company included.' He grinned that wicked grin of his and I found myself smiling back. 'I'm lucky to be making a good living doing what I love.'

I must have looked doubtful because he added, 'I mightn't make a lot of money by your standards, but I'm comfortable. I can pay my bills and my mortgage and I'm doing okay. Don't make the mistake of thinking that because I live simply I don't live well.'

Although he was still smiling at me, his tone left me in no doubt that I was being put in my place – along with the assumptions I'd made about him.

I nodded and said, 'I'm sorry,' surprising myself with the words. 'What about luxuries?'

'Like what?'

I hesitated. Luxuries for me were shoes, handbags and the brands I wore to keep up with the likes of

Ainsley. I supposed that Matt would have similar items on his list – without the handbags, of course. But Jake? He wouldn't have need of those things. Jake was like no one I'd met before; and he'd managed to quash every judgment I'd previously made about him. So rather than answer, I shrugged.

'A luxury for me,' he went on, 'is a surprise upgrade, or when a client wants to me to review somewhere five-star. What I do like is to splurge occasionally on a really good meal somewhere.'

I spluttered the beer I'd just taken a sip of. 'But didn't you say –'

'That I love street food and don't need the foams and smears and some of the other unnecessary stuff they do to food?'

'Yes. That's what you told me in Hong Kong.'

'And it's true. Street food for me gets to the heart of the place I'm in. I love it all – the noise, the crowds, the smells, sitting shoulder to shoulder with someone on a stool meant for a five year old at a communal table in the street. But I also like blowing a ridiculous amount of money occasionally on a starred foodie experience complete with the dress-ups and the pretension.' He laughed at the look on my face. 'Having problems keeping me in the box you'd put me in?'

'Yes,' I said simply. What I didn't tell him was that my first instincts about him were proving to be correct: he was trouble, both in bed and out of it.

CHAPTER TEN

The rest of the afternoon flew in a whirl of banter, photos and food. Our next stop was down at the St Kilda end of Chapel Street where we sampled bahn mi – a Vietnamese-style baguette sandwich; mini bowls of pho bo – aromatic beef noodle soup; and fried chicken wings in a chilli sauce. And more beer. I continued to snap the photos, my confidence growing with every shot – and, I suspected, every beer.

At one point I struggled to hold in a beer burp and Jake roared with laughter. 'You're not normally a beer drinker, are you?'

I considered coming back with a smart retort but decided that the whole idea of me both drinking and belching beer was actually pretty funny – as long as I didn't happen to run into anyone I knew.

In between restaurants we caught trams, getting off when Jake thought there was some place interesting I should see, or a great example of street art. He said he was considering putting together an article on street art, so I captured the images for him. We walked, we talked, and we laughed. At one point he threw his arm around my shoulders and I didn't shake it off.

We didn't stray into personal territory until we were relaxing at our final restaurant in one of the alleys in the city near Bourke Street Mall. I'd given up on the beer and was sipping at a white wine. Jake was flicking through the images I'd taken.

'These are great, Tiff. Really great.' He paused and looked across at me. 'With raw talent like yours you could probably have turned it into a career. What happened?'

His eyes bored into mine and it felt as though he had a spotlight trained on me and could see right into my soul. I didn't know whether it was the beer and the wine, or the food, or the fact that we'd been walking and talking all day, but where I would normally have avoided the question or come back with a smart comment, I did neither of those things.

'I always wanted to be a photographer; all the way through high school it was what I was going to do. Then just before I finished my final year my parents separated. Mum took an important job in Perth, and because there was no question of me leaving before I finished my exams, I stayed in Brisbane with Dad. I wouldn't have gone anyway – my friends were in Brisbane and my father was devastated. He couldn't look after us, so I had to. He used to sit in his studio every day and stare at blank canvases.'

'You obviously get your creativity from him.'

I managed a half-smile. 'Maybe. But I get my business savvy and my practicality from my mother. Dad fell apart, you see. When she left he was unable to work because his emotions were too closely tied into his art. I know that's why he's as good as he is, but that knowledge doesn't help when there's no money coming in because there's no work going out. He wasn't as well-known back then, of course. I think that was the real problem – Mum wanted more than he could offer. She was ambitious and he wasn't. She planned for the future and he didn't. She fell in love with the creative free spirit that he was, but he wasn't who she needed, and he couldn't make her happy. I think he knew that she'd looked at him and their life together and found it wanting on so many different levels.'

'What did that have to do with your career choice though?'

'I knew that if I wanted the nice things in life I'd have to pay for them myself; and that wasn't going to come from photography – at least not in a hurry. I vowed that I was never going to allow myself to care so deeply about someone that I gave them the power to break me. Mostly though I never wanted anyone to look at me with the disappointment that Mum must have felt with her choice.'

'Don't you mean that you didn't want your mother to look at you with disappointment?' Jake said softly.

I stared at him, unsure whether it was his insight that rattled me or the fact that I'd told him as much as I had about something I'd never even discussed with Alice and Callie. To this day I didn't think they knew why I'd put my camera away.

'I don't know,' I finally admitted.

'Are you still in touch with your mother?'

'Absolutely. She did what she needed to do to get to where she wanted to go. As I've gotten older, I've understood it more. She's super busy so we don't talk much – maybe every few weeks, once a month. It's been a while since I've seen her.'

'What about your father?'

'Dad met someone else about a year after Mum left. Mary's so different to Mum. She's a bit like Dad – totally free-spirited. She's a potter and makes those ceramic keep-cups to cut down on coffee cup waste. She's been making them for years, way before they became fashionable. Together they're absolutely hopeless with money so it's fortunate that Dad's paintings began to sell well. Once he fell in love again, the work flowed and sold. Maybe knowing that he could never be enough for Mum had held him back – I don't know. He and Mary finally got married a couple of months ago. I don't know who was more surprised – Mary, that he'd finally got around to asking her; or Dad, that she actually said yes. The last I heard they were in one of the Channel Islands. I have no idea when they'll be home. That's Dad, I guess.'

I didn't tell him how disappointed Dad had been when I turned my back on my creativity. It was only with the hindsight of maturity that I understood he'd probably seen my switch from visual arts to business as a similar slap in the face to the one my mother had dealt him. While he'd never said anything to me, it must have seemed to him that I'd also declared his life and his work not good enough.

'Anyway, none of that matters now,' I said. 'It's all been for the best, and I haven't looked back.'

'Haven't you?' Jake asked.

I shook my head. 'Absolutely not. I've worked hard to get to where I am, and my next promotion will be the one I've worked all these years to achieve. I'll be going to Masters at the end of July – that's an all-expenses-paid conference I desperately want an invite to – and then I want my boss's job. And I intend to get it. No, I have no regrets at all.'

He raised his eyebrows at my vehemence. 'I get it: you have no regrets about your career choice. But what about love?'

'What about it? It's not something I want or need. I manage quite well without it.'

'How can you not want love? Surely everyone does.'

'What for?'

He grinned at first, as if he thought I was joking. Once he realised I was serious the look in his eyes changed to something else – something I couldn't read.

'I don't know,' he said, 'for connection, discovery, adventure, partnership, warmth. That feeling that there's one person in the world who you want to see – or at least talk to – each day. The rush when they call; the knowledge that they're the first thing that comes to your mind each morning and the last thing to leave it at night. Someone to celebrate the good with and to share the crap of the bad. All of that – and more.'

There was something in what he'd said, the way he said it, that left me speechless and muddled. That's the only excuse I can find for my response; for the way I laughed derisively and said, 'You didn't mention sex in that list, and yet that's the only thing my friends can't give me. Everything else is a short cut to heartbreak, and I don't have the time or the energy to deal with that. Take my friend Alice as an example – she fell in love and the next thing you know she's lost her job. Then there's Callie – she's always in love, or what she thinks love is, which usually involves her crying her eyes out while the man she's been trying to hold onto cheats on her. Cal's a smart woman but love turns her into someone who puts everything on hold – her career, her hopes and dreams, everything – for whichever man she's with at the time.'

'But you know better?' There was something in his tone that I should have heeded.

'Yes, I think I do.'

'It sounds like you don't believe in love.'

I shook my head. 'I don't think I do. I get the lust

thing, but that passes. Well, usually.' I chanced a smile at him, but he wasn't smiling back.

'Have you ever been in love?' he said.

I deliberately avoided the question. 'It's just that I have a goal, and men tend to get in the way of goals – so I don't let them.'

'Has there been anyone … umm, regular?' he persisted.

'Recently?' He nodded. 'Well, Alice's brother Matt – in Hong Kong. But that seems to have petered out.' I shrugged to let him know that I didn't care it had.

'So, let me get this clear,' he said. 'You don't date, and you don't believe in love. It's just about a series of hook-ups for you – preferably with men who won't get attached and won't distract you from your main purpose.'

'I wouldn't put it quite that way,' I started.

'Wouldn't you? If that is the case, what are you even doing out with me today? I thought we'd had a good time. Has that all been an act?'

'No. Of course not. I … I've had a good day … with you. I've eaten more carbs than I'd usually eat in a month, but it's been a good day.' I smiled to let him know I meant it, but the twinkle was still missing from his eyes. I tried again. 'What about you? Have you ever been in love?'

'Absolutely.' His eyes bored into mine.

I wanted to ask him who with and what was she like. I wanted to ask him how fast he'd fallen for her, or whether it was something that grew over time. I wanted to ask whether he was over her, but none of those words came out. Instead I told him I was tired. 'It's been a big day. I think I might go home.'

He nodded. 'Yes, I think that's a good idea.'

In the cab on the way to my place he was quieter than I'd ever known him to be. There was none of the banter we'd had during the day. None of the teasing glances and accidental touches that had set my pulse racing. He sat on the other side of the seat from me and looked out the window. I deliberately let my hand stray towards the middle of the seat, hoping he might stretch out his pinky finger to meet mine. But the space between us remained.

At my block he asked the driver to wait while he walked me to my door. When we got there, I waited for his wicked smile, for him to suggest running back to pay the driver and tell him to be on his way – but neither came.

'I really have had a good day,' I told him.

'So have I,' he said finally with a half-smile.

I stepped closer so that my breasts touched his chest. 'Do you want to come in?'

He shook his head. 'No. I don't.'

'But …?'

'Don't get me wrong, Tiff. I want you – very much. But I said I wasn't sleeping with you tonight and I meant it.'

'But why? I thought you were joking.'

'I know you did, but I'm serious.'

I stepped back and looked into his eyes. Yes, that twinkle was still gone.

'I like you, Tiff – and I know you well enough now to know that even saying that is likely to send you running. The thing is, I think you like me too – so the way I figure it, I have three options. One, we don't sleep together any more but stay friends so we can take fabulous photos together. Two, we treat this as a relationship – as in we date and get to know each other just like normal people do – and take fabulous photos together. Or three, we never see each other again – which would be a great pity indeed.' He bent down and kissed my lips. 'You think about it.' Then he pulled back and turned to leave.

'Will I see you tomorrow?' I said, then grimaced as the words sounded almost desperate to my ears.

Jake turned back towards me. 'That's up to you.'

'And if I don't call?'

'No problem. I'll go to the football with Todd, the friend I'm staying with.'

I felt strangely disappointed that he had a back-up plan, that he hadn't banked on spending the day with me.

'And I really can't tempt you to stay tonight?' I took a couple of steps towards him until there were mere centimetres between us, and felt his body drawing mine closer as if we were caught in some type of magnetic field.

He closed the gap and took my head in his hands, allowing me to feel just how much he wanted me too. He kissed me again, hard and fast. 'Oh, you can tempt me alright. But I'm not giving in – as much as you know I want to. It's not just about the sex any more for me, Tiff. I enjoyed the time we spent together in Hong Kong, and I've really enjoyed today. I want to get to know more of you – all of you – but that's up to you.' He released me and stepped away. 'I have the feeling though that you don't really want to get to know me in case you find that you like me too much.'

'It's not like that,' I protested.

'Isn't it? Goodnight, Tiff, sleep well. Hopefully I'll talk to you tomorrow.'

With that he turned and walked back to the waiting taxi, and I let myself into my empty apartment.

It *had* been a good day until the conversation took that serious turn. I'd tried to lighten things up again and he'd stepped back. There was a message in what he'd said, but I'd missed it – and something I'd said had made him pull away from me. I wished I'd been able to tell him what he wanted to hear – that I liked him too. If I had done, he'd be here with me now. And even though no man had ever spent the whole night in my bed, I would have let Jake stay.

I remembered what he'd said about thinking I had

talent, and even now his words warmed me. Maybe I could take up photography again, just as a hobby.

In my spare room I pulled the suitcase back out from under the bed and opened it. Under the camera was a cardboard folder. Sitting on the bed, I opened it. Inside were enlarged prints of some of my favourite photos, all of them bright and full of life. There were the images I'd taken at the Ekka, Brisbane's annual agricultural show. Here was a photo of the ferris wheel at night, taken using a tripod and leaving the shutter open for long enough to create a brightly coloured blur. I'd done something similar with the sideshow-alley game where people tried to get balls inside the mouths of a row of clowns. There were photos of Callie and Alice laughing as they whirred around in one of the rides; and a close-up of a border collie maintaining eye contact with the sheep he was intent on mustering into the yard in the sheepdog trials.

There were other pictures I'd taken in and around Brisbane – the Story Bridge at all times of the day; the bright pink of the bougainvillea in the Grand Arbour at South Bank – and a whole wad of photos taken one spring when we went to Toowoomba for the annual garden show. I must have been sixteen or seventeen and it was probably one of the last day trips we'd taken together as a family. I couldn't remember the day itself clearly now, but imagined that I'd probably sat resentfully in the back seat of the car until the colour of the blooms and the call of the lens distracted me. In those days I was rarely without my camera. I wondered now whether I would have appreciated the day more if I'd known it would be the last time we'd all be together like that, but doubted it. That's not how you think when you're that age.

At the back of the folder was a separate envelope. I knew without looking inside what it held – my final-year art project for school, the one I'd planned my future on. I took a deep breath and opened it.

There were suitcases on the luggage carousel at Brisbane airport; an old man sitting on a park bench with all his worldly belongings in garbage bags; a battered backpack with hiking shoes tied to the straps; and a window display of old-fashioned Louis Vuitton travelling chests, like those you'd see wheeled onto the Orient Express or the first-class cabin of a cruise ship. The story behind the images was that bags contained their owner's baggage – whether it was the excitement of a holiday, the adventure of the trail, the joy of coming home, the hope of a new home, the hopelessness of no home. All those emotions.

Even as I put the finishing touches to the project that had consumed most of the last two years of my school life, I knew it would be the last time I showed my photography. I'd added the final image the day before the work was due to be submitted – the bag Dad used to transport his paintings in, with blank canvases peeking out the top, a blank canvas on his easel, and clean brushes on a paint-free palette. I'd printed it in black and white because it felt to me as though Mum had taken all the colour in the world away with her. There wasn't any left for Dad's canvases and there wasn't any left for my photographs.

As I looked at the glossy images spread out on the bed, their colours bright and almost jarring against the white quilt cover, I wondered what Jake would say if I asked him to look at them. But how could I when I'd already lied to him about keeping any of my work?

Shaking my head, I shoved all the pictures back into the folder and piled everything back into the suitcase. I should have gotten rid of these years ago.

Jake had said that what happened next was up to me. He'd said that I didn't want to get to know him in case I decided I liked him too much.

In that respect he was very wrong. I had the feeling I was already there, and it terrified me.

CHAPTER ELEVEN

I didn't call Jake, yet spent all day wishing I had. Which, I figured, only went to show that I'd made the right decision not to phone.

Alice rang mid-morning to fill me in on the trivia night she and Callie had been to.

'There were parts of it that were hilarious. The announcer – who called himself the Quiz Master – thought he was on afternoon television and spoke in exclamation marks all night. Tommy hadn't told me we needed to bring our own snacks, so I was completely starved by the time we finished. Cal was on fire though. There were a few questions about boy bands and eighties' music trivia –'

'Cal would have been in her element,' I cut in.

'She was. There was one thing though – she ran into Jamie. He was there with a group from his work, I think. He told Cal how good she was looking and that he owed her an explanation. You really shouldn't have taken her for that haircut.'

'I was just trying to help with her confidence,' I

said. 'A good haircut and a style makeover will do that.'

'Anyway, he's asked her out and they're having dinner on Thursday night.'

'Crap. How was she about it?'

'She claims she said yes because of Project Yes, but I think she just needs to know. Do the whole closure thing, you know?'

'Hmmm, I hope she's careful,' I said. 'I don't want to be picking up the pieces again.'

Alice groaned. 'You know Cal's never had any self-control where Jamie's concerned. How was your date?'

'I told you yesterday, it wasn't really a date. I was just meeting him because he was in town. Project Yes and all that – I couldn't say no.'

'You called it a date the other night.'

'Did I? Anyway, I won't be seeing him again I don't think.' I scratched at an itch under my watchband that had been irritating me all morning. 'He says he wants to get to know me, even though right from the start I told him this thing, whatever it was, was just about sex.' I took my watch off and rubbed at the red welt I'd created with my nails. 'Besides, I don't want to talk about Jake Stewart any more.'

'Don't you? Then you won't want to know that he credited you with a photo in his article today. You didn't tell me you'd picked up the camera again.'

'I haven't. He handed his over a couple of times during that tour we met on, that's all.'

'Really?' She sounded sceptical. 'Well, he obviously considered the image good enough to include with his story – unless he's trying to tell you something?'

'I don't think so.' My other wrist was itching now. 'What about you? Did you end up going home with Tommy last night?'

'I sure did.' I could hear her smile.

'How was it?'

'Great. I'd forgotten just how much I missed sex. Stella wasn't really happy to have him there, but other than that it was all very nice indeed. All that tapping on keyboards has made him, umm, quite dextrous. Anyway,' she said with a laugh, 'I'd better go. Mac's due to pick up Kevin.'

It was only after she rang off that I realised I still hadn't told her about seeing Luke. I debated calling back, but decided the information could wait until next time. Maybe by then she'd be distracted enough by Tommy to not react to the news that I'd spoken to Luke.

I pulled out the travel lift-out that I'd studiously avoided looking at all morning. There it was: Jake's review of the tour we'd done, and underneath the photo of the beach fisherman were the words: *Photo by Tiffany Samuels*. It was ridiculous but seeing my name on his article sent a rush of pride through me.

I picked up my phone to call and thank him, then put it down again. No, I wasn't going to call. I might text later. Maybe. When he couldn't mistake it as being anything other than a thank you text.

By early afternoon, calling Jake was all I could think about. That and the weird itch that felt as though it was crawling all over my body. I contemplated doing another Bikram class but, being Sunday, my usual yoga studio was closed. Instead I took myself shopping in Chapel Street. A new pair of shoes might help take my mind off both Jake and the itch.

In the end I spent a ridiculous amount of money on two fitted sleeveless dresses – one in black and white and another in a textured pale grey. To go with them I bought two tight-fitting zip-fronted jackets – one black with a cute little peplum, and another in the same textured grey as the dress. As I was paying for my purchases, I spied a pencil skirt in a blue so deep it went beyond navy into ocean blue. Over the top of the navy was a floral lace design in the same blue and emerald green, with a narrow red stripe piped up the side seam. It was the type of skirt that I'd never normally wear in the office, but it was beautiful. I recalled Jake's comment yesterday about how I could replenish my wardrobe of black, grey and neutral suits if I went to Vietnam with him – and on impulse added the skirt to my pile. I even allowed the sales consultant to talk me into a sleeveless silk blouse in the same red as the stripe. Bloody Jake.

As I walked back home with my bags, I was distracted by a sign in the window of a travel agency. It was advertising package holidays to Vietnam. Before

I could talk myself out of it, I'd gone inside and asked for a brochure. After all, it wouldn't hurt to look.

I'd just left the shop when I heard someone call my name. Looking around I spied my friend Andi sitting alone in a coffee shop. I hadn't seen her in a while – not since our mutual friend Abby's birthday drinks back in early April. At the time, Andi had just finished with her married lover and Abby had broken up with Brad, the man we all thought she'd be with forever.

I waved and Andi waved back, indicating for me to join her.

As she kissed me hello she said, 'Are you going somewhere?'

'Sorry?'

'The travel brochure,' she clarified.

I shook my head. 'No, I don't think so. A friend mentioned Vietnam, but ... Anyway it's great to see you. It's been ages.' I rolled up the brochure and poked it inside one of my shopping bags.

'I know. Abby's birthday drinks back in April – we were heading off to Bali the following day. Both of us were more than a tad worse for wear on that flight.'

'You'd just broken up with Jason, and Abby –' Andi's face fell as I mentioned Jason. 'What is it?' I said.

'Jason and I got back together after that – he called me when I was in Bali. But we've broken up again, for the last time. He's never going to leave his wife for me.'

'No, Andi, he isn't.'

Andi was a lawyer and an intelligent woman, but another of my friends who wasn't so smart when it came to men. She had a talent for falling hard and fast for men who, it later turned out, already belonged to other women. Then when she did find out, she was already in too deep and waited around for them to leave their wife – which, of course, they never did. Either her radar was deficient, or subconsciously she deliberately fell for men she couldn't have.

'Next time I'm going to insist on a full background check before I get involved with anyone,' she said.

I laughed and asked about Abby. 'How's she doing? Did you guys have a great time in Bali?'

'We did.' Her face clouded over. 'I just wish she and Brad would sort themselves out. I can't believe it's over completely for them. If ever there were two people meant to be together it's them.'

I nodded in agreement. Abby and Brad had known each other when they were children and reunited many years later. Abby, like me, was single-minded when it came to her career yet somehow had managed to make it work with Brad – who was a landscape gardener – and still stay on partner track at her firm. I didn't know what had gone wrong between them, but hoped that when Brad came back from Denmark, where he was doing some sort of landscaping sabbatical, they'd be able to make things right again.

'What about you?' Andi asked. 'Are you seeing

anyone at the moment?'

I shook my head, 'No, not really.'

'You know, I admire the way you can separate the whole sex and love thing,' she said. 'I tend to do the opposite – fall in love so I can justify the sex. But you seem to just manage it. Abby and I always say that the day you meet someone who ticks none of your boxes yet makes you laugh will be the day you fall hard.'

'What do you mean, ticks none of my boxes?'

'On that checklist of yours.' As I went to open my mouth, Andi laughed. 'Don't deny it, Tiff. You have a checklist that's so impossible to comply with no guy will ever be able to meet all your conditions – and that's exactly the way you like it. That way you can stay in control. It's why you keep things to sex only – in case you actually get to know someone and find that you like him, or worse might fall in love with him.'

'I don't do that. Do I?' Wasn't that almost exactly what Jake had said to me last night?

Andi grinned. 'Maybe not deliberately, but that's exactly what you do. You form an opinion of someone at your first meeting, then prefer not to get to know them in case that opinion doesn't turn out to be right.'

'My first impressions are rarely wrong,' I said, but even as I said it I thought how wrong I'd been about Jake.

'You don't give them a chance to be wrong,' Andi said. 'Look, I'm sorry, Tiff – it probably sounds like

I'm having a go at you and I'm really not.' She smiled an apology. 'It's definitely me today and not you. It's been so long since we caught up and here I am being all judgmental because you've been smart enough to stick to your guns and look after your heart when I've thrown mine away.' She paused. 'Maybe I'm a teeny bit envious of you because of that.'

I smiled back to let her know she hadn't upset me. 'It's okay, Andi, I get it. And it's been great to see you – but I'd better get home.'

On the way back to my apartment I thought about what Andi had said. It was true that once I formed an opinion about someone, I didn't give them an opportunity to change it. Why would I? I was normally right. But Jake had managed to sneak through that net somehow, and was continuing to surprise me. I might kid myself I'd kept him at arms-length, but he'd already gotten under my skin – why else would I have told him private things I'd never even told the girls? Even the way he'd left me last night was unexpected. I'd thought I could change his mind, or, rather, seduce him into changing his mind; by walking away he'd proved that he liked me for me, not just for how we were together in bed.

I thought about yesterday – that frisson of excitement every time we touched or our eyes met; the way he knew exactly how to leave me dizzy from his kisses and boneless with desire – but there'd also been a really simple enjoyment in sharing the experience of the day. Finally, there was his generosity in giving me a photo credit on his article. He didn't have to do that – no one except me would have known any different – yet he'd obviously felt it was the right thing to do.

I didn't know what this was with Jake yet – and I definitely wasn't going to fall in love with him – but I wasn't ready to let go of him either. Not yet.

I sent him a text: *Thanks for the photo credit – that was a lovely surprise to wake up to.*

His reply came back quickly: *You're welcome. How was your day?*

Good. And the football?

Great. The Tigers won!!!!

I'm pleased for you. I hesitated before typing my next message: *I have to be in Sydney on Thursday and Friday. If I stay for the weekend, would you like to catch up?*

Like in a date?

Yes. Like in a date.

In that case I'd like it very much.

As I put my phone down, I realised that I was smiling – widely.

CHAPTER TWELVE

Jake took my message as encouragement to ring or text me each day through the week. I supposed that was what people did when they were dating, but it wasn't something I was used to. But as much as the pinging of my phone was distracting, it didn't stop me from smiling each time I saw his name on my screen.

On Thursday morning he texted when I was in a meeting with Ainsley and the Sydney-based branch-closure project team. Ainsley had been in town all week and I'd flown into Sydney that morning.

I'm booked to do a story on Cockatoo Island and the shipbuilding history. I was thinking I could do it on Saturday when you're here. What do you say? Interested in shooting the images for me?

Ainsley was in the middle of delivering a lecture to Shannon, the project lead, about the communication plan for one of the closures in suburban Melbourne. 'I don't think I need to remind you about our zero media tolerance on this matter,' she said. 'I don't want to read about this in either mainstream or social media.'

That sounds great. I've never been to Cockatoo Island. Do we catch the ferry over?

Yeah … unless you want to go the other way.

I coughed to hide the giggle that escaped. It was an island – of course we got there by water. I sent back a line of laughing face emoticons.

Ainsley's attention suddenly turned to me. 'Is everything alright, Tiffany? I trust you're completely across the communication plan?'

'Absolutely,' I said. 'Shannon's done a great job coordinating the change management for this. All the clients should receive letters this week advising them of the closure and where their nearest branch is. The closure leaflets have been posted at the branches too and –'

She cut me off. 'What about the staff? Are they aware of what they shouldn't say?'

I smiled thinly. 'That's a little more difficult to control given some of them will be losing their jobs as a result of this.'

'I don't care how difficult that is to control. Shannon, what's the latest date we can communicate to the employees?'

My phone pinged again. *We can be like Jack and Rose on the ferry.*

Jack and Rose? Who are they?

'The employees will need to be told at the same time as we communicate to clients,' Shannon said. 'We can't risk clients finding out before the employees do.'

Titanic, you heathen.

'Do you find this funny, Tiffany?'

'No, not at all, Ainsley.' I told myself to get a grip. This was why I didn't date – the potential for unprofessional distraction was too great.

'Do I need to remind you that this stops with you?' she went on. 'To be crystal clear – anything adverse in the media and … Well, I don't think I need to spell it out, do I, Tiffany?'

'Actually, as general manager of this division the buck stops with you, Ainsley.'

As soon as the words were out, I knew I shouldn't have said them. I heard sharp intakes of breath around the room as everyone else suddenly became very interested in the paperwork in front of them. But now the words were out …

'Maybe you should spell out the consequences for the minutes,' I added. 'Just so we're all as clear about this as you are.'

'I'm sure we'll be fine with the employees,' Shannon said awkwardly as Ainsley and I continued to stare at each other. 'They've been kept updated through the process, and all redundancies are voluntary. Perhaps we can draft a communication to remind them what they can and can't say on their social media accounts?'

Ainsley's eyes dropped from mine. 'You do that,' she said. 'And make sure you're clear about their responsibilities. Remind them we have a team in the background who constantly run searches on all social media.'

'What are you going to threaten them with if they breach that communication?' I asked. 'They've already lost their jobs.'

I deliberately ignored Shannon who was trying to catch my eye to warn me to hold my tongue.

'That's not my problem, Tiffany, it's yours,' Ainsley said tightly. 'As the senior manager in change control, if any of this hits the mainstream media you'll be the one looking for another job. Are we clear?'

Ainsley was making it clear that this wasn't over, not by a long shot. My words today had been tantamount to an open declaration of war. I should have been concerned, but I wasn't. What I did know was that from now on I couldn't afford a single misstep – but then nor could she.

'As crystal,' I said.

'Good. Now, Shannon, tell me how you'll be dealing with the removal of the branding on the site. What's our timeline there?'

Shannon took me aside after the meeting finished and Ainsley had swept from the room. 'What the absolute fuck was that about?'

I didn't pretend to misunderstand her. 'I was just making my position clear.'

'Oh, it was clear,' she said with a short laugh.

'Ainsley is not a good enemy to have, Tiff.'

'I know that, but neither am I – and I'm tired of watching how she treats people in this company. Everyone in this office is operating under ridiculous amounts of stress just to keep up with her reporting requirements and whatever else she chooses to spring on them. She over-manages to the degree that very few people are confident to do their job – which is exactly how she wants them. I happen to know my job, and so do you. You've project-managed how many of these closures?'

'I hate to think,' said Shannon.

'Exactly. So tell me why you're now questioning your ability? Because you are, aren't you?'

Shannon dropped her head. 'I guess I am.'

'Which is what she wants. It keeps you in your place. That's why she's brought me in to consult on change management when you guys have a strategy that's worked every other time. Not only does it make you question whether that strategy is right, but it gives her a scapegoat – me – if it's not. Sure, I probably shouldn't have said anything to her, and I don't really know why I did, but now I have at least we both know where we stand.'

'Just watch your back, hey?' she said quietly. 'You're the only one brave enough to stand up to her, so if you're gone, we'll have no one.'

A lump rose to my throat and I swallowed it back. 'You'll be fine,' I said, hearing the gruffness in my voice.

'Just keep doing your job and you'll be okay.'

Shannon gave me a quick smile as if she knew that she'd embarrassed me. 'I have to say, that skirt you're wearing is next level,' she said. 'It's completely business-like, especially with the white blouse, but that red stripe up the side is kick-arse. Maybe,' she added with an arch look, 'you channelled that red stripe to basically stick your finger up at Ainsley.'

I grinned back at her. 'Maybe I did.'

I called Jake when I got back to the hotel that night. We chatted about the day – as we'd done each night this week – but hadn't made plans to see each other before Saturday.

Just before he hung up I took a deep breath and said, 'Do you want to meet for dinner tomorrow night? After work?' When he didn't say anything I added, 'It's okay. I understand if you're busy. I just thought you might like to, and I might like to … And, god, this is hard!'

'Tiff! Enough already. I'd like to meet you for dinner tomorrow night. Okay?'

'Okay.'

We arranged to meet in the lobby of my building in George Street and from there we'd walk to the restaurant – an Asian place that had earned itself a couple of stars for both its authentic street food and its creativity. I hoped Jake would see that I'd tried to choose somewhere that suited both of us – a little bit of him in the street food, and a little bit of me in the status.

The next evening, I looked at myself in the office bathroom mirror before going down to meet him. I took my glasses off and let my hair out of its high ponytail so it looked more casual, but couldn't hide the kink from where I'd had it up all day. I compromised and put it back in its elastic, but lower so it wasn't so businesslike and perky. I hadn't been this nervous about meeting a man since … well, since I could remember. It was no wonder I didn't date. Sex was so much easier.

Jake was sitting in one of the chairs in the lobby. When I stepped out of the lift, the grin that caused me so much trouble spread across his face.

He kissed my lips lightly in greeting. 'No dreadful business suit?'

I was wearing a pair of tailored black skinny pants, a white shell top, black heels and the grey textured jacket I'd bought the other day.

'Casual Friday,' I said.

'That's casual?'

'As casual as I'll ever get for the office.'

'At least you've ditched the glasses you don't even need,' he said, grinning, 'so I suppose I can't complain. I really don't like those glasses.'

'I would never have known.' I smiled at him, suddenly feeling happier than I had all week.

When I led us across the road and up the little

alley into the restaurant, he recognised it immediately and laughed. 'A little bit of me and a little bit of you. Great choice, I love it!'

Once we'd ordered drinks, I fiddled with the menu and the chopsticks, suddenly finding it difficult to speak. 'This is nice,' I managed, looking around the space so I didn't need to look into his eyes. 'I like how they've left some of the walls exposed. It's a real boho mix of grunge and luxe, don't you think?'

He smiled and reached across the table for my hand. His thumb traced the red line where I'd scratched at myself. 'What's this?'

'I don't know. Just a rash or something.'

His head tilted to the side as he searched my eyes. His thumb had moved on from my irritated skin and now drew circles on my wrist, relaxing me, yet at the same time sending shivers of sensation running through my veins. I dropped my eyes from his.

'It's okay,' he said. 'Just because we've called this a date doesn't mean we need to be different with each other. Besides,' his grin turned wicked, 'I fully intend sleeping with you tonight, so the pressure's off to impress me. I'm pretty much what you'd call a sure thing.'

A laugh escaped me. 'Thanks for that, but I haven't told you yet about Alice's three-date rule.'

He frowned dramatically. 'Three-date rule? Please tell me that's not what it sounds like?'

I lifted one shoulder and adopted a look of mock resignation. 'Yes, it's exactly as it sounds – we can't sleep together until we've been on three dates. That's the rule according to Alice – and she makes all the rules.'

'Wow, if I'd known that before I suggested we date ...' He thought for a few seconds. 'Don't we get some sort of special dispensation for already having had a few one-night stands?'

'I don't know,' I said slowly, as if I was seriously considering his request. 'I don't make the rules.'

'What if we say that last Saturday was a date, and we know tonight is one, and we've already agreed that we're calling tomorrow an official date as well – so we only need to wait until tomorrow. In fact, we could call the dumpling night in Hong Kong a date too, which means we're actually ahead of the game.'

I sat back in my chair and took a sip of the martini that had been delivered during our conversation. 'You have a point, although you did make a big deal last week of telling me that Saturday was absolutely not a date – just as you did the dumpling night. I'm sorry, Jake, but you seem to be hoist by your own words.'

He reached for his beer and made a show of turning his eyes to the ceiling as if searching for inspiration. 'You're right.' He sighed deeply. 'There's no way around it. Unless – and I'm not sure how you'll feel about this – we just don't tell Alice.'

'Now, why didn't I think of that?' I said. 'Besides,

seeing as how the girls and I are doing Project Yes, if you ask me to sleep with you, I have no choice but to agree. Then if the subject comes up, I can tell Alice it was completely out of my hands.'

'Now there's an idea. Do you have to say yes to everything?'

'As long as it's safe, legal and consensual.'

He grinned. 'Naturally.'

'It's designed to help Alice and Callie push their boundaries a little,' I explained.

'And you?'

'I'm just along for the ride.'

That wicked twinkle was flickering in his eyes. 'Oh, I think we can manage a little boundary-pushing of our own.'

When we left the restaurant to walk back to my hotel, he reached for my hand to hold it. 'Can I?' he asked.

'Only because it's Project Yes,' I replied.

He didn't let go of my hand the whole way back to the hotel. It felt so nice I even rested my head against his shoulder when we stopped at the traffic lights.

CHAPTER THIRTEEN

The rain started while we were on the ferry to Cockatoo Island. Just a drizzle to start with, but enough to (thankfully) prevent Jake's plan of re-enacting Jack and Rose on the *Titanic* on a Sydney ferry. By the time the ferry pulled in at the dock, the rain was pelting down and we had to run for cover.

'Okay,' I said, peering at the rain. 'What do we do now?'

'Well,' Jake looked around, 'we need to get to the shipyards and the tunnels, and they're both across there.' He pointed across the exposed tarmac. 'Given there's no shelter between here and there, and neither of us have an umbrella, I figure we either make a run for it or stay here until it stops – which doesn't look like it's going to be anytime soon.'

'You know what?' I said. 'Let's make a run for it. How wet can we get?'

I couldn't remember the last time I'd been out in the rain without cover. It felt as though I was ten years old again – although there was nothing childlike about the way Jake was looking at me.

'The tunnel?' I said.

'The tunnel. On three ...'

We were off and running, splashing through puddles, our backpacks bouncing around. I reached the tunnel entrance marginally before he did and leaned against the wall, panting from the effort of the sprint, drips from my ponytail making my jumper wet.

When he reached me barely seconds later, I said, 'Nice of you to finally join me.'

He said nothing, just leaned in to kiss me hard, taking away what breath I had left.

'God, you look beautiful,' he said. 'Wild and wet and –'

I cut off his words by kissing him back, walking him backwards until he came up hard against the other wall.

'We have photos to take,' he managed when I finally let him come up for air. 'And you have that new baby of yours to try out.'

'You're right,' I said, pulling reluctantly away from him. I'd spent my lunch break on Wednesday buying a new digital camera and lens that I was aching to try out. 'What's the plan of attack?'

'The piece I've been commissioned to write is on the history of the place, so let's concentrate on the sheds where they built the ships. Some of the old machinery is still in there and with the skylights we should have enough light. If it fines up, we'll head up the stairs to the convict buildings – and there are some more factories up there too.'

'Okay. And if it doesn't fine up?'

'We go home and make love instead.'

A quiver ran through me as I recalled how hard it had been to get out of bed this morning. Thankfully Jake had thought ahead and brought a change of clothes and his camera with him last night, so we didn't need to go via his place this morning. I looked at him watching me as if he could see the thoughts and images racing through my mind and wondered again what it was about this man that had gotten so far under my skin.

He held my face and kissed me again. 'I know,' he said. 'I have no idea either, so let's not think too hard about it, hey? Thinking too much is when the trouble starts.'

There was an edge to his voice, and I searched his face to find a reason for it. When I couldn't, I nodded and stepped away from him. Outside the tunnel, the rain had eased to a soft drizzle. 'Okay, the shipyards it is.'

A couple of hours later, we were sitting under cover in the café, eating a late lunch and looking at each other's photos.

'What is it that you have that I don't?' asked Jake.

'Is that a leading question?'

'Oh, ha ha. No, seriously, Tiff – I'll have a proper look when I get the images onto the computer, but yours have something that mine don't. It's the same photo, but it's also not the same at all.'

I felt my cheeks grow warm and looked around for distraction. The rain was coming down hard again, dripping through the gaps in the plastic screens. At the only other occupied table a birthday party was taking place. It felt a little as though we were intruding.

'Where's your family, Jake?' I said.

His eyes widened, but he didn't express his surprise in any other way at my asking such a personal question. 'My parents live on the family farm in Armidale, in the New England region of New South Wales. Do you know it?'

'I know of it. It's a university town, isn't it?' He nodded. 'What do they farm?'

'Beef cattle – Angus, or Aberdeen Angus as some people call them.' At my blank look he clarified, 'They're black and produce amazing steaks.'

'Okay.' I was none the wiser. 'What about brothers and sisters. Do you have any?'

'I do – one of each. I'm the baby of the family though. My brother Rob helps Dad out on the farm. He's married to Sharon – they have three kids. My sister Melinda is also married, to her high-school boyfriend, Jarrod – they're pregnant with their second child. She's a teacher and came back to Armidale a few years ago.' He smiled as he spoke about his family. 'Jarrod lost his first wife in a car accident, so they also have his daughter from that marriage with them. I think Mel had a few problems with her to begin with – understandably so – but it all seems to have settled down now.'

'You sound close,' I said. 'Are you likely to end up there too?'

'No. I love going home – it's a great town and really beautiful country, although dry at the moment – but I don't belong there. Almost as soon as I could I popped a backpack on and headed out.' He grinned. 'What about you? Any siblings?'

'No, there's just me.'

'That must have been lonely growing up?'

'No. I had Alice and Callie. We always seemed to be at Alice's place with her family.'

'That's Matt that you were talking about before?' There was that edge to his voice again.

'Yes. And their older sister, Laura.' I tilted my head to look at him. 'Don't be jealous, Jake.'

'Of Matt? I'm not.' I continued to hold his gaze. 'Okay, maybe just a little.'

'Please don't. We're not like that.' I didn't know whether I was telling him that Matt and I were no longer like that, or I didn't want Jake to think he and I were like that. I scratched at my wrist again and shook my head slightly. It was time to change the subject. 'Let's get out of here, hey?'

We went to Jake's apartment after Cockatoo Island – or

rather, the apartment he was staying in – so he could change his clothes and drop his gear off. I was hoping for a shower and a clothes dryer. Located near a railway station on the lower north shore, the apartment was as I'd expected – rather drab, without style, features or colour.

'I know,' he said, correctly reading the look on my face. 'It's pretty dismal, isn't it? It's okay as somewhere to stay, but I'm looking forward to getting back to my own place.'

'When is that happening?'

He shrugged. 'A few weeks. The tenants will be out in a fortnight, but I'll be away pretty much through until the middle of June.'

'Where are you this time?'

'New Zealand first. I'm heading to Wellington.'

'How do you keep track of it all?'

He shrugged. 'I just do. I spend one day a month planning six months in advance. Most of the publications I write for have long lead times so six months is about right. I always have some gaps for when commissions drop into my lap – they're the stories that I don't need to pitch. They're usually what we call "famils" – where I'm being paid to review a resort or a hotel, whatever. If I get any of those I try and combine them with other stories. That's what the Wellington trip is: I'll be reviewing a new hotel and combining it with pieces on restaurants and where to go, what to see. The usual.'

'It's not how I imagined,' I conceded.

'You mean you thought I flew from job to job with no idea where my next pay cheque was coming from?'

I nodded but didn't meet his eyes. 'Yes, something like that.'

'At first it was, but I soon worked out that I'd have a very short career if I carried on that way. No, I schedule everything out so I can even out both the income stream and the deadlines. The biggest challenge is keeping track of the invoices – and whether they've been paid. Most of the publications I work with operate on payment thirty days after receipt of copy – that's what they call the article. Some of them, though, pay thirty days after publication. They're also the ones who pay on published words rather than the words commissioned.' He grimaced. 'There's a difference. Thankfully I don't need to work with those publications too much these days.' He reached for me. 'But I didn't bring you here to talk about the business side of my work.'

'What did you bring me here for?' I was already reaching for his head to pull his mouth down to mine.

'To get you out of those wet clothes, of course.'

'I wouldn't want to catch a cold,' I agreed, gasping when I came up for air.

'I'll keep you warm,' he promised.

This time when he kissed me it was as if I'd drunk the smoothest whisky in the world – its liquid heat rushing through my veins, warming the very core of me, and leaving me light-headed and disorientated. I toyed briefly with the idea of trying to dredge up some semblance of control from somewhere until he murmured, 'Don't fight it, sweetheart.'

So I didn't.

CHAPTER FOURTEEN

'You're really not going to say anything about it?' Callie asked, disbelief and suspicion in her voice.

She'd called me yesterday and asked me to meet her for Saturday brunch. Given Alice had already told me she was back with Jamie I'd figured that was the reason for the brunch – so Cal could tell me herself. Normally she'd have roped Alice in as well to make sure she had moral support.

I'd said as much to Jake when he called last night.

'Why would she need moral support? Isn't she one of your best friends?' he'd said.

'Yes, but she knows I won't approve of her being back with Jamie.'

'Do you have to approve?'

'Well, no, but he's already hurt her before, and I know he'll do it again. He's like kryptonite to her – she knows it'll hurt but she still goes there.'

'Which surely is her decision?'

'Yes, but he holds her back and saps her confidence. She'll stop doing the things she wants to do and spend all her time waiting around for him.'

'Which again is her decision,' he said.

'So I just sit around and wait for it to happen?'

'Yes, you do. You need to allow her to work that out for herself.' He was silent for a few seconds. 'It's great that you care, Tiff, but you can't stop her from being hurt. Besides, if you make too big a deal of it, she might stay with him longer just to prove to you that she hasn't made a mistake going back to him.'

I pondered that. 'I hadn't thought about it that way.'

'And now you have?'

'You could be right.'

Now I looked across the table at Callie. Her chin was firm and her shoulders tight, as if she was bracing herself for my judgment.

'Would me saying anything make any difference?' I asked.

Being back with Jamie was what Cal had so desperately wished for over the last few months. Jake was right – reminding her that he was bad news wouldn't make any difference to her. Not only would she ignore what I'd said but I also risked losing her. While I didn't support the relationship, at least I could make sure I was here to pick up the pieces when it was over.

'No, not at all,' she said.

'That's what I thought. You know how I feel about him, but at the end of the day the only one who has to like him is you.'

I forced myself to make my voice warm, although the idea of Jamie breaking her heart into little pieces all over again made me feel anything but warm. I trusted Jamie Aldridge about as far as I could throw him.

'And you really don't mind that we're back together?'

Inwardly I cringed. What sort of friend was I that Callie felt she needed my approval?

I smiled at her. 'It really is none of my business and I just want you to be happy. If Jamie makes you happy that's good enough for me.'

I watched her shoulders and jaw relax once it became obvious I wasn't going to try and talk her out of her new-found happiness.

'In fact, if he's going to be around for a while this time maybe you can organise for us all to get together,' I added.

'I'd like that. Alice can maybe bring Tommy and you can bring Jake.' She paused. 'Are you still seeing Jake?'

'Oh, we're not like that. We're not having a relationship or anything.' I screwed up my nose as if the idea was something I hadn't considered until that moment. 'Besides, he's away again and I'm not sure when he'll be back.'

'Really? When did you last see him?'

'Last weekend in Sydney.'

Although I hadn't seen Jake in a week, we'd spoken

most days. At first, I thought they were calls for phone sex, but Jake made it clear that chatting was all he had in mind. I was going along with it – for now.

'It's moved on from just sex then?' Callie said.

'I'm mucking about with photography a little and he's helping me.'

'More than a little, I'd say. Alice showed me the picture he credited you with the other week. I can't believe you didn't tell us about that.' Cal was watching me for my reaction. 'I'm really glad you've picked up the camera again – I never really understood why you gave it up in the first place. Alice said that next thing we know you'll have an Instagram account.'

I ducked my head so she couldn't see the colour come to my cheeks.

'Oh. My. God. You've got one already! Does Ally know?'

I shook my head. 'Not yet. It's not important.'

'Not important? You're the one who said she'd never have a social media account – that it's too intrusive on your privacy. That's what you said.'

'Perhaps, but this is just a few photos – it's not giving anything away.'

Cal picked up her phone and opened the application. 'What's your username? I'll follow you.'

I hesitated before answering. 'It's sammytii – with a double "i".'

'Very clever. Oh, here you are.' She was silent as

she flicked through the pictures. 'These photos are fabulous, Tiff. Where did you take these?'

'Cockatoo Island.' I found myself leaning over Cal to point out the images. 'Last weekend. It was raining most of the day, but that just made the light really even. Otherwise I would have had harsh shadows – especially in this one.' I indicated a picture of some abandoned machinery. 'It helped me bring out the textures in the metal and contrast it with the fragility of the glass from the skylights.' I looked up from the phone to see that Cal's eyebrows were raised. 'Not that there's anything special about it,' I added quickly. 'It's just some old shipyard in the rain.'

'Is that Jake in the photo too?' Cal asked.

I shrugged to show that it was nothing special; just an ordinary photo of an ordinary man taken on an ordinary day. 'Yes, that's him.'

'He's really very cute, isn't he?'

'I suppose he is.'

'And absolutely not your type.'

I heard a smile in her voice, but when I raised my eyes from the image of Jake Cal's expression was one of pure innocence.

'No, he's not my type,' I agreed.

'But you've spent time with him out of bed?'

'I guess, but don't read anything into that. We're friends, I think, with benefits. I've told him I don't do relationships.'

'That's okay then,' said Callie with a grin. 'As long as you've told him that. Is he looking for a relationship?'

I shrugged. 'I don't know.'

'But you think he might be?' When I didn't answer she added, 'Because if he is and you're not, take care not to hurt him, Tiff.'

I looked up from the remains of my omelette. 'I can't control how he feels.'

'Maybe not, but you can choose to encourage it.'

'I should end it, shouldn't I?'

Her eyes widened in surprise. 'I'm not saying that, Tiff. Why don't you take a chance on him and see where it goes?'

'Because if it goes nowhere and I've allowed myself to be distracted, I could end up missing my chance at Masters.'

'And you could end up hurt the way you were that summer when we finished school,' she said gently.

It was my turn to be surprised. 'What do you know about that?'

'Nothing really. I know you were upset by your parents' divorce, but something more than that went down too, didn't it? What happened to you, Tiff? What made you so determined not to let any man close to you?'

The backs of my eyes were burning. 'Nothing happened,' I said quickly. 'I just saw how Dad collapsed on himself once Mum left. That's what happens when you fall for the wrong person. I wouldn't like for that to happen to Jake.'

'Or are you scared it will happen to you?'

'I won't let it,' I said firmly.

'What if it's too late to stop it?' Callie asked the question so quietly that I pretended I hadn't heard it.

Since my mini showdown with Ainsley she'd done everything possible to pile the pressure on me. Her latest play had been to assign Shannon's project assistant to another piece of work and then insist on daily checkpoint meetings complete with status reports. Without someone to help her prepare the reports Shannon was struggling to keep her head above water. I was trying to help her out as much as possible by completing the communication piece myself rather than overseeing it as I normally would.

I was still on top of my objectives and still confident of a place at Masters, but it was taking every ounce of my concentration to stay there – and most of my energy as well.

Jake was still away, and while we'd exchanged texts, I hadn't actually spoken to him in over a week. I knew he was busy and on the move, and told myself I should be relieved he was no longer ringing me daily, but even so I missed seeing his name come up on my phone. I also missed the sound of his voice – not that I would have admitted it to anyone. It had taken the best part of a week to admit it to myself.

My relocation in Hong Kong was progressing well and the clients I'd been having issues with were now convinced that the move would end up being in their favour. By the time I'd finished with them I was sure they'd be thinking that the entire move was their idea in the first place. Ainsley, however, had attended my last teleconference and asked a question of the project team in such a way that the client was now concerned about the security of their data.

While I seethed, Ainsley had shrugged her bony shoulder and said, 'It looks like you'll need to get back over there and sort it out, Tiffany.' She'd tutted. 'Your only job is to manage the change and it seems you're not managing that very well. This client has always expressed their concerns about data security and now it seems there's an issue with that. I'd suggest you increase your visits to fortnightly for the next few months, starting with attending the project meeting in person this week.'

I'd gritted my teeth and said, 'Perhaps you're right, it certainly won't hurt. At least that way I can control the messages they're getting. There are too many people who don't understand the change who can manipulate what the client hears.'

She searched my face, looking for an accusation behind my words. 'Just to be clear, you need to do this within your current budget.'

'Don't worry, Ainsley, you've made yourself crystal clear on that front.' I'd turned to walk out but then a piece of mischief made me turn back. 'I've been meaning to ask, what colour bikini are you taking to Fiji? It's just that I don't want us to either match or clash.' Then I'd smiled sweetly and left her office.

A few days later I was sitting down to a drink with Matt in our usual bar. This time there wasn't even the pretence that there could be anything else involved. We really were just two old friends catching up for a drink. It still felt strange having a man as a friend without even the possibility of sex, but I quite liked it.

'How long are you here for this time?' he asked.

'Just a few days. It's hardly worth the flight to be honest, but I needed to be here for a meeting this morning that it turns out I really didn't need to be here for, so I figured I'd bring forward a review that I did need to be here for. Two birds, one stone, that sort of thing. I'm heading home tomorrow night.'

'I should feel grateful then that you found the time to have a drink with me,' Matt said with a grin. 'What's happening at home? Mum tells me Alice has a new boyfriend – have you met him?'

'No, but Callie has. She said he seems nice and different to Alice's usual type. Not that that's a problem – her type has landed her in trouble in the past. I think she's trying on a different type for size.'

Matt laughed. 'Typical Alice. Does she still have

that ridiculous three-date rule?'

I nodded.

'What's the rationale behind that one again?'

'Something about how most men – and women, I suppose – are on their best behaviour for the first date, beginning to relax a little at the second, and might slip into their normal mode of behaviour by the third. She thinks that if she sleeps with someone on the first date and the sex is good, she could end up putting up with the parts of his personality she doesn't like for longer than she would if they hadn't had sex before she worked out she didn't like him.'

He tilted his head slightly to the side as he thought it through. 'I suppose it makes sense in an Alice sort of way. Wasn't there also something about one of the dates being in daylight hours?'

'Uh huh. That's to guard against the potential of beer goggles – you know, when you've drunk enough that you can overlook traits you'd normally find really unattractive?'

Matt laughed. 'Oh yes, I know that one!'

'I just wish Callie had listened to those rules before she fell back into bed with Jamie,' I said, not really knowing why I was mentioning it to Matt.

'Is this Jamie the guy you were telling me about last time?' he asked. 'The one you said is bad news?'

I nodded. 'He's definitely trouble for her. They were together for about five years and he cheated on her. I'm sure it wasn't the first time – he even put the moves on me one time – but this time he got caught. Let's face it, guys like that never do it just the once. He begged her to take him back and she did, but once he had her where he wanted her again, he broke up with her because he said she was too clingy and didn't trust him. She was just starting to get over him and now he's back in her life again.'

'Why did she take him back?'

I shrugged. 'She says she loves him. Personally, I can't see the attraction. To be honest, I think she's more in love with the idea of him than the reality.'

'What does Alice say about it?' I couldn't see Matt's expression, but the tone of his voice sounded different – as if he was forcing neutrality into it.

'That I can't control what happens and Cal has to make her own mind up and blah blah blah. But she's taking Cal away next weekend to the Sunshine Coast to your brother-in-law's party. She deliberately hasn't invited Jamie to go with them, and from all accounts he wasn't happy when he found out. If I know Alice I'd say she's done it to get Cal away from his influence and cause some trouble between them.' I grinned. 'It's so typical of Ally – I just hope it works. Cal still needs to make the decision for herself.'

'Laura sent me an invite to that party,' Matt said thoughtfully. 'I don't expect she really thought I'd come, but I haven't been home in a while and it would be good to see Callie again too.'

'Really? You'd go all the way over there for a birthday party?'

'Why not? It's as good an excuse as any.' He said it as if he figured he might as well get the visit home over and done with. 'Laura's named her latest baby after me so I probably should go and meet him.'

'If you do decide to go, maybe you could give Callie something else to think about,' I said, smiling so he'd know I was joking.

But he didn't smile back. 'What makes you think she'd appreciate that?'

'Maybe she wouldn't, but Callie has no idea what it is that she really wants. And I need to show her that what she thinks she wants isn't what she needs.'

'And you think you know what Callie needs?'

'Of course I do. Much better than she does. That's why I've instigated Project Yes.'

He sputtered his beer. 'Project what?'

'Project Yes. It's designed to push Alice and Callie into exploring new ideas. Rather than sitting at home on their butts, if someone asks them to do something, they have to say yes.'

'Does the same apply to you?'

'Sure, but it's just a bit of fun for me. After all, I know exactly what I want.'

He hesitated briefly, as if choosing his next words carefully. 'You seem so keen to fix Callie's love life but what about your own?'

I shook my head. 'We had this discussion last time. I don't believe in love. Love doesn't pay your bills. All I'm interested in is getting to Masters and knocking Ainsley off her perch. Until then nothing and no one is going to distract me.'

'That was said with some force. Is there something – or someone – you need to tell me about?'

'Absolutely not.' I could hear his scepticism in the silence. 'I mean it, Matt. There's nothing to see here.'

'If you say so.' He didn't sound as if he believed me but he changed the subject.

I should have been relieved, but I wasn't. Part of me wanted to tell him about Jake and hear him laugh at the idea of us together – at me together with anyone. He'd tell me that Jake was a distraction I didn't need, and remind me what was really important. My fear, though, was that Matt wouldn't laugh and he wouldn't remind me that my career was all I should be focusing on. My fear was that he'd tell me to follow my heart and see where it led.

I didn't want to hear that. And I didn't want to listen to my heart either. I already knew what it would say.

CHAPTER FIFTEEN

My flight home was delayed: firstly because some passengers obviously felt that scheduled departure times were too mainstream for them to follow; and secondly because of a heavy downpour. To make matters worse there was a baby in the row to my left who began crying the minute we were seated, but was (thankfully) stopped mid wail by its mother's boob. For now.

Forty minutes after our scheduled departure time, the doors had finally been closed and the cabin crew were demonstrating the safety procedures. I'd heard it all before so I tuned out.

'Cabin crew, please be seated for take-off,' requested the PA.

'Thank god for that,' I muttered under my breath. Christ, it was hot in here. I lifted my blouse out from the waistband of my skirt and fanned my skin. The man sitting beside me looked at me and smiled in what I assumed was shared discomfort.

Across the aisle from me an older Chinese woman pressed her call button. She mimed the act of drinking.

The steward nearest her said, 'I'm sorry, madam, but I can't serve you until we're in the air and levelled out.'

The passenger clutched at her chest.

'Are you unwell?' the steward asked.

The woman nodded and patted her chest again.

I heard another steward grab the phone and tell someone at the other end, 'Suspected heart problems, will need to abort.'

Then came the PA announcement: 'Ladies and gentlemen, due to the health of a passenger we've had to abort our take-off. We'll be back underway as soon as we're sure they're okay, and as soon as air traffic control can find another slot for us in the queue.'

'Oh, for fuck's sake,' I said, a little too loudly.

The man beside me was laughing soundlessly. '*Merde*,' he agreed in a rather delightful French accent. I smiled back at him.

In the meantime, someone in the row behind the old lady had acted as translator and established that she wasn't having a heart attack, but was just thirsty and would be heartily grateful for some water.

And, if I wasn't mistaken, the aroma coming from the baby in the row to my left was definitely one of *merde*.

I looked at the man beside me. 'It's going to be a long flight,' I said.

He shrugged in a nonchalant Gallic way. '*Oui*, and

a long night. Perhaps we can find something to talk about to pass the time.'

His eyes held mine, letting me know in no uncertain terms that he was flirting with me and talking wasn't all that might be on offer.

He was quite good-looking, and judging from the laptop he'd tucked into the seat pocket he was travelling for business. It would be very easy to say yes to him, especially in the spirit of Project Yes. The problem was, I didn't want to say yes. He was exactly my type – or rather, he would have been if he was sitting further up the front of the plane – yet I didn't feel even a glimmer of attraction. Instead, an image of Jake came into my head.

That spot under my watchband was itchy again. I scratched at it, and made a mental note to take the band into the jeweller when I got home to see if they could change it for something that didn't irritate me.

My travelling companion was still watching me.

'I'm sure we can find something to talk about to pass the time,' I finally said. 'But I also need to get some work done. What do you think is the likelihood that the woman in front is about to push her chair all the way back?'

I added a smile so he wouldn't take my comment as a rejection of the offer we both knew he'd made.

My flight landed on Friday morning after yet another

sleepless night. I turned my phone on and saw missed calls from Ainsley (two), Shannon (three) and Drew (three). Only Shannon had left a message, so while I was waiting for my luggage I called her.

'What's up?' I asked.

'We've received a complaint about the branch closure from the aged-care home in the suburb.'

'And?'

'Ainsley's having a fit about it and needs you to fix it.'

I sighed and yawned at the same time. 'How does she expect me to do that? The aged-care customers were, if I remember correctly, called out in the initial impact assessment that Ainsley completed before the decision was made to close the branch. That was all over and done before we became involved. It's all in the impact assessment.'

'But the complaint has gone all the way up the line so that means someone needs to be made responsible.'

'Let me guess – Ainsley's decided that's me.' I rubbed at the back of my neck. God, I was tired.

'She told me to remind you that you're in charge of change management.'

'I'm sure she did. I guess there's no point reminding her that change management relates to the actual implementation of the change, not the assessment that occurred prior to the change being decided?'

'No, I don't think there's any point.' Shannon

paused. 'You know, I thought I saw Ainsley's name all over that impact assessment too. But she's telling anyone who'll listen that she gave that task to you, and you told her you'd spoken to the care home and arranged for a weekly bus to run the residents to the next suburb.'

'Interesting.' I spied my bag and reached for it, balancing my phone in the crick of my neck.

'What does that mean?' Shannon said.

'Just that she obviously thinks no one has a signed copy of that impact assessment.'

'And you do?'

'I learned long ago to save anything that has Ainsley's name on it,' I said. 'Tell her I'll come straight into the office.'

'But you've flown all night – you must be exhausted.'

'Somehow, I think that's her point.'

In the taxi, I leaned my head back against the headrest and resisted the temptation to shut my eyes. Instead I checked my Instagram to see if Jake had posted anything in the time that I'd been in the air. He'd left New Zealand and was now in the US and, judging by the photos he'd posted over the last few days, doing a road trip.

I clicked on the location of his last picture to see what else was in the area he was travelling through. Given the time difference between us I figured it was the next best thing to being able to hear his voice. The first image that came up was the one he'd posted, and the next was a photo he'd been tagged in – with a woman. She was pretty in a laid-back surfer-chick sort of way – the type of woman who would go hiking with him and camping with him and not worry about hopping into a car with no fixed plans for that night's accommodation. She was exactly Jake's type and the stab of pain that shot through me at the realisation of that took me by surprise. All this time I'd been reminding myself that Jake wasn't my type. It hadn't occurred to me that I mightn't be his. What if the reason he hadn't called me was because he didn't want to? What if he'd decided I was too much trouble? This woman, whoever she was, didn't look as though she'd cause him any trouble. Where I was high maintenance, she was the exact opposite.

He wasn't touching her, but they were leaning against the dusty side of a car and he was laughing – probably at something she'd said. The caption said something about how the best friends were old friends, and they certainly looked as though they were comfortable with each other. I hadn't known I was capable of jealousy – and if anyone had told me that I was I would have laughed at them – but there was no denying that the bitter taste that rose into my mouth was exactly that.

I was saved from spending too long with that idea as the taxi pulled up in front of my office. I sat there, tired suddenly in spirit as well as body – until the driver turned around and asked if I was alright. I sighed heavily, paid the bill and stood on the pavement outside our building with my suitcase beside me. Okay, here we go again.

When had my job changed from something I enjoyed into an ongoing power struggle with Ainsley? These days I accomplished very little of value; every day was about staying ahead of the game. And when I got to Masters, what then? Even if I managed to beat Ainsley there'd be another to take her place, and then another. Alice once said that she thought there was a conveyer belt in the bowels of head office in Sydney turning out copies of Ainsley St James one after the other. All of them in designer labels with only their hair colour and names to tell them apart. I'd laughed at the time but now, as I rode the lift to my office, I wondered if she wasn't right. And what if I was one of them – an Ainsley? Too busy making sure no one was threatening my position on the ladder to actually get any real work done?

As the lift doors opened, I wondered for the first time whether my mother ever felt this way. Had she ever regretted the choices she'd made, or was she still fulfilled by them? We'd never spoken about why she left. I didn't even know if there'd ever been anyone in her life other than my father. Mostly, though, I wondered whether she was happy.

•

I spent most of what remained of Friday agreeing on a plan to resolve the complaint that had been received. I'd deal with Ainsley's part in it later, but for now it was about putting in place the transport plan that Ainsley had promised the director of the aged-care centre but done nothing about.

When Ainsley complained about the cost and threatened to have it hit my budget, Shannon stepped in and told her that it would be absorbed by the division that had made the decision in the first place. It would have been the perfect time to raise the impact assessment and call Ainsley out on it, but I was too tired to be bothered.

It wasn't until later that evening when I was home, showered and in clothes that didn't smell of Hong Kong humidity that I allowed myself to think about Jake and the photo.

We might be dating, but no one had mentioned anything about being exclusive, although I suppose I'd assumed that if I wasn't seeing anyone else then neither was he. I was sure he wasn't like Jamie, but I still spent ages scrolling through the woman's Instagram to find more pictures of him. Then I compared her posts with the locations tagged in his and essentially drove myself mad trying to link their locations.

I'd always thought a long-distance relationship

would suit me. The idea of him doing his thing and me doing mine and us coming together every so often for great sex sounded like the perfect scenario – in theory. But my reaction to the photo had shown me that I had no idea how to deal with a long-distance relationship and the inevitable silences and worries that came with it. Yet, if Jake and I were to continue to see each other that was the way it was going to be. Maybe I should end this before either of us were in too deep. I refused to consider the possibility that I was already out of my depth.

I flicked back to the photo of him with the surfer girl, who I was now thinking of as Gidget. A reasonable person wouldn't jump to conclusions and, I told myself, I was known for being reasonable. A reasonable person would show that she trusted her boyfriend, if indeed that's what Jake was, by showing him she didn't feel ripped apart at the sight of him laughing with someone who wasn't her.

To prove my reasonability I clicked on the heart to show I liked the photo and added a comment: *Looks like fun. Aren't old friends the best?*

It was only after I'd closed the application that I realised he'd now know that I'd been on Gidget's profile and wonder whether I was Insta-stalking him. This was why I shouldn't be in a relationship. I was absolutely hopeless at them.

CHAPTER SIXTEEN

On Saturday evening I met up with Andi and another mutual friend Lisa for some drinks. We were onto our second martini when Todd Reynolds, a friend of Abby's ex, Brad, turned up with some of his mates. I hadn't seen Todd since the night Lisa, Andi and I were out for Abby's birthday drinks, just before she and Andi went to Bali. By the sounds of their conversation, though, Andi and Todd had been seeing each other fairly regularly – something that surprised me given that in the past they'd clashed.

I said as much to Andi, who actually blushed. 'We're united on the cause of getting Abby and Brad back together,' she said. 'That's all.'

Looking at her face, and the way Todd looked at her, I didn't believe her.

'Anyway,' she added with a smile, 'he's too single to be my type.'

'What about you?' Lisa asked me. 'Are you seeing anyone special?'

'Me, no.' I almost had to shout to be heard over

the music.

'Tiff has a checklist that you'd need to be Superman to jump over,' Andi told Lisa. 'But one day she's going to fall in love with Mr Wrong and he'll be perfect for her.'

I laughed and shook my head. 'You know me – I don't believe in love.'

'That's bullshit.' Andi waved her drink around for emphasis, spilling some of it. 'Everyone believes in love. You believe in love, don't you, Lisa?'

'I sure do, although sadly I don't think love believes in me.'

'I believe in love even though I know that most men – at least the ones I fall for – are cheating bastards,' said Andi.

'That just means you're not giving the others a chance,' said Todd, joining the conversation. 'Hey, Tiff. Good to see you.'

I raised my glass in his direction and settled back to watch the banter between him and Andi.

'It's pretty obvious, isn't it?' said Lisa.

I laughed. 'It certainly is.' I raised an arm to push back my hair. 'Surprising yet obvious.'

She saw the movement and frowned. 'What have you done to your wrist?'

I lowered my hand. 'It's nothing, just an allergic reaction to who knows what.' I cast my eyes around the room. 'You know what? I need to dance. Feel like dancing with me?'

She nodded and the two of us hit the floor. At some point Lisa backed out and returned to where Andi and Todd were. I stayed, smiling and dipping and curving, my hips swaying to the beat, the music and the alcohol pushing away the picture in my head of Jake and his surfer girl driving in a convertible along a desert road somewhere on the other side of the world.

I caught the eye of a man at the edge of the dance floor and found myself recklessly holding it. He smiled slowly and made his way towards me until he was dancing with me, moving closer and closer, pushing me further away from my friends and nearer to the toilets at the other end of the room. Eventually we were at the edge of the dance floor and into the dark.

He took my hand and led me further into the shadows. 'You look pretty good out there,' he said into my ear.

'Thanks.' I smiled back at him and flicked my hair behind my ears.

'What's your name?'

'It doesn't matter.'

'Aren't you going to ask me what my name is?'

'Nope.'

His smile didn't slip, but his face showed his confusion.

'I don't care what your name is,' I said, leaning forward to kiss him, 'and you don't need to know mine.'

He reached for my waist and pulled me roughly

towards him, his tongue driving into my mouth, his hardness pushing into my belly.

'Get a room,' someone said, knocking against us as they went through to the toilets.

'Good idea,' he said. 'The disabled loo is just down that corridor. I'll go in first and you follow?'

He didn't wait for my assent, just smiled in a way that I think he thought was seductive but came across as arrogant.

As soon as he'd turned his back, the bile rose to my mouth. What on earth was I doing? I didn't want to be with him – whatever his name was. Even though I'd started it, I'd felt invaded when he pushed his tongue into my mouth.

I scratched again at my wrist and almost ran back to the table where Lisa was talking – or, rather, shouting – to one of Todd's friends and picked up my handbag.

'I'm not feeling great,' I said. 'Can you let Andi know I've gone?'

'Sure,' she said. 'Is there anything I can do?'

'No.' I nervously looked back towards the toilets. 'It was good to see you, let's not make it too long next time.'

'Agreed,' she said. 'Did you know your wrist is bleeding?'

I looked down and saw that somehow I'd scratched it raw. 'I must have hit it against something,' I said. 'I'll put some antihistamine on it when I get home.'

I was in the taxi when the text came through from Jake. *Hi there, just wondering how your Saturday night is going.*

I laid my hand against my forehead and closed my eyes briefly. If I'd gone into that toilet, I would have been having rushed and dirty stranger sex at the exact minute he was texting me.

Hi yourself, I replied. *All good. I've been out with a friend but heading home to get some sleep – it's been a big week.*

Sleep well Jx

The heaviness that slipped over me was something I hadn't felt in many years but recognised. It was guilt. I'd had sex with people in the past who I knew probably had girlfriends or even wives at home and hadn't felt a single twinge of remorse. Any guilt was their problem, not mine. It's why I could never understand how Callie had been able to twist Jamie's cheating around to blame herself for it. She believed that if she'd loved him more, doted on him more, made herself even more of a doormat, he wouldn't have had to stray.

A memory came into my head. It was about two months after Mum had left and I'd come home late from somewhere or other and seen the light on in Dad's studio at the back of our Brisbane home. He was sitting there staring at some portraits he'd painted of Mum when she was pregnant with me, her belly round and full, the contented look on her face one I'd never seen in real life.

'I'd always hoped we'd be enough for her,' he said,

tears streaming down his face. 'But she always wanted more than I could give her.'

'Did you even try?' I said. 'Mum put her career on hold for us; the least you could have done was tried to be more of a success. You could have gone and got a proper job at any time to help out, but instead she's had to work jobs she's hated to keep the money coming in. You've always known how ambitious and driven she is, and you haven't cared that she was unfulfilled as long as you were doing what you wanted, sitting in here and playing with your paints. I don't blame her for going.'

I'd spat the words out, my pain at her leaving directed squarely at him, and watched my father dissolve in front of me. I'd put the bitter taste in my mouth down to disgust at his lack of self-respect and selfishness over the years, but now, almost two decades later, I knew it for what it was – guilt.

Neither of us had ever spoken of the incident, and over the months that followed, before I left to go to university in Sydney, we fell into a pattern of me going to work during the day and coming home to cook him dinner. Ironically it was during those months that he painted his first commercial works, as he went from staring at blank canvases to emptying his despair onto them.

I knew now that I'd blamed Dad for Mum leaving because I couldn't admit that it was myself I blamed. She used to say how like Dad I was, that I was creative like him. For many years I thought that was why she'd left me behind – because I wasn't enough like her. If I'd been more like her, she might have stayed. I knew it was illogical – in exactly the same way Callie knew it when she was justifying Jamie's behaviour. But it was how I'd felt, what I'd believed.

Now, I'd very nearly cheated on Jake – all because I'd allowed my bad day at work, lack of sleep and a photo of a surfer girl to send me into a tailspin. I felt sick at the idea of it. I had no idea whether Jake had slept with the girl in the photo, but somehow I knew that he hadn't.

I picked up my phone and tapped out another text. *Miss you x*

Then I erased it before I could send it.

Over the next week or so I tried as much as possible to put all thoughts of Jake from my mind – and for the most part managed it during working hours. I threw myself into the projects Ainsley had foisted on me, and was aware that I was being overly demanding in my need to micro-manage each of them. I worked late most evenings to keep everything else on target and was tracking to budget and schedule in all of my objectives.

It was only in the mornings and late at night when I allowed myself to think about Jake. At those times I'd check his Instagram account to keep up to date with where he was and what he was doing.

It was also at night when he'd text me. Often it was just a *hello, how are you*, but sometimes it was more, and sometimes he didn't text at all. It was enough to know that he was thinking about me.

After the night out with Andi and Lisa and my failed attempt at being with someone else, I spent the next weekend walking around with my camera. On Saturday I strolled up Lygon Street into Brunswick, detouring into the university to photograph the cloisters and the halls. I then wandered through the cemetery, playing with light, shadows and highlights, before stopping for pizza and red wine, and coming back via Brunswick Street and Fitzroy for the street art. I posted some of the images to my account, and checked it hourly until I saw a like and a comment or thumbs-up from Jake.

On Sunday I walked in the opposite direction – down Chapel Street as far as Balaclava – snapping pictures of Sunday morning in Melbourne. People meeting for coffee, for brunch, to read the paper. The skies were grey, and the occasional drizzle made the colours of the umbrellas stand out and gave my images a definite European feel.

When I got home, I played with the images on my laptop, adjusting the exposure and saturation, changing the contrast, adding brightness.

As I looked back through the files, I could see how my work had improved even in the last month or so. Those initial photos I'd taken were almost dispassionate in style; the capture of an image in isolation. Technically everything I'd learned when I was younger about light, shade and texture had come back to me, but the pictures I'd shot on Cockatoo Island and since were more alive than those I'd taken in Hong Kong. They had a context and a liveliness that was missing before – as, I feared, did I.

CHAPTER SEVENTEEN

Jake arrived back in Australia on Tuesday morning and called me to say that he was home and moving back into his apartment. I, however, was in Sydney. Hearing his voice for the first time in weeks almost brought tears to my eyes. I told myself it was a combination of tiredness and frustration that he was there and I was here, but it was more that I was relieved he was home. I'd memorised his schedule and had been embarrassed to find myself tracking his flight on the app I'd downloaded to my phone, relaxing only when I knew he had safely landed.

'I can't believe you're there and I'm here,' he said.

'I didn't realise you were home already,' I lied. 'I'm on an evening flight back on Friday. I won't be home until late.'

'I have to fly out again on Sunday morning. Can we spend Saturday together?'

I told myself to hesitate, to make it sound as though I had other things I wanted to be doing, or should be doing, but I couldn't.

'I'll look forward to seeing you,' I said.

'I've missed you,' he said.

I felt it, but I couldn't say it back.

I tried to play it cool when I opened the door to him on Saturday morning, but failed dismally. His smile was so wide, his eyes were so bright, and his arms were so open. I fell into them and into his kiss.

He pulled away just as things were getting interesting. 'God, I've missed you, Tiff, but I promised you breakfast.'

'Let's call it brunch instead,' I murmured, my hands reaching for his belt.

Later, we walked up Chapel Street to one of my favourite places, chatting as we walked, his arm around my shoulders as we waited at traffic lights, his hand occasionally reaching for mine.

Once we'd ordered, he told me about going out with his friend Todd the previous night. 'He's the one I stayed with the other week when I was in town.'

'Oh yes, I remember,' I said.

'Since then he's fallen for someone who's been under his nose for years.'

'What do you mean?'

'This is confusing, but she's the best friend of his best friend's girlfriend – although his best friend and his girlfriend have recently split up. Maybe that makes her the best friend of his best friend's ex-partner? Anyway, Todd's known this woman for years and they've always clashed. Now, all of a sudden, they're working together to try and get their friends back together and it's *wham.*'

As he spoke, I was putting two and two together. 'Are you by chance talking about Todd Reynolds?'

'What the fuck? Do you know him?'

'A little. I'm friends with Andi Shaw and Abby Brentnall – who I suspect you're talking about. In fact, I was out with Andi the weekend before last. Todd was there too. I wondered if there was something brewing between the two of them. And you're friends with Todd. Wow, it's a small world.'

I wondered if Jake had spoken of me to Todd, and if Todd had made the same connection. After all, there weren't that many Tiffanys in Melbourne. My tummy took a dive as I recalled how the evening had ended. Had Todd seen any of that? I hoped not.

After brunch we caught a train down to Brighton and wandered back to St Kilda via the coast path. The day was grey and windy and Port Phillip Bay was only a few shades darker than the sky so we had the beach almost to ourselves. We stopped and took photos of the beach boxes, then lingered over pizzas in St Kilda, watching people walking and cycling by, braving Melbourne's winter.

It was late in the afternoon by the time we made our way back to Jake's place. Just when I didn't think Jake could surprise me any more, his apartment rendered me speechless. I'd thought it would be something like the place he'd been staying in Sydney – but the reality was a stylish warehouse conversion in Richmond.

'It used to be the top floor of a garment manufacturer,' he explained. 'The developer opened the space up and there are three one-bedroom loft-style apartments in this complex.'

The space was mostly open plan, with the original tall sash windows retained. The bricks had been left exposed in most places, with remnants of previous paint jobs allowed to come through. At one end of the large room was the kitchen. What appeared to be recycled cabinets with timber tops framed a modern free-standing cooktop and wide oven. Repurposed vintage dressers held plates and glasses, and a large timber island bench had a deep Belfast sink in the centre, with open shelving at either end. It looked like an amalgam of a few different pieces put together. I said as much to Jake.

'That's because it is,' he said. 'I have a friend who makes cabinets and furniture from recycled timber.'

'I've never seen anything like it. It's beautiful.' I ran my hand over the timber benchtop, marvelling at the colours and textures within the wood.

Towards the centre of the room was a large wooden table with mismatched chairs, and beyond it, a modern brown leather lounge suite and television. A bathroom and laundry sat under the loft that held Jake's bed and workspace.

He watched me as I took it all in. 'Not what you'd

expected?'

I shook my head. 'Not at all. But I love it – it's very you.'

It was Jake all over. That casual, laid-back almost grungy style with an underlying practicality that was easy to miss if you weren't looking for it.

'I'm glad you like it. I don't get to spend as much time here as I'd like, but it's still home.' He pulled me in for a kiss that was quicker than I wanted it to be, and moved into the kitchen. 'I thought that rather than go out I'd cook you dinner,' he said.

'I didn't know you could cook.'

'Why would you? I bring recipes home from wherever I've been – they're a lot more use than most souvenirs.' His grin was wide. 'When I'm someplace new I like to do the occasional cooking class or food walking tour, and you already know how I feel about street food.'

I nodded.

'The recipe I thought I'd cook you tonight is a Malaysian dish called kapitan chicken or ayam kapitan, which loosely translates to captain's chicken. Apparently, it got its name when the Chinese chef on a British ship in Malacca – back when the British were running the spice trade through there – got flustered when he was asked what was for dinner. "Ayam, Kapitan," he said, meaning "Chicken, Captain".' He smiled again at me. 'I have no idea whether the story's true or not, but I like to think it is. Anyway, I love this curry – it's not too spicy, but at the same time has layers and layers of flavour, which is just the way I like it.'

He paused in his fridge forage and grinned at me and I wondered whether he was comparing the curry to me.

'That sounds great.'

I didn't know what else to say. No one had cooked for me since Mum left. It made me feel comforted, but also deeply uncomfortable.

'I can't stay here tonight,' I blurted. 'I don't do the stay-over thing.'

'That's okay. We'll have dinner and discuss sleeping arrangements after that.' His tone was even, and he didn't look up from his chopping board. It was almost as if he'd expected a comment like that from me.

'Or we could skip dinner and go straight to bed,' I suggested.

He looked up then, those wicked eyes of his twinkling. 'Nope, we prepare this first, go through the photos, and then discuss sleeping arrangements. You see, Tiff, once you're in my arms tonight I won't be letting you leave them. That means we either stay here or go to yours – whatever you're most comfortable with.'

I knew I should have stood my ground, asserted myself, said that I didn't like decisions being made for me. Instead I nodded. 'In that case, what can I do to help?'

'You can get us both a drink while I chop these spices and the chicken. There's beer and wine in the fridge – I'll have a beer, please. Then you can sit right there,' he indicated one of the bar stools at the island bench, 'and listen while I amaze and astound you with my prowess in the kitchen.'

'As opposed to your prowess in other parts of the house?'

'As well as.' His blue eyes twinkled again, and I laughed with him.

He roughly chopped ginger, galangal, chilli, turmeric, garlic and shallots, telling me about each of the ingredients as he sliced. There was some particularly foul-smelling stuff that he sliced to put into the mini-blender with everything else.

'What on earth is that?' I wrinkled my nose as he double-wrapped it in foil before putting it back in a sealed container. 'It smells off.'

He let out a short laugh. 'It's belacan.' He pronounced it *belachan*. 'It smells disgusting but wait till you taste the extra something it gives to this sauce.'

'I'll take your word for it.'

I sipped at my wine and watched him blitz the paste. He was methodical in the kitchen – in both the preparation of the ingredients and the way he cleaned the bench as he went. When I commented on it, he just smiled and said he was used to working in a small space so didn't have the luxury of mess. For half a heartbeat

I allowed myself to imagine us doing this regularly – cooking together, having a drink and talking through our days. Seriously, Tiff?

'Do you cook?'

His question pulled me out of my ridiculous mini-fantasy. I waited until he'd finished rinsing out the bowl of the processor before I answered.

'Not really. I can, I just don't have any call for it these days. When Mum first left, I had to cook for Dad and me – he was pretty hopeless – but since then there's really been no one to cook for.'

'You don't cook for your friends?' He scraped the curry paste into a bowl and took the chicken from the fridge.

'No. We mostly eat out or order in.'

'And … men?' He didn't look up from the chicken he was chopping.

'No.'

'Is that no, you don't cook for them, or no, there aren't any, or no, I don't want to talk about it?'

'Probably all of the above. Are you sure there's nothing I can do to help?' I scratched at my wrist.

'You keep doing that,' he said. 'Scratching your wrist.'

'No, I don't.'

'You do, you know. Whenever I ask something you don't want to answer, or suggest something you're not comfortable with, or start to get too personal.' He looked up from the board and met my eyes. He wasn't smiling. 'Do I make you feel uneasy?'

I had no idea how to answer the question so I told him the truth. 'I don't know. I'm not used to … umm, any of this.' My hand swept around the room to encompass the kitchen, the cooking, the domesticity.

Sex I could deal with – but I could no longer kid myself that Jake was just sex. I wasn't sure he'd ever really been just that. From the minute I looked in his eyes and he handed his camera over on that first day it had been personal – much more personal than sex ever was.

'How long has it been?'

'Since I cooked?' I deliberately misunderstood him.

'Since you were in a relationship.'

He turned away to begin to fry off the curry paste. It gave me the space to consider my answer – or whether to avoid the question. The air filled with the fragrance of the spices.

'Is that what this is?' I said eventually.

'Isn't it?'

I got up from my seat at the kitchen counter and went to the fridge. 'Do you want another?' I asked, holding up a bottle of beer.

'Please.'

I poured my wine and took the top off his beer, placing it on the bench beside the cooktop where he was working.

'Thanks.' His smile was brief.

I sat back down and took a sip from my glass. 'Not since I was eighteen. He was a bit older – just a couple of years – one of Matt's friends. Not that Matt knew about it. No one did. I thought I was in love and I thought he was in love with me. I wouldn't say that he supported me as such, but when my parents split, I think I was looking to hold on to anything. I remember Cal went with Alice to the Delaneys' holiday house in Mooloolaba – where her parents live now – and I stayed back in Brisbane. I said I had to work, but it was mostly because I wanted to be with Shane. Also, because I'd just realised I'd skipped a period.' I heard his sharp intake of breath. 'Of course Shane wanted nothing to do with me – or the baby, not that I even knew if there was one. He told me how stupid I was and said I couldn't prove it was his because a little whore like me had probably been sleeping around – which was ridiculous given that he was my first, we'd only had sex once and even that hadn't been entirely consensual.'

'Oh, Tiff,' Jake said.

I pretended that I couldn't hear the concern or sympathy or whatever it was in his voice. 'He said how I'd been just a bit of fun, but it wasn't fun any more and nor was I. Looking back, I cringe at how desperately I tried to hang on to him. It was like a perverse game to him – the harder I tried to hold him, the more he pushed me away.' I took another sip of my wine. 'Anyway, he needn't have worried. Before I could even take a test, let alone decide what to do about it if it was positive, my period arrived.' I laughed ruefully. 'It was probably for the best – I would have made a shit mother.'

'What did your friends say?'

'I didn't tell them. I was too embarrassed about the whole thing. I'd made a fool of myself with Shane and didn't want anyone else to know about it. Besides, they were an hour or so up the coast and having a fabulous time. They didn't need me raining on their parade.'

'Did you love him?'

'At the time I convinced myself that I did and he'd broken my heart, but I think that was more a reaction to my parents splitting up and Mum leaving.'

'And you haven't been in a relationship since?'

'No. After that I focused on my studies and then my career. There have been men, but on my terms, not theirs.' I saw his back stiffen as he stirred the onions in the paste. The smells coming from the pan were amazing. 'I know that makes me sound selfish,' I added, 'and I guess I am. One thing that both Shane and my mother taught me is I can't expect anyone to give me what I need – it's my responsibility to get it for myself. So I do. That way I have no one to blame for my disappointment or whatever else.'

'Have you forgiven your mother?'

'Yes. I understand her, I think. We don't talk a lot – but that's because we're both busy.'

'Have you forgiven Shane?'

'I don't know. I don't think about it any more if that counts as forgiveness.' I shrugged one shoulder. 'I don't even know why I told you.' I heard the surprise in my voice.

'I'm glad you did. I wish you hadn't been through it, but I'm glad you told me.'

He proceeded to fry the chicken in the curry paste. I heard it sizzle and spit in the pan.

'There was a photo of you with a girl,' I said.

He didn't pretend to misunderstand. 'That was Ginny. I went to school with her and she lives in the States now.' He paused with his stirring to look at me. 'Did it upset you?'

I shook my head, then nodded slowly.

'I'm sorry for that, Tiff. She really is just an old friend.'

I nodded again and he turned his focus back to the pan.

'I don't want to sleep with anyone else,' I said. 'But you, I mean.'

'That's good. Because I don't want to sleep with anyone else but you either.'

I heard the smile in his voice, but he didn't look at me. He opened a tin of coconut cream and emptied it into the pan, stirring it through.

'I tried to,' I said. 'The other night on the plane home from Hong Kong, and then again on the weekend when I was out with Andi.'

'On the plane?' He slowly and deliberately put the lid on the curry before turning to face me.

I shrugged. 'It sounds kind of desperate, doesn't it? But yes. He was French and quite cute. I would normally have been tempted.'

'And when you were out with Andi?'

'I wanted to, but I couldn't. I hadn't seen you in a month and I thought you might be out of my system, but I'd had a bad week and then I saw that photo. It shouldn't have hurt, but I wondered about you and her and it did. I thought sex might make the week better and prove it was only my pride that was hurt, but when it came to it, I couldn't do it. I didn't want to do it, and I didn't want to do it to you.'

'Would you have told me if you had?' he asked.

I nodded.

'So I could leave you?'

I hesitated, and nodded again.

'I see,' he said, his tone indicating he understood more than what I'd said.

'It was the first time that it mattered – how you would have felt, and how I would have felt afterwards, you know.' I had no idea whether he understood me or not, but he nodded as if he did. 'This is a relationship, isn't it?' I added.

'It is to me.' He left the cooktop and came and sat on the bar stool next to me. 'And I think it is to you too.'

Taking the hand that I hadn't realised I'd been scratching again, he lifted it to his mouth and kissed my wrist, soothing the irritated skin.

'I don't want to trap you, Tiff.' He turned my hand and kissed the palm. 'I don't want you to feel trapped. This, the rash on your wrist – I'm not putting handcuffs on you –'

I attempted a weak smile. 'Not even if I ask?'

'Sure, if you wanted to try it, I guess I would, but I think I'd prefer something soft and loose so you don't feel restrained.'

'What do you want?' I almost whispered the question.

'What do you think?'

My eyes dropped to his groin and I placed my hand on him, watching him half-close his eyes as I squeezed him gently. 'Aside from that, I mean.' I said when his breath hitched.

'I want to share a meal with you, and then I want you to spend tonight here with me in my bed.' He looked deep into my eyes and I was lost again. 'The whole of the night.'

'I'll think about it,' I said, but we both knew I'd be waking up beside him tomorrow morning.

The curry was special, the night was special, and so was waking up in Jake's loft. But watching him pack brought me back down to earth with a thud.

'Where did you say you're off to this time?' I tried to make my voice sound interested rather than needy – even though I wanted nothing more than to hold on to him. Maybe it was a good thing he was going.

'It's a big few weeks,' he said. 'I have Singapore this week, and a ferry across to Bintan Island where I'm reviewing one of the resorts. Then I'm booked to go hiking and camping in Hong Kong for a week –'

'I didn't even know Hong Kong had places you could hike to or camp in,' I said.

He leaned in and kissed me. 'Yes, but until we did that tour you didn't even know there were beaches.'

'I knew, but I didn't know.'

He grinned to let me know that he understood the distinction and continued to roll clothes. 'Then I'm in Taiwan, and will be in Vietnam by the middle of August.'

'So you'll be away for the next four weeks or so.' I allowed my disappointment to sneak through.

'I will.' He disappeared into the ensuite, emerging with a shaving bag that he put straight into his case. 'When are you next up in Hong Kong?'

'Next week. Why?'

'I can arrange to come in a few days earlier and we can spend the weekend together if you like?'

'I won't get in until Saturday evening, so we'd only have Sunday together, but if you can make that work I'd like it.'

'You're not even going to pretend that it's something I need to talk you into?'

'Nope. Project Yes, remember.'

He grinned. 'Why do I get the impression that Project Yes is something you remember only when you want to do something that you want me to think you don't want to do?'

'Whatever.' I stretched languorously, a delicious warmth seeping through me as his eyes followed my movement. 'Besides, who knows when we'll see each other if I don't.'

'I'm home in September,' he offered. 'But I can't wait that long to see you. I've missed you too much these last few weeks.'

At his words I felt my smile fall. 'It's always going to be like this, isn't it? We live in the same city, but this relationship is always going to be long distance.'

'You're admitting that it is a relationship now?' His tone was teasing but I was no longer in the mood to be teased.

I sat up straighter in bed and wrapped the sheet around me. 'Yes, maybe, but how can it be? We'll be seeing each other by appointment when we can fit it into our diaries. I don't see how that's any different to hooking up when it's convenient.'

He screwed his eyes tightly shut and looked to the ceiling – in exasperation or in search of inspiration?

'Tiff, is this you running scared again?' He left his

packing and came to sit on the edge of the bed beside me. 'I know it was weird for you last night with me cooking and then the stuff we talked about and you staying over. It really felt as though we'd made some ground, but now you're running again?' Taking my head in his hands he kissed me deeply. 'This is a relationship and I know there'll be some challenges, but I'd really like to see if we can make it work.'

'I don't see how,' I said. 'My diary is dictated by Ainsley. What happens if you're home for a week and I have to be in Sydney or Hong Kong? There might be months in between, and as good as you are at it phone sex gets boring really quickly. And we can't even do that when you're on the other side of the world.'

'You know how I usually schedule my stories and my travel six months ahead?' I nodded. 'There's no reason why I can't change the way I travel so I can spend longer periods at home in the future.' He brushed his thumb across my lips. 'I have some other ideas about that too – but I'll need you to be prepared to meet me halfway on them.'

I shrugged a shoulder in what was supposed to be a don't-really-care gesture but which I feared looked more obstinate or sulky.

'How about we talk next weekend, hey?' he said.

'In other words, you have a flight to catch now.'

'Exactly – even though I'd far prefer to be staying in bed with you.'

'Have you finished packing?' I asked.

'I think so.'

'Well then,' I let the sheet slip, 'if you're quick …'

When he left his kiss felt more tender than it usually did. I went to get up and he shook his head.

'No, stay here – at least for a little while. I want to picture you still in my bed, and I want you to think about me picturing you in my bed.' He smiled as he watched the images play across my face. 'I'll see you next weekend?'

'You will.'

'And we'll talk?'

I nodded slowly. 'Yes, we'll talk.'

The look that passed across his face could have been relief, but it was gone quickly.

After he'd left, I rolled over to his side of the bed and burrowed into his pillow. It smelled of his aftershave, and even though I had things I should have been doing, I snuggled in and went back to sleep.

CHAPTER EIGHTEEN

Two things happened on Monday: my father phoned me, and I received confirmation that I was off to Masters. The former was a surprise – I hadn't actually spoken to Dad since he and Mary left about six months ago; and the latter was, after everything I'd gone through to get there, an anticlimax.

Dad called when I was on my way into work. 'Tiffany, love, we're home.'

'Is that Brisbane home or Australia home?' I asked.

'Australia home. Mary and I want to duck over and have a look at Tasmania so we're in Melbourne for the night.' I must have hesitated because he added, 'It's okay, love, I'm not asking if we can stay with you – we've booked into a hotel in the city – but I would like to see you. We'd both like to see you.'

'Ummm, well, I'll probably be working late,' I started, then pictured Jake's face when he'd told me about his parents. I was an adult; it was about time I acted like one. 'There's a fabulous Italian restaurant up the Spring Street end of Bourke Street. It's casual, laid-back and the pasta is excellent.'

'That sounds great, love. When do you think you'll be able to get away?'

'I'm guessing you two still like to eat early so let's say six thirty?'

'We'll look forward to it,' he said.

The news about Masters arrived during the morning. Because I was in meetings I hadn't had a chance to read my emails, so the first I knew about it was when Ainsley glared at me in the team meeting before announcing through clenched teeth that I'd been awarded a seat at the conference. Given that I'd been working towards this for over a year I should have felt more elated than I did. Instead there was just a quiet sense of satisfaction.

As my colleagues applauded me, Ainsley sat expressionless. When the meeting broke up soon after she hissed, 'My office.' Shannon grinned and Drew gave me the thumbs-up as soon as she'd swept from the room.

Ainsley didn't wait for me to shut the door before saying, 'I want you to know that I argued against your inclusion.'

'I wouldn't expect anything less,' I said. 'But this is based on performance against objectives and the data tells the story.'

'You might be on that plane, but don't get too comfortable,' she warned. 'Any more slip-ups on this relocation project and I'll have you on performance management.'

'Any more slip-ups? That implies there's already been one.'

'Yes.' Her mouth smiled as much as her frozen muscles would allow. 'The aged-care transport debacle. That costing should have been included in the business case for the branch closure.'

'You know I wasn't responsible for that.'

'Do I?' She sat back smugly. 'Unfortunately, the executive I sent that impact assessment off to has left our employment so no one can find a copy of the assessment or the accompanying business case.'

I nodded slowly. 'I see. Isn't it fortunate then that his assistant sent me a copy in case I needed it during the implementation? Would you like me to forward it? It's no trouble.'

'That won't be necessary,' she bit out. 'You might have a ticket this year, but you'll find that next year's objectives won't be quite so easy for you to achieve. I'm not as easily influenced as my predecessor was.'

She said it as if I'd somehow convinced Mike, my previous general manager, to go easy on me when in fact those targets had been hard but fair. Just as Mike had been before he'd been forced into an early retirement and Ainsley took over.

Rather than pointing that out, I decided that I wasn't going to allow her to tarnish the moment for me and smiled thinly. 'You've certainly made that clear, Ainsley.

Now, if you'll excuse me, I have another meeting.'

My other colleagues all seemed happy that I'd made it onto Masters, although to be fair, given that all congratulations were expressed when Ainsley was absent and all discussion about it ceased as soon as she was within earshot, I suspected their pleasure in my triumph was more about Ainsley's displeasure.

Alice almost screamed down the phone when I called her. 'Oh my god, Tiff, that's great! I bet Ainsley was pissed off.'

'You could say that.' I told her what Ainsley had said to me.

'I'm really happy for you,' Alice said. 'You're well on your way to getting her job.'

'I certainly am,' I said, attempting to put more enthusiasm than I felt into my words. After all, that was the plan, wasn't it?

Dad and Mary were already at the restaurant and had secured a table outside under the heaters when I arrived. I watched them talking for a few seconds before they caught sight of me – their heads close together. Dad was holding Mary's hand, his other hand idly tracing a pattern on hers. He said something and she tossed her head back and laughed. It struck me that I'd never seen him that relaxed or happy with my mother. Although perhaps I'd been so wound up in my own teenage self that I wouldn't have noticed if they had been like that.

Mary saw me first, a wide smile breaking across her face. She nudged Dad and he turned and gave me the same grin and stood to walk the few steps to hug me.

'It's good to see you, love,' he said.

'You too, Dad. You're looking well. Both of you.'

'Never felt better,' he said. 'Now come and see Mary.'

As we settled down with drinks and menus, they kept me entertained with stories of where they'd been and what they'd seen. It was no wonder I hadn't been able to keep up with them.

'Any ideas for new series?' I asked my father.

'Absolutely,' he said. 'I sketched all the way around, of course.' I smiled at that – Dad's sketchbook rarely left his side. 'I've got an exhibition booked in for the summer for a series of Channel Islands landscapes. They have their own microclimate, you know, and the colour of the ocean needs to be seen to be believed.'

'It sounds great,' I said.

'Mary's come up with a new range as well, based on the colours. She's going to launch it on the same night.'

Mary's pottery keep-cups and tableware had been featured in some of those style magazines.

'You'll have to come,' Dad said. 'I'll send you an invitation.'

I smiled and said, 'I'll try,' but knew I wouldn't go.

The look in his eyes told me that he hoped rather than believed I would. I saw the same on Mary's face and suddenly felt the need to drop my eyes to the table.

There was silence as the waiter delivered our meals. Dad and Mary gushed over their respective pasta dishes, and I pushed my salad around the plate wishing that I'd ordered pasta too and reminding myself of all the reasons why I couldn't. Top of that list right now was the need to be seen in a bikini beside Ainsley.

It was Dad who broke the silence. 'Are you seeing anyone special at the moment, love?'

He asked the same question every time we caught up and I always gave him the same reply. Tonight, I felt my cheeks warm as I struggled for the right answer.

'Sort of,' I finally said. 'But don't get excited, it's not serious.'

Mary placed a hand on Dad's arm to stop him saying anything. 'Tell us about him,' she encouraged.

I pressed my wrist into my lap to ease the prickle. 'There's nothing really to tell. He's a travel writer I met in Hong Kong. I don't think it'll come to anything, but he's encouraged me to pick up the camera again.'

Dad's eyes lit up as I knew they would. It had been the lesser of two evils – to talk about Jake or to disclose the fact that I'd been taking photos again.

'I'm so pleased,' he said. 'You had such a talent.' He turned to Mary. 'I never understood why she put the camera away.'

'Yes, well, it's just something I'm playing with again.' I shifted in my chair and rubbed my wrist against my skirt. 'I don't have any time to do more than that. Did I mention that I'm going to Masters?' When he looked blank, I explained further. 'It's an all-expenses-paid trip to Fiji for the top performers in each of the departments.'

'Congratulations, love. I'm sure it's a real triumph for you. Your mother would be so proud.' There was less excitement in his voice than there had been at my earlier announcement. 'Have you told her yet?'

I shook my head. 'No, I'll call her.'

'How's she going?' he asked. 'Is she happy?'

I frowned, unsure how to answer. It was the first time that Dad had mentioned Mum in years. I supposed he knew that I'd stayed in touch with her, but it wasn't something we talked about.

'It's okay to talk about her,' he added.

I nodded slowly. 'I see,' although I didn't really. 'Umm, she's good, I think. We don't talk a lot – she's busy, I'm busy.'

'You're both always busy.' I looked for a hidden meaning in his words and his smile but couldn't find one. 'As long as you're looking after yourself and you're happy. You are happy, aren't you?'

'Of course I am,' I said. 'I've just got what I've been working towards all year.'

'And what's next?' he asked.

'My boss's job, of course.'

'Other than work?'

When I looked blankly at him, Mary stepped in. 'What about travel, relationships, things like that?'

'I'll have time for that when I get to where I'm going,' I said. 'I can't afford the distraction at the moment.'

Dad looked away from me, but not before I saw something in his eyes that could have been pity.

It was Friday night and Alice was insistent about the three of us getting together. Because I was flying to Hong Kong again the next morning for another week, I'd made them promise not to lead me astray. Jake had been commissioned to do a story on hiking trails and the islands in Hong Kong and would be meeting me there. He'd be leaving on Wednesday, and I had to go into work on Monday and Tuesday, but we had all of Sunday to spend together and a few glorious nights and it was all I could think about. *He* was all I could think about.

Callie seemed preoccupied. I had the feeling that Alice knew more – or suspected more – than she was letting on, but for whatever reason, Callie hadn't confided in me. I didn't blame her – I'd been distant the last few weeks. I'd thought I could keep it all together – work, Jake, friends – but at the moment I was flat out finding room in my head for anything other than Jake and what he'd said he wanted to talk about. While I now knew that I wanted to be with him, I also knew that I couldn't do a long-distance relationship, or compromise on my career. If he needed me to do either I'd have no choice but to walk away and I didn't know how I could bear to do that either. The thought that this might be my last weekend with Jake was eating into me and outweighing any excitement associated with Masters and Fiji.

'Okay, girls, I'm trusting you both not to lead me astray tonight,' I reminded them. 'There's nothing worse than being hungover in economy. Bloody Ainsley.'

'As opposed to being hungover in business class?' asked Alice, smiling.

'If you're not happy there, why don't you leave?' Callie said. 'It's obvious she's going to win, so I don't understand why you don't just cut your losses and get out of there.'

I felt my mouth drop open as I stared at Callie. She never passed judgment on anyone – that wasn't her style.

'Cal,' Alice warned softly, casting a worried glance towards me. 'Maybe that's not the most helpful thing you can say at the moment.'

'Why not? Tiff's never backward in telling us what she thinks about anything. Perhaps it's time she listened to some straight talking from one of us for a change.'

'So says the woman who couldn't wait to run back into the arms of someone who cheated on her before and is probably cheating on her again now,' I said.

'Oh, yes. You're very quick to dole out the advice and pass judgment when it suits you, but you can't handle it when it comes back your way.'

Callie's chin had jutted out and I could see it quivering slightly. I knew I should have stopped it right there, but my frustration about my feelings towards Jake, as well as the anger I felt towards Ainsley – all of it was bubbling over in that moment and being directed towards Cal.

I took a deep breath. 'So why don't you tell me what you really think.'

'I just don't think you need to destroy Ainsley in order to prove that you're top bitch in the kennel. I thought you were there already.'

Callie's words hit me like a blow to my belly. I struggled not only for breath, but to keep my face impassive.

'Just look at the way you've been playing with Jake – pretending Matt's the perfect man for you when anyone can tell it's Jake you really want.' She paused and drew breath. 'Then there are the photos you've been taking. I've known you for a long time – we've known you for a long time.' She looked at Alice, who'd managed to catch the eye of a passing waiter and was mouthing 'And hurry, please!' to him. 'We haven't seen you like this for years. When you showed me those photos you'd taken at Cockatoo Island, it was like you were coming alive from inside. You were the Tiff we knew and loved from school, before you decided to ditch photography for corporate warfare. It's the same with the images you're sharing on Instagram – it's like you've got your mojo back. But when you're talking about work, or taking a call from Ainsley, the light goes out of you. You're tired, Tiff – and I don't think it's just physical. I think you're tired of pretending to be someone else, and that's why you've been avoiding us. Or is it because you're still seeing Jake on the side? You never did tell us how that date went. Are you still seeing him?'

I blinked and swallowed, and reached for my glass. My hand shook slightly as I did, so I put it back into my lap. But Callie wasn't finished.

'You are, aren't you? That's why you haven't been around. So, you're what – playing with him to amuse yourself while you chase the big prize, and then as soon as he gets too close, you'll dump him and move on to someone else? Nothing gets between work and climbing that ladder of yours – didn't you say that? What about love? Oh, that's right – love doesn't belong in your world, does it. You don't believe in it.'

As hurtful as they were, Callie's words had too much truth for me to accept them without fighting back. I felt a red mist descend over my eyes, blinding me to all logic.

'Maybe that's a safer attitude than being such a total romantic that you don't think you're worth anything unless you've got a man. Think about your dating history, Cal – you've gone from the love of your life to the love of your life, and they've all been variations of Jamie. Think about how much he's held you back – from travelling, from progressing at work. You would have gone so much further if you hadn't let him convince you that you weren't ready. And now you're making the same mistake again. He's going to hurt you, Cal. Mark my words, men like Jamie don't have isolated flings.'

'Don't stop there, Tiff. Next thing you'll be telling me that he cheated on me with you.'

I didn't know how to answer that. Jamie had made a pass at me. It was just before they split last time, so I didn't think Cal would ever need to know. I'd told Alice and we'd agreed that nothing good could come of her knowing, not now they'd finished. When Cal went back to Jamie this time, I'd wondered if I should tell her, but Alice had argued that if I did I might lose her.

As all of this ran through my mind and the seconds of silence ticked away, Cal's eyes began to well. 'Oh my god, you didn't!'

'No, I didn't, but he certainly tried it on. I'm sure he tried it with Alice too.'

'Don't involve me in this,' warned Alice.

'Well, did he?' Callie turned on her.

'Not so I noticed,' Alice replied. 'Sweetie, we love you – we'd never do that. Besides, that was a long time ago. He's changed now – you said he has.'

'Why didn't she tell me then?' Callie demanded, gesturing towards me. 'Is that why you've never liked him?'

'How could she tell you?' Alice said. 'She warned you at the time, but you were so in love with him that if she had told you, you'd have taken it out on her. And we both knew that at some stage you'd need us.'

Alice rubbed at Callie's arm in a gesture of support. Callie brushed it away.

'He has changed,' she insisted.

I was getting tired of this conversation very quickly. Why couldn't Cal see Jamie for who he really was?

'Men like that don't change,' I told her. 'They just go into hibernation for a few months until they're sure of you again. They let you think they'd be lost without you and that you're the centre of their universe – until *they're* the centre of *your* universe. Then they back away. You try harder and harder to make things right, and they withdraw more and more until your whole world is built around trying to keep them happy. Just a little more love, you think. You stop going out and you sit at home and wait. That's how it was last time, and that's how it'll be this time too. That's why I've never liked him – I've seen too many of his type before, and I knew how it would end.'

'And what about men like Matt?' Callie demanded.

I rubbed at my brow to smooth the furrow I felt

there. What was it with Callie and the subject of Matt? 'That's the second time you've mentioned Matt. We're not having a relationship. Men like Matt Delaney don't do relationships until they're ready to do them. It's a commitment thing. Sorry, Alice.'

Alice cast a quick glance at Callie. 'No offence taken. I know exactly what my brother used to be like.'

'You act like Matt is some prize you want to win,' Cal went on. 'I know you haven't said as much, but I think that when you decide to settle down, your intention is to do it with Matt. But you don't just get to decide that. You don't just get to say he's perfect and expect he'll be waiting for you when you're ready to take him back from whoever he's moved on to. That's not fair to her – or him.'

I stared at her. I'd never seen Callie like this. She had never uttered a cross word to me in all the years we'd known each other.

'What is with you tonight?' I asked her. 'Number one: Matt Delaney is not the type of guy you can decide to win – it's exactly the opposite. He's the type of guy who decides who he wants. He'll shag around until he finds her, and he'll stop shagging around once he does. But it won't be me – I've always known that. Yes, we've hooked up in the past, but it was just casual – there was no expectation of anything else from either of us. I'd say it ended months ago, except there was nothing to end. We just stopped having sex and started being friends instead. We're way too similar to be together, and I've never wanted us to be anything more than we were. I might joke about how he ticks all the boxes, but that's all it's been – a joke. Happy now?'

Callie looked at the floor.

'Why are you so interested in me and Matt anyway?' I said.

She looked up at me and then down again, and then it hit me. Maybe all of this was from back when Callie had that enormous crush on Matt – when we were in high school. It was about the same time that Mum and Dad separated, so I was wrapped up in my own problems. Surely, though, she wouldn't still be going on about that all these years later? There was only one way to find out.

'Hang on, didn't you used to have a thing about him way back in school? Please tell me that's not what this is about?'

'No,' she said. 'It's not about that. It doesn't matter. Look, I'm sorry – obviously I'm not great company tonight. I shouldn't have said what I did, and I don't know why I did. I'll see you later.'

She kissed Alice and me on the cheek but couldn't meet my eyes. I couldn't meet hers either. What she'd said, wherever it had come from, had cut way too close to the bone for my liking.

I noticed Alice whispering something in Cal's ear as she left, but it didn't seem to cheer her up.

'What was that about?' I asked Alice.

'I think she's dealing with some stuff at the moment.'

'Maybe, but that's no reason for her to go off at me the way she did.'

I waited for Alice to defend me, but she didn't.

'Oh, Tiff, I love you both, but maybe what you both said needed to be said. You know you can be judgmental at times.' I grimaced at that. 'And I can't count how often you've told Callie that she needs to stand up for herself. Perhaps that's what she was doing tonight. This mess she's in with Jamie – she needs to sort it out herself. Just as you do whatever's going on with you.' She looked at me keenly. 'Are you sure this is about work and Jake and nothing to do with my brother?'

'Of course it is. What's with this fascination about me and Matt tonight? No offence, Ally, he's hot as hell, but these days we truly are just friends.'

'So, there's no more random sex taking place?' Alice had leaned forward slightly, as if my answer was extremely important for some reason.

'Isn't that what I just said? Hang on, Matt was talking about going to Queensland last weekend for your brother-in-law's birthday – did he actually go?' Alice looked away briefly and muttered something about snacks. 'And Callie went with you.'

No, it wasn't my imagination. Alice was looking everywhere but at me.

'Oh. My. God! Callie and Matt hooked up! They did, didn't they?'

'I wouldn't call it a hook-up. Look, I don't know about you, but my tummy's going to start rumbling very soon. Can we get some food?'

'You're such a bad liar, Alice Delaney. Jesus, no wonder Callie's messed up – and no wonder she was going off at me. Callie doesn't do random sex – she makes love – and right now she must be feeling like she doesn't know which way is up and which is down. What's she going to do about Jamie?'

'She was going to finish it with Jamie. As you say, Cal's never been able to separate sex and love – and Matt was pretty full on with her over the weekend. You've seen what he's like when he's going after something?' I nodded. 'Well, multiply it by about a hundred. Callie never stood a chance.'

The more I thought about it, the more Callie and Matt made sense. If anyone was going to tame Matt Delaney, I would love for it to be Callie. And if he'd fallen for her, I had no doubt he'd treat her well.

'Is he serious about her?' I asked. I knew with absolute certainty that if Matt hurt her, I'd cause him bodily damage.

Alice must have seen it on my face and giggled. 'Yes, the same thing crossed my mind. He tells me he's never been more serious about anything in his life – and yes, I told him I'd have his balls on a plate if he hurts her. The problem is, she's come home and Jamie's booked a romantic holiday to Phuket and is telling her that he loves her. Matt's a million miles away in Hong Kong, so I have no idea how it will pan out.' She hesitated. 'I think Callie will work herself out. The one I'm really worried about is you.'

I felt myself grow warmer, but it was a prickly warmth that itched around my neck and made me feel as though I was wearing a collar or a high-necked top that needed loosening.

'Don't be ridiculous.' I didn't mean to snap, it just came out that way.

'When did you last see Jake?' Alice asked.

'Oh, I can't remember.' I busied myself filling our wine glasses.

'So the photos he posted during the week where he gave credit to someone he hash-tagged #ithinkwerealonenow had nothing to do with you?'

'I don't have time to be checking Jake Stewart's Instagram,' I said dismissively. 'Besides, what made you think it could be me?'

I'd seen the pictures – and the comments and feedback from Jake's audience. It had given me a thrill of pride that I hadn't felt in … I couldn't remember when.

'Really, Tiff? How stupid do you think I am? Remember that old eighties' pop song by Tiffany, "I Think We're Alone Now"? I thought you said you were finishing it?'

'Well, it would appear that I didn't. Besides, there's nothing to finish. It's just casual.'

Alice nodded as she flicked through Jake's Instagram. 'Of course it is. But these photos are fabulous – and this picture was taken by someone who is definitely serious about her subject.'

She showed me the photo I'd taken of Jake down at Brighton Beach. I'd forgotten it was on the memory card I'd given to him to upload to his laptop. He was sitting on the steps of one of the beach boxes, his eyes squinting into the wind. I'd looked at him through the viewfinder, and the minute I'd clicked the shutter I knew that no matter how hard I tried to keep him at arms-length, Jake Stewart was the only man I wanted. It was also the exact minute that I'd realised he was the one man I probably couldn't have.

As I remembered the kiss we'd shared immediately after I'd taken the shot, Alice said quietly, 'You're in trouble, Tiff – aren't you?'

I nodded. 'Yes, I think I might be.'

'Are you seeing him this week?'

I nodded again. 'I'm meeting him in Hong Kong tomorrow, and we'll spend all day Sunday, and Monday and Tuesday evening together. After that he's going hiking or island-hopping or something. I'm back here on Friday morning, and then it's off to Fiji for Masters next Monday. I'm going to finish it with Jake. I have to finish it.'

'You don't, you know.'

'I do. Remember what happened with Mum and Dad? It doesn't work when one person is artistic and the other is ambitious. Everything gets fucked up. I always swore that I wouldn't wind up like them, Ally. I saw what it did to Dad when Mum went to Perth, and I don't ever want to hurt someone like that. She was only doing what she'd always said she wanted to do – he was the one who didn't believe her. Then there's the long-distance thing.'

'But you're not your parents, and Jake isn't your father.' She paused, then said softly, 'And try as you might, Tiff, you're not your mother.'

I attempted a derisive laugh, but it came out as something that sounded almost like a sob. 'Of course I am. I'm my mother's daughter – and I'm going to make it to the top, just as she's done.'

Alice shook her head. 'You'll make it to the top if that's what you really want, but don't do it at the expense of your happiness. Tiff, I think you're more like your father than you've ever wanted to believe. You're a different woman to your mother: you're warm and passionate and intense, and scared of being left – just like she left you.'

I rubbed at my wrist to avoid scratching the raw skin there. 'You know what – I don't think I'm good company either tonight.' I bent and picked my bag up from the floor under the table, then smiled at Alice. 'I think I'd better go home too, before you start telling me that this is typical Scorpio fear behaviour – or something like that.'

'If you already know it, there's no reason for me to remind you,' she said, hugging me in a way that made my eyes itch as well.

'I saw Luke the other week,' I blurted out.

She pulled back and searched my face. 'And you're only telling me this now?'

'There hasn't been a right time,' I mumbled.

'Since when has that ever stopped you? Christ, between you and Callie, you'll be the death of me. I'm with Tommy now and well and truly over Luke, so nothing you could tell me about him would hurt me, okay?'

I nodded. 'Okay.'

There was a pause, then she asked, as if she didn't care what the answer was, 'Did he have anything to say?'

'Not really.'

She waited for me to expand on that, and when I didn't she said impatiently, 'Okay, so what did he say?'

'I thought you didn't care.'

'Tiff,' she warned.

'Honestly, he said very little. He said that he'd heard you were in Melbourne and wanted to know what you were doing and if you were dating anyone. I told him it was none of his business and he said to say hi to you.' I forced a tight smile. 'So this is me saying hi from Luke.'

Her eyebrows raised slightly and she half-shrugged one shoulder. 'When you see him next say hi back from me.'

'Are you sure you don't care, Ally?' I asked softly.

'Absolutely. Just as sure as I am that you don't believe in love.' She waited for her words to hit home. 'Not that it matters. I'm with Tommy now and he's a sensible decision.'

'Jake isn't,' I said.

'No, I don't suppose he is.' She lightly patted the side of my face. 'But that doesn't necessarily make him the wrong decision.'

I chewed at my lip to stop it from trembling and pressed my wrist hard against my thigh. 'I really am going now.'

She nodded. 'Promise me that you won't push Jake away because you're scared.' My eyes flew to hers as she went on, 'You know I love you, Tiff – Cal and I both do. Stop worrying about us and all the other "shoulds" that you fill your brain with and listen to your heart for a change.'

'That sounds like the lyrics from a really bad pop song.'

'Maybe.' She grinned then. 'Cal would know who sang it.'

'And she'd sing it for us very badly.' I felt the lump rise to my throat again. 'Oh, Ally, I really owe her an apology, don't I?'

'You'll both sort it out, I'm sure.' She kissed my cheek. 'Now, get that skinny arse out of here. I'll talk to you when I'm back from Bali.'

I squeezed my eyes shut as I remembered. 'God, I'm sorry. I completely forgot you were going away.'

She waved my apology away with a smile. 'It doesn't matter, Tiff. I know you have other things on your mind. Just have a great time with Jake, and kick Ainsley's arse at Masters.'

CHAPTER NINETEEN

I didn't sleep well that night. It was as if my brain had the argument with Callie on replay, over and over again. I'd had plenty of opportunities to shut it down and I hadn't. Alice had said that we each obviously had things going on in our lives and the words had needed to be said, but in all our years of friendship it was the first time I'd ever seen that look in Callie's eyes and heard that tone in her voice. It took me until the early hours of the morning to determine what it was – disappointment. Callie was disappointed in me. For what though? Putting my head before my heart? For passing judgment on her? For not telling her about Jamie when I had the opportunity? For not sharing what was happening in my life? I suspected it was all of these things.

I turned over in bed and punched my pillow into submission for about the hundredth time that night. She had no right to be disappointed in me. How I chose to live my life had nothing whatsoever to do with her. At least I went after what I wanted and didn't fall in love constantly with men who would cheat on me and hold me back. Callie could have achieved so much more if it hadn't been for her choice in men. Jamie was the worst, and I couldn't understand why she couldn't recognise how he drained her confidence and manipulated her into doing what he wanted – especially now that she had Matt interested in her. Why wasn't she running straight to him? He was perfect for her.

Hours later on the plane I was still replaying the conversation. What was I supposed to do? Sit back and watch her ruin her life? I wouldn't be a very good friend if I did that, would I? Although if I really was a good friend, maybe I'd support her decisions and be there to catch her when I was proved right – as, inevitably, I was.

But *was* I always right? When it came to matters of business, absolutely. But when it came to matters of the heart? I was beginning to think that I didn't have a clue.

Cal had said that I was always quick with my opinions whether they were welcome or not; and I supposed I was. My first impressions were never wrong. Yet I'd been so wrong about Jake. Based on what he was wearing and his profession I'd built an image of Jake that had proved to be way off the mark. In fact, the only thing I'd been right about was the knowledge that he'd cause me trouble.

If I'd been so wrong about Jake, maybe I was also wrong about Cal – and possibly even Jamie. What if he really had changed and what I'd said to her last night made her question that? What if I pushed her towards Matt and he broke her heart too? What if my ridiculous Project Yes had compelled her to say yes to something she absolutely should have said no to? What if I'd been manipulating Callie all these years to do what I wanted her to do? What if I was no better than Jamie? Then came the worst thought of all: what if I knew nothing about anything?

Andi had told me that she and Abby had joked about me having such a clear image of who my Mister Right was. They'd said that one day I'd meet someone who had completely the wrong job, the wrong look, the wrong income, the wrong car, who lived in the wrong suburb, came from the wrong family and had gone to the wrong school, and that would be the day I'd fall hopelessly in love.

They'd probably say that was what had happened with Jake, but they'd be wrong. I wasn't in love with Jake. That's not what any of this meant. The jealousy I'd felt seeing him with another woman, the way I couldn't wait to see him again, the way I couldn't stop thinking about him – none of that was love. It was hormones and it would pass.

It had to. Because unless Jake had a foolproof plan for dealing with the distances resulting from both of our careers, at some point over the next few days I needed to find the strength to end this. Before he had the chance to break my heart.

•

By the time we landed I'd managed to convince myself that I had the strength to break things off with Jake. I repeated it to myself as I showered and changed into a fresh set of underwear and the hotel's white terry-towelling bathrobe, and even as I walked across to the door to open it to Jake. But then he smiled at me and it was like every logical thought that had previously been in my brain flew out the window.

His eyes moved slowly down my body, lingering where I'd loosely tied the bathrobe together. Reaching for the end of the sash, he pulled me towards him and kissed me.

'What do we have under here?' I could feel the smile in his voice as he nuzzled his way down my throat. Pushing the robe off me, he pulled back to look at me when his hands met the filmy fabric that barely covered my breasts. 'Nice,' he said, bending his head to suck at my nipples through the fabric.

Gently turning me around, he unclipped my bra, reaching his hands around to catch my breasts, his body pressed against my back. When I would have turned to face him again, he moved my hair away and whispered into my ear, 'No, sweetheart, just stay still.'

I could feel him looking at me and my breath came faster, heat pooling between my legs. Then his finger traced my spine, so lightly it felt like a feather, up and down, around my buttocks and back up again. Just one finger, back and forward, up and down. Soon his finger was replaced by his tongue, the touch just as light, his breath warm on the skin he'd wet. One hand rested gently against my hip, holding me in place, while the other played with my breasts, tracing a line under them, then over my hip, across my buttock, between my legs, back over my hip. Oh god. Moaning, I opened my legs further in a silent plea to touch me where I most needed it and gripped at the edge of the desk. Out the window I could see Hong Kong Harbour stretched out below me, but it only vaguely registered as Jake continued his teasing.

'Please,' I groaned.

'Please what?' he asked into my skin, his finger straying tantalisingly close to where I needed it to be.

'Please touch me.'

'I thought I was.'

He dropped to his knees on the floor, his tongue now tracing circles over my bottom. First one cheek, then the other. His hand trailed up the inside of my thigh. He paused for long enough to turn me around and blew lightly on my undies.

'These are so pretty it seems almost a shame to take them off.' He leaned forward again and tongued me through the flimsy fabric.

'Please, Jake.'

He lifted his head to look up at me, that slow smile

spreading across his face as he watched me fight for breath, my hands itching to push his head back where I needed it so badly. Without taking his eyes from mine he slowly pushed the pants down my legs, taking his time, lifting first one leg and then the other until they were gone.

Just when I thought I'd go mad with all the teasing and waiting, he placed his hands on my hips and pulled me forward so he could taste me properly.

When my legs couldn't hold me any longer and I fell into him, he continued to hold me long after the wave had passed. It was only then that I realised he was still fully dressed.

'You have too many clothes on,' I said, pulling away so I could reach for his hand and lead him over to the bed.

'Maybe you should do something about that,' he suggested, the twinkles in his eyes making my breath catch all over again. Christ, I was in so much trouble with this man.

I must have slept because when I woke it was completely dark outside. The curtains were still open, and the room was momentarily lit by the colours of the laser show that flashed from the buildings close to the harbour each night. I rolled onto my back to see Jake lying on his side watching me.

I turned to face him. 'I'm sorry. I must have been

exhausted.'

He trailed a finger down my arm, smiling into my face. 'You went out like a light.'

'I seem to be making a habit of that with you – the snoring and dribbling thing.'

'It's okay, I dozed off too.' He hesitated before asking, 'Is everything okay, Tiff?'

'Of course, why wouldn't it be?'

He shrugged and his smile seemed tighter, as if he was worried about my answer. 'I don't know. You just seemed really tightly wound up tonight – more than usual.'

'Well, I'm certainly not now.' My skin grew warm at the memory of exactly how he'd relaxed me.

'I'm pleased to hear it.'

I turned onto my back to escape the question in his eyes. 'Jake, do you think I'm overly opinionated?'

He let out a short laugh. 'What?'

'You heard me. What about cold? Do you think I'm cold?'

'You certainly weren't this afternoon. You were like molten lava in my arms this afternoon.'

'I'm serious.'

In the darkness I could feel his eyes on me. 'O-kay. And this isn't some sort of trick question? One of those there's no right answer to? Like "Does my bum look fat in these jeans?" It's not one of those?'

'Do you think I'm putting on weight?' I said. 'I

wouldn't be surprised. I've been travelling so much my exercise routine has suffered, and since I met you it's been nothing but carbs and way too many dumplings. That's the problem with street food, it's –'

I didn't get a chance to finish my sentence before he'd pulled me back towards him and covered my mouth with his.

'I have no idea whether you've put on weight,' he said when we came up for air. 'And nor would I care if you did. I love watching you eat. I love watching *you*. You look fabulous to me – all the time. Although, if I'm being honest, I much prefer you now to when you're in those serious business suits of yours.'

I lightly punched his arm. 'Of course you prefer me like this, you idiot. Any man would prefer a naked woman to a clothed one.'

'I didn't mean that. Well,' his grin was wolfish, 'I absolutely do – especially when that naked woman is you. And I adore you in that little flimsy whatever it was I took off you earlier.' He lifted the sheet and peered beneath it. 'No, I take that back. I prefer you exactly like this; and if it was up to me, I'd keep you like this forever.'

'That would get very boring,' I said, although the prospect of never leaving this bed and not having to go into work on Monday was suddenly a very attractive one.

Not having to go into work again was an attractive thought – where had that come from?

'I don't think I'd ever get bored with you.' He leaned forward and kissed me again. Although he was still smiling, the conversation felt as though it was going somewhere deeper. 'I'm serious though, Tiff. When you're dressed in those work suits with your hair up or straightened, you're still beautiful, possibly more so, but at the same time you seem remote and detached, and yes, cold. It's like you put those clothes on and you're suddenly Tiffany and all business; not the Tiff I met and not the Tiff I … Just not the woman I know.'

It sounded like he was going to say something else but changed his mind.

'So you do think I'm cold.'

He sighed. 'What is this, Tiff? Are you trying to start an argument by putting words in my mouth? Where is this coming from?'

I turned onto my side and faced the window again. A pink light flickered through the room. 'It's something that Callie said last night. She said I'm quick to judge people and tell them what I think regardless of whether they want to hear it or not.'

'Aaaah, I see.'

'Cal's never spoken to me like that ever. It was more than her words though, it was the look in her eyes as though she was disappointed in me or with me or something. And she's got no right to think that. Not about me. I've spent my whole life making sure that people can't be disappointed with my performance or my life choices or …' My voice trailed away. 'I don't make mistakes. Not the sort of mistakes that Cal makes anyway. You know, she's about to go away with Jamie – remember I told you about him?'

'Yes, I remember.'

'Well, apparently she's now going to Phuket with him – even though I'm sure he's only booked it so that a) she won't get to go to the interview for the dream job she's been asked to go for, and b) so he can have her under his control again. That's what men like Jamie do. They're all over you until you can't see straight, and then just when you've completely fallen for them, they start to pull back. Just a little bit at first, then a bit more, and before you know it you've stopped seeing your friends, your work is suffering, and then he pulls back completely and you're left with nothing but a broken heart. That's what happened before and it's what will happen again. I know it, and I think deep down she knows it too.'

'Are we still talking about Callie and Jamie?' he asked softly.

'Of course we are,' I snapped. 'Who else would we be talking about?'

'I don't know … you tell me. You and Shane? Your parents maybe? I hope you don't think that's what I'd do with you.'

I flipped back to face him. 'Don't be ridiculous.' His eyes widened at my tone. 'I'll be there to support Cal when it happens again – as it will. This time, though, she has the opportunity to make a more sensible choice. Apparently she and Matt – that's Alice's brother –' My gaze moved away from his.

'The one who lives here who you catch up with occasionally? Yes, you've mentioned him a few times.' His voice sounded so innocent that I searched his face for another meaning.

'I've told you, we're just friends.' I pretended to be fascinated by the colours dancing on the ceiling. 'Okay,' I conceded, 'we might have been a bit more for a while, but that was just a sometimes thing and we're not any more and haven't been for months, so that's beside the point.' I knew that I sounded defensive.

'I wasn't suggesting it was anything more,' Jake said.

'Yes, but …' I shook my head in an effort to bring my thoughts back on track. 'Anyway, as I was saying, Matt and Callie hooked up and Matt apparently wants to take it further. And yet she's going to Phuket with Jamie! She's mad. Matt is absolutely perfect –'

'For who?' Jake cut in. 'Who is he perfect for? Callie or you?'

'Callie of course!'

'There's no "of course" about it, Tiff. From what you've told me he would tick every box on the checklist you say you don't have.'

I turned to look at him. He was also lying on his back staring at the ceiling, the line of his jaw firm. A little pulse beat there and I longed to reach out and smooth it away, but something stopped me. Instead I sighed deeply.

'You're right. Matt does tick every box on my checklist, but that doesn't make him right for me. We had some fun – I won't deny that – and now I think he's a friend. But Cal? I think she loves him – she can't do the shag-and-forget thing so she must. I wouldn't be surprised if she's always loved him. Plus, he's a nice guy and will treat her well. He won't play those games with her that Jamie does, and he won't stand in her way.' I paused, then added softly, 'That's why I'm so angry with her. I want to grab her and shake her and wrap her up so she doesn't get hurt by Jamie again, but I can't. Instead I have to wait until it happens and then pick up the pieces knowing that if she'd only listened to me it wouldn't have happened.'

He turned to face me again and ran a finger down the side of my face and across my lips. 'Oh, Tiff, you can't control everything. But you can do what you're doing now – be a good friend and care about her.'

My eyes suddenly felt hot and a lump formed in my throat. 'That's the thing – I don't think I have been a good friend. If I was, Cal would have told me about Jamie when they first got back together, and she would have told me about Matt. But she didn't because I think she was worried about what I'd say. Cal was right to say what she did to me – it was a long time coming – but I reacted badly and was mean to her when she's the last person on earth that anyone should be mean to. She was right – I am quick to pass judgment but can't take it when it comes back at me. I'm just as cold and hard as Ainsley is – it's a wonder I have any friends left.'

'I only know Ainsley from what you've told me about her, but you're far from cold, my darling. And those people you let see beyond the business suits? They're very lucky indeed. Let's just say that I don't ever want to get on the wrong side of you.' He laughed, but it was a short laugh and didn't match the intensity in his eyes.

I knew I should have got out of the bed, made up some excuse why he couldn't stay the night, and told him to leave – all the things I should have done that first night. But I couldn't. All I could do was let myself be wrapped in his warmth.

'I don't think you ever will,' I whispered as I kissed him.

I didn't know if he'd heard me, but our lovemaking felt different, as though we'd moved to a new and even more terrifying level. I could almost hear the click as the lock turned, and even though I knew that escape was more impossible with every kiss, I let myself go willingly.

CHAPTER TWENTY

I slept deeper and later than I had in … I couldn't remember how long, and when I woke it was to the smell of coffee being waved under my nose.

'Come on, sleepyhead,' Jake said. 'Half the day has gone while you've been lying there.'

I stretched luxuriantly and smiled when I saw the look in his eyes at my movement, so I did it again. 'What time is it?'

'Just past nine,' he said, his gaze stuck on the breast that had somehow escaped from the sheet.

'Mmmmm, what's the rush?' I pretended I'd just seen the coffee. 'Oh, you've bought coffee – I can't let it go cold after you've gone to the effort of getting it for me. And is that a Portuguese tart?' If I could see my own face, I was sure it would be the picture of innocence.

'I can always go out again for coffee,' he said, lowering the sheet until both breasts were exposed. 'But while you're lying there …'

Much later, after shared custard tarts and fresh

coffee, we were on the subway and heading to Kowloon and the mainland.

'Where are we going?' I asked.

'Kowloon,' he answered with a grin.

'I know that, idiot. But what are we going there for?'

'There's a temple over there that I want to write about.'

'A temple? Seriously? We're going all the way over there for a temple? Aren't there plenty on the island?'

He laughed. 'Ah, my unbelieving beauty, this isn't just any temple. This temple contains a magical garden where wishes made with the right intent come true.'

'Really?' I said sceptically.

'Uh huh. They can't help it – it's written in ... Well, it's written down somewhere – that's some of what I have to find out. I'm writing a piece about fortune-tellers and that's part of what this place is famous for.'

'Fortune-tellers? Like what Alice does?' Despite my scepticism I was interested.

'No, nothing to do with astrology. Besides, haven't you told me that what Alice does is nothing to do with fortune-telling?'

I returned his grin. 'At least you've been listening. So if they don't use the stars, what do they use? A crystal ball?'

'Nope. Nothing so esoteric. They use sticks called chim.'

'Really? How does that work?'

'You'll need to wait and see, won't you?'

'Does this temple have a name?'

'It does. It's the Sik Sik Yuen Wong Tai Sin Temple.'

I laughed. 'I bet you can't say that too many times in a row after a few beers.'

'I can't say it more than once even completely sober.' He grinned and our eyes met, and for a few seconds I felt as though we were alone in the crowded train carriage.

The jolt of the train pulling into a station broke the spell and I forced my eyes away from his. 'How much longer before we get to this temple of yours?'

'You really are always this impatient, aren't you?' I nodded. 'We get off at the next station.'

The walk from the subway was lined with stalls selling incense and other offerings. We ignored them and made our way through the decorative gate and into the temple itself. Inside was a village of coloured roofs, intricate lattice work and red pillars painted with gold characters. The air around the temple hall was heavy with the smoke of countless sticks of incense; and worshippers kneeled on rows of cushions facing the hall. There was something about the scene that stirred me in a way I hadn't expected and couldn't explain.

To hide my discomfort, I pointed out the portable metal fencing. 'What's that? Temple crowd control?'

'Actually yes, it is,' Jake said. 'This is one of the

busiest temples in Hong Kong, so they quite often need help with queuing.'

'Oh.' I looked again at the people kneeling on the cushions. 'What are they doing? Praying?'

He followed my glance. 'Yes and no. They're shaking chim or fortune sticks. Each of the sticks has a number and a Chinese character on it that corresponds to a fortune. What you do is get your box of sticks, kneel on the cushion and think of a wish.'

'Any wish?'

'The only proviso is that it must be truly meant – so not what you think you should wish for, but what you want from the bottom of your heart. This is about what your heart wants, not your head.' He paused and rubbed at his jaw. 'At least that's how I think it goes. Anyway, you kneel, you think of your wish and then you gently shake the box until a stick drops out. You take the stick to the pigeonholes around the back and find the one with your number on it. In it will be a little slip of paper, which you then get read by a fortune-teller. So,' he pulled his cap off his head, 'are you going to have a go and make a wish?'

'Why not?'

'Okay, I'll get you some sticks, but be careful what you wish for – you might just get it.' He smiled at me, but it seemed forced.

'Are you going to make a wish too?' I asked.

'I'm not sure I can ask for what I truly want without

breaking some of the rules. You see, that's the other thing about your wish – it has to be one that doesn't impede anyone else's free will, or force anyone else to do something or feel something they don't already feel.'

He looked away from me and focused his gaze on the rows of people kneeling before the hall. It felt as though there was a meaning hidden behind his words that I hadn't quite grasped – but suddenly very much wanted to.

'Maybe if you tell me what it is, I can help you put it into words?' I said.

He shook his head slowly. 'No. If you tell someone your wish, it won't come true.'

'Is that written somewhere too?'

'I have no idea, but it's what I'm afraid of.' He turned and met my gaze.

'I see,' I said, although I didn't understand what he was trying to tell me. 'Best you don't tell me then – give your wish the best possible chance of coming true.'

We each got a set of chim and kneeled beside each other on the cushions.

I clinked my box against his. 'Here's to our wishes coming true.'

He nodded but said nothing.

I looked up at the temple hall before us and the altar full of offerings, needing their inspiration. I knew I should be wishing for a successful Masters and Ainsley's job, but every time I thought I had a grasp on the wish it drifted out of my head.

I looked at Jake. Like me, he'd made no move to shake his sticks.

'I know,' I said, 'let's go on the count of three.'

'You're on. One. Two. Three.'

His eyes held mine as he shook the container of chim. I did the same. I tried to picture Ainsley, I tried to picture the awards ceremony at Masters, but my mind could only see Jake. It was all Jake. He was my wish.

I felt, rather than heard, the single stick fall from the canister. One fell from Jake's container at the same time.

'I've got thirty-eight,' I said.

'Seventy-eight.'

'Any idea what that means?'

'Not a clue.'

'Shall we go find out?'

'Yes, but first I want to offer some incense.'

Just like on that first day in the temple on Lantau Island I watched Jake light the incense from the flame burning in the cauldron. He held the sticks in his hands for a few seconds before raising them to the sky in offering to the gods. Then, still holding the incense, he bowed to the temple and stuck the burning sticks in the cauldron of sand that was already holding the hundreds of other sticks that filled the air with smoke and fragrance.

'Just making sure the gods got my message,' he

said, the grin back on his face and the twinkle returned to his eyes. It was as though I'd imagined that moment of uncertainty or fear I'd seen while he was kneeling with the chim.

Without speaking, we made our way to the passage lined with pigeonholes, found our respective numbers and each took the slip of paper containing the meaning of our fortune in Chinese characters.

'What happens now?' I asked.

'Now we take it to one of the fortune-tellers in those booths over there. There should be some English speakers who can interpret these slips, but if we want to pay more, they'll tell us our fortune.'

'Okay, but let's look at the gardens first,' I suggested.

'Delaying the inevitable?'

'Perhaps,' I conceded. If my wish wasn't going to come true, I didn't want to be told that right away. The problem was, I was still no clearer about what it was that I'd wished for, just that Jake was involved. 'Actually, no, let's get it over with.'

At the booths I chose a little dried-up man who was wearing so many sets of beads that they clinked in time with his movements. He grabbed the paper, looked at my palm and began talking in riddles – or what sounded to me like riddles.

'You've had one life,' he said, 'and will start another soon. A proposition will come with the blessing of the fates. Forget the lessons of the past; the teacher of the present and your future is wise and brings with him love. To take one road means you will leave another behind.' Just as I was trying to work out what that meant, he started rhyming. 'A roving life will be your lot, you'll smile and seldom moan, and gather wealth sufficient to fool the rolling stone.' He let go of my hand. 'You will soon receive important news that will change your residence – a surprise and a strange bed.' He smiled, showing me the gaps in his teeth. 'You will get your wish.'

Then he waved me away, indicating that the reading – if, indeed, that was a reading – was over.

Jake appeared soon after, his smile wide. 'How did you go?' he asked.

'I'm going to have strange news and a surprise bed. Or was that the other way around? I couldn't really make much sense of it all – maybe I'd need to pay for the full reading for that – but apparently I'll get my wish and seldom moan. What about you? You're looking pleased with yourself.'

'That, my dear, is because I'm going to get my wish soon. Actually, it's better than that – my ardent hope will soon be realised. Apparently, though, it won't run completely smoothly and there'll be a step back before my wish makes its way to me over land and sea.'

'Do they always talk in riddles and rhymes?' I asked.

'I have absolutely no idea, but I like that they do.'

•

After the temple we made our way back to Hong Kong
Island and down to the area called So Ho, being south
of Hollywood Street. It was a neighbourhood known
for its art and its antiques, but I especially loved walking
through the Cat Street markets and the stalls of bric-
a-brac – as I called it – and other people's junk, as Jake
referred to it. He and I both knew that I'd normally
turn my nose up at what the hawkers were selling, but
something about the mood of the day elevated the
wares from tourist tat to potential finds.

'You know these were probably made yesterday
and most likely in a factory in Shenzhen,' Jake said
when I lingered at a table of 'genuine antique' porcelain
vases.

'I know, but they're very pretty,' I replied. 'I love
these chopsticks though. I might take some home for
Cal and Alice.'

'Do you normally buy them presents when you
travel?'

'No, but there's a first time for everything. And
when else am I going to find chopsticks made out of
whatever this black stuff is – jet maybe?'

'Plastic, I'd say,' Jake replied with a grin.

'Okay, plastic, but they have little silver engravings
of the birth year animal on them.'

'Also plastic.'

'I don't care what you say – it's the thought that counts and I'm getting them. A set for each of us.'

Not that a set of black plastic chopsticks with dodgy plastic silverwork could possibly make up for my behaviour on Friday night, but it was a start.

'And what about a set for me?' Jake said. 'When I'm at your place.'

'Even though they're plastic?'

'I was born in the year of the dog,' he added helpfully; then: 'It's the thought that counts.'

I nodded slowly and rummaged in my wallet for longer than I needed to for the cash to buy the chopsticks.

When the rain came down, we ran for cover and huddled in shopfronts.

'I don't know if I'm soaked from sweat or from rain,' I laughed.

'Me neither,' said Jake.

I peered out at the rain. 'So why are we even bothering to shelter when we're wet anyway? It's not as if we can get any wetter.'

'Excellent point.'

He grabbed my hand and we walked back out into the downpour.

CHAPTER TWENTY-ONE

By the time we got back to the hotel we were both soaked to the skin. My hair hung limply down my back and my clothes clung tighter than decency would normally have allowed. In the hotel lift Jake's eyes lingered on my breasts in a way that sent all the heat in my body somewhere way south.

'Don't look at me like that,' I whispered, desperately wanting him to continue to look at me like that forever.

'Like what?' He whispered it back, the promise in his voice making all the goosebumps in my body wonder where they should be.

'Like you want to eat me up.'

My eyes followed his to my breasts where the nipples were clearly standing to attention. As the doors opened and more people squeezed in, I shuffled back until I was wedged delightfully in front of him.

'Oh, but I do want to eat you up,' he whispered, nipping at my earlobe and pulling me closer into his body. I thought I heard him moan into my ear; or it could have been me as his hand brushed at the edge of an already very sensitised breast.

'That had to be the longest lift ride in history,' I said when the lift doors finally opened at our destination.

'It sure was.' He pushed me back against the door to our room to kiss me, then kissed his way down my neck. 'Hurry up and open the door.'

'You have the key,' I gasped.

'Do I?' He ground himself against me.

'Uh huh. Do you want me to check your pocket?'

'Yes – no. If you touch me at the moment, I'm not sure we'll make it into the room.'

I pushed him away and leaned against the wall. 'Hurry up with that key.'

His eyes didn't leave me as he fiddled in his pocket for his wallet and then the key, somehow managing to get the key into the slot on the door, and a condom out of his wallet almost at the same time.

'What about a shower?' I asked as the door finally opened and he pulled me into the room behind him.

'Later.'

When I woke sometime later, Jake was at the desk with his laptop open. I didn't know if he was going through the photos we'd taken or jotting down notes for the story he'd be writing. He was dressed just in a towel and I lay there propped up on one elbow and watched him work. As if he felt my gaze, he turned to watch me watching him.

'I had fun today,' I said.

'Me too.'

'Have you got what you needed?'

'No,' he said, shedding the towel and walking towards the bed. 'Not yet.'

'I was talking about the story,' I managed.

'I wasn't.'

And then I didn't think again until the alert of an incoming text interrupted my moans.

'Ignore it,' Jake urged.

'I can't,' I replied, tipping my head back to allow him easier access to the arch of my neck. 'It could be work.'

'But it's the weekend,' he protested. His hand cupped one aroused breast and he dipped his head to taste my nipple.

Another text came through and I summoned what was left of my willpower to push against his chest. 'I'm never off work and there's a branch closure happening this weekend that Ainsley is just waiting to go wrong. I can't ignore it.'

'Tonight? It's a Sunday.'

'Yes,' I replied as I pulled his T-shirt on to cover my nakedness, then reached for my phone on the bedside table. 'Normally they'd do it on a Friday – and we did cease operations on Friday – but they're doing the clean-out and pack-up this weekend. My responsibility is the communication and change piece, so if these messages relate to that there's a problem.' I scrolled through the messages on my phone. 'Oh shit. That's all I need.'

'What's happened?' Jake moved behind me to kiss behind my ear, his hand under the T-shirt and tracing lightly down the line of my spine.

Ignoring the tingles it gave me, I shrugged his hand away. 'It's from Ainsley and she doesn't sound happy. Apparently an employee has tweeted that they're going drinking to celebrate the closure.' I pressed two fingers into my brow as I forced my brain back to where it needed to be. 'Fuck, fuck, fuck, fuck,' I muttered under my breath.

'I don't see what the problem is,' said Jake, a look of confusion on his face. 'So the staff are heading out for a drink – surely they're allowed to do that? In fact, if one part of their life is finishing, I would have thought they'd need to do that for closure – or isn't that allowed?'

'They can go out for a drink,' I said, scrolling through the email Ainsley's text referred me to. 'I agree, they need to do that. But we can't be seen to be paying for it, and they certainly shouldn't be using the term "party" or "celebrate", especially not on social media and especially not in the same sentence as "branch closure". Can you see the headlines? "Community loses branch while bank staff celebrate." The paper would find someone to say that the bill was being picked up on someone's corporate card and the whole thing would be a current affairs show's dream come true.'

I left the bed and stalked around the hotel room in the too-big T-shirt and no underwear. 'They'll haul out some little old lady with a walking frame to say in a quavering voice how she's been going to this branch since she was a girl and now she'll have to order a taxi to take her to her nearest branch to access her pension. No, wait,' I held one finger in the air as I thought aloud. 'Better yet, she can't afford a taxi and her only option is a tram, and we all know just how unsafe that part of town is for little old ladies. Maybe they'll show her turning up at her old branch to find that everything's closed and there's an empty office where she used to sit and have a cup of tea while she waited to be served.' I stopped pacing. 'And Ainsley will have the reason she needs to fire me.'

The look on Jake's face became more disbelieving. 'Babe, let's get some perspective here. You're not denying that you've closed the branch?'

'Of course not.'

'And you would have had to let people in the community know you were doing that?'

'I approved the communication plan myself.' My chin pushed out to its most haughty.

'Where's the problem then? None of this is exactly a surprise to anyone. From tomorrow, everyone's going to know the site is empty and that little old lady is going to have to catch a tram. I'm assuming that was factored into your business case?'

'I wasn't involved in the impact analysis, but it was,' I said, choosing to ignore the sarcasm in his voice as he referred to the bank's business case. 'But by tomorrow morning, there'll be no evidence left that there was ever a branch there.'

'What do you mean? Surely you'll leave the ATM?'

I shook my head. 'Nope, if the team does their job properly, every last piece of branding will be gone by now, including the ATM.'

'Wiped clean? Like a murder scene?'

I nodded. 'Something like that.'

'Man, you guys are good!'

'Thanks. I think so. We've improved the execution of the plan over the years.'

'It wasn't meant to be a compliment,' he said, moving to the edge of the bed to pull his clothes on.

'What do you mean by that?'

'You're so hung up on protecting your brand, you've forgotten about the human impact of the decisions you've made. Just listen to yourself, Tiff. It's okay for that little old lady to have to change her whole routine at a time of her life when the tiniest change has a huge impact – as long as it doesn't hit the media. And it's okay for the staff to have a few drinks to commiserate with each other for the fact that some of them mightn't have a job tomorrow and, at the least, their team is breaking up, as long as they don't call it a celebration and aren't seen to be smiling.'

'No,' I corrected him. 'As long as they don't hashtag our name.'

That look on his face – was it pity or disgust? I couldn't be sure.

'It's my job,' I said weakly.

'I get that, but you don't have to buy into it to that extent. You're not a heartless bitch, so why pretend you are?'

His words hit too closely to the wounds that Callie had left on Friday night. I scrambled to find the higher ground.

'How dare you tell me what I am and what I'm not? It's my job and it pays for my life, and whether or not I agree with the decisions that are made, I'll do what I need to do.'

'To get to the top?'

'Exactly.'

'So you can spend the rest of your career looking back down the ladder to knock anyone off who's climbing up behind you? You're prepared to compromise what I know you believe in for that?'

'Who are you to tell me what I believe in?'

'I don't need to,' he said quietly. 'Your photographs do that for me.'

I was silent for a few seconds, shifting uncomfortably under his gaze. 'You have no right to criticise my ambitions – you've never had any yourself.' I hated myself as soon as the words sprang from my mouth.

'What makes you say that? I have ambitions, but they're different to yours. And,' he held a hand up to stop me interrupting him, 'there's absolutely nothing wrong with wanting to get to the top – as long as your heart is in it.' He paused and looked steadily at me. 'And I don't believe yours is, Tiff. It might have been once upon a time, but that's not the Tiff I know.'

'I'm not letting that bitch destroy what I've worked for,' I declared, my eyes glittering with moisture I refused to allow to flow.

'Perhaps not, but you seem to be prepared to destroy yourself in the process.' He walked across to the bench and picked up the camera to display the photographs from today. 'Look at these, Tiff. Really look at them. There's an integrity in your photos that's missing from your work. This is who you are. You said it yourself – it's what you wanted when you were younger. Why not now?'

'Are you saying that you think this is what I should be doing?'

He nodded. 'And us, me, what we have. You mightn't want to admit it, but you want that too.' He took my hand and led me to his laptop. 'Just look at that. That's your work.'

I looked, remembering the way the picture in my eye froze as I clicked the shutter on the beaming stall-holder. Then I shook my head. 'No, no, it can't be. That's not happening.'

'Come with me, Tiff.'

'Where?'

'To Taipei next week, and then to Vietnam and to wherever else after that. We're the perfect package, you and me. My words, your images.'

I was shaking my head but the words I knew I should be saying wouldn't come out.

Jake reached for my other hand. 'I know you haven't wanted to hear it, Tiff, but I love you. I've loved you from that first afternoon.' He smiled into my eyes and just for a second I allowed the warmth of his words to curl around my heart. 'You opened your eyes and smiled at me through the dribble and just like that I was gone.'

'But you never said,' I managed.

'How could I? You were so keen to let me know that we were for one night only – and I wanted you so badly that I'd take anything from you that you were prepared to give.'

'I thought we'd shag each other out of our systems,' I said.

'But we didn't.' He hadn't let go of my hands or my eyes.

'No, we didn't.' I spoke so softly I could have been whispering.

Then I was pulling my hands away and shaking my head again. 'No, no no,' I repeated as if it were a mantra. 'No, this can't be happening. I'm going to

Masters – I've worked all year to get there. I can't go with you to Taipei.' I forced a smile. 'I know – I'll go to Fiji for Masters, and you can go to Taipei, and we'll catch up when you're back. Nothing has to change.'

He shook his head sadly. 'But it does have to change. It's what I wanted us to talk about. I love you and I want to be with you – all the time. Not every so often when we're in the same city at the same time.'

'But on your terms,' I said.

'I can see how it could come across that way. But I truly believe this is what you want too. I've watched your face when you see a shot and compose it in your head, as if you know how it's going to look when you squeeze the shutter. I've watched you come alive over a simple dumpling that squirts soup into your mouth, and a bowl of noodles eaten on the side of a street. You wear those suits and heels of yours as if they're battle armour, yet that day on Cockatoo Island when we were soaked to the skin – well, I don't think I've seen anything more beautiful in my life. And today, with sweat dripping from everywhere it shouldn't be, you were remarkable. You were radiant, Tiff – and it was coming from inside of you and had absolutely nothing to do with getting to go on any Masters trip. You know you felt it too.'

Jake watched me as I wavered.

'Look me in the eye and tell me you don't love me too and I'll walk away now,' he said.

When my gaze remained focused on the laptop screen, he lifted my chin so my eyes met his. 'Tell me, Tiff. Tell me you don't love me.'

I met his eyes then and the intensity in them stopped my breath in my throat. 'I can't,' I said when I could breathe again. 'You know I can't.'

'You can't tell me that you don't love me, or you can't tell me that you love me, or you can't come with me?'

'All of it,' I said miserably. 'It would never work – don't you see? We don't want the same things, you're too –'

'Too what? Too different to what's on your checklist? Don't deny it, Tiff – I'm the wrong type, I have the wrong occupation, I wear the wrong clothes, I drive the wrong car. Who am I kidding? I don't drive a car. The thing is, I don't tick any of the boxes on your checklist.'

'You make me sound like a shallow bitch.'

'Perhaps.' He smiled and I smiled weakly back. 'Yet for all that, I'm right for you – you know that. You just need to admit it to yourself.'

'I'd have to give up everything I ever wanted,' I said.

'For everything that you really want.'

I screwed my eyes shut. 'Don't ask me to do this, Jake. Let's just carry on as we were. We'll go to bed now and make love, and tomorrow morning I'll go to work and you'll go island-hopping or hiking or whatever it is you're doing.'

'No, Tiff. I'm going to leave now and sleep at the hotel I'm being paid to review, and you can think about my offer. Go to work, do your job, go home on Thursday and pack, and come back here and meet me next week. Don't go to Fiji, come with me instead. We'll go to Taipei and then see what happens.'

I shook my head again. 'I can't do that – the see-what-happens thing. I need to know where my next pay cheque is coming from. I've got a mortgage to pay –'

'Lease your apartment.'

'And shoes and handbags –'

He grinned at her. 'You won't need many where we're going.'

'But I've been working towards Masters for ages.'

'Then go.'

I stared at him. 'If I do, I lose you.'

'And I lose you.' He paused and drew in a deep, long breath. 'But that's better than only half having you.' He stepped closer and rested his forehead against mine. 'I love you, Tiff – and I think you love me. All I ask is that you think about my offer – the whole package, the possibility and not just the things that can go wrong.'

He raised his head and looked deeply into my eyes, and just like that first time I was undone. 'Promise me?'

'I promise,' I whispered.

And then he kissed me. Gently at first, as if he was savouring the taste of me to file it away in his memory in case it was the last kiss. Then he pulled me even closer and kissed me with everything he had in him – and I kissed him back with everything that was in me. If it was to be the last kiss, it was one that neither of us would ever forget.

When he lifted his head, we were both breathing raggedly. 'Think about it, Tiff.'

'After that kiss, how can I think about anything else?'

'That's what I'm counting on.' He smiled and touched my cheek gently. 'I'll see you soon?'

I met his eyes and gave a half-shake, half-nod. 'Perhaps. I don't know.'

'Yes, you do.'

He grinned, kissed me hard and fast, picked up his laptop, and left.

I sat back on the bed and gave way to the tears that my heart had been holding in forever.

CHAPTER TWENTY-TWO

I have no idea how long I sat on the bed and cried after Jake left. I was vaguely aware of another text coming through but ignored it. When the tears continued to drip down my face I stood under a hot shower and let the water stream over me, mingling with my tears and washing them away.

It was dark outside by the time I was ready to deal with the texts and emails and whatever else Ainsley had sent through in the interim. Jake was gone and nothing else seemed to matter, but still it was my job and if I didn't have Jake then that was all I had.

Reading through the email and the tweets it became obvious very quickly that Ainsley had overreacted. The employee in question had resigned some months ago, and the party they'd referred to was a family birthday. Chartered Pacific hadn't even been mentioned. It appeared that a mutual friend from the project team had mentioned to someone else that they were posting party pictures on social media, and someone else – who had probably been ordered by Ainsley to report anything she overheard about celebrations – had jumped to conclusions. The whole thing had nothing to do with the branch closure and I was positive that Ainsley knew that. So rather than dealing with it regardless, I decided not to respond at all.

I stalked across the room to the minibar and eyed off the contents before choosing the bottle of red wine, my eyes widening when I saw the price. With a snort I wrenched the screw-cap off and filled a large wine glass.

If those texts hadn't come through when they did, Jake and I would still be tucked up in bed. We wouldn't have argued, he wouldn't have said the things he'd said, and I wouldn't be faced with the choice now facing me: Jake and our relationship; or Masters and my job. If it wasn't for those texts everything would be as it had been. I refused to listen to the little voice in my head that reminded me it had been my decision to pick up my phone.

Tears now completely gone I gulped at my wine. It was Ainsley's fault that Jake had told me he loved me, it was Ainsley's fault that he'd left, and it was Ainsley's fault that I now felt as though something inside me was tearing in two.

I drained my glass and poured another, slopping some drips onto the desk. The more I thought about it, the more the anger inside me grew and the more I was convinced that Ainsley was to blame for everything. Even our initial meeting on that blasted bus trip was down to Ainsley and her spiteful budget changes. I took another large mouthful.

If I hadn't met Jake I wouldn't have come up with Project Yes, Callie wouldn't have gotten back together with Jamie, and she and I would never have argued on Friday night. Sure, Alice wouldn't be with Tommy, but for Ally it was always going to be a matter of time before she replaced Luke. Come to think on it, it was Ainsley's fault that Alice had lost her job too.

I drained my glass for a second time. As I poured yet another, I pondered that last idea. If Alice were here, she'd be quick to tell me that the bright side of her losing her job was that it meant she wound up in Melbourne with Callie and me, at a time when she needed her friends the most. She'd probably go as far as saying that she owed Ainsley her thanks for that. In fact, if Alice was here in the room with me now she might even say that I owed Ainsley my thanks for meeting Jake in the first place; and even for giving Jake an opportunity to tell me how he felt about me.

And I'd tell Alice that meeting Jake was one of the worst things that could have happened to me – even though I knew deep down that it was also one of the best.

I'd also say that I hadn't wanted to know how he felt about me, but I couldn't deny the rush of warmth that had settled around my heart when he told me he loved me.

Even now, as my heart felt as though it was crumbling into so many pieces it might never be made whole again, hearing him say those words in my head brought the ghost of a smile to my face. He'd said that he loved me, that he'd loved me from the start and that he wanted to be with me. No man had ever said that to me before.

As I took another big mouthful of wine, I acknowledged two truths: I'd never given anyone the chance to say that to me before; and until now there'd been no one I would have wanted to hear it from.

Then there was that kiss. What right did he have to give me what had felt like the best kiss in my life as a goodbye kiss?

I pressed my fingers to my mouth and shut my eyes. If I tried really hard I could remember how it felt, the look in his eyes, the words he'd said, the promise I'd made to think about his offer even as my head was telling me otherwise.

I shook my head. No, I couldn't think about it. Not now, not before I finished this bottle, and certainly not until I'd numbed the pain. And maybe not even then. What he'd proposed was unthinkable.

Matt was already seated on a low lounge in the corner of the bar when I arrived, a beer in front of him, his jacket off, his tie loosened and his sleeves rolled up. I allowed myself a few seconds to look at him before he noticed me. Why couldn't I have fallen in love with him? He was everything I'd thought I wanted in a man. Physically he was exactly my type – tall, lean, with great taste in clothes. He ticked every other box too – good job, jet-set lifestyle, professional, ambitious. Although I'd never asked, I was sure he had his superannuation and investments all sorted too. Yes, Matt was perfect for me in every way. Except that he wasn't Jake and I wasn't in love with him. The person he really was perfect for was Callie.

He looked up and noticed me, a grin spreading across his face. He stood as I walked towards him and pulled me in for a light hug.

As I sat on the lounge beside him, he signalled the waiter to take our drinks order. 'I'll have another beer, thanks, and … Tiff? A martini?' I nodded. 'A classic martini please – gin, shaken, super dry. Thank you.'

Then he turned to me. 'How's your form? You've been here over the weekend and I had to find out about it from my sister.'

'Yeah, sorry about that.' I lowered my eyes to the table as I told the lie. 'Things came up – you know how it is. My boss doesn't understand the concept of personal time.'

'You're a terrible liar, Tiffany Samuels,' he chided gently.

I looked up and grimaced. 'I know. I'm sorry, I don't know why I lied.'

Matt laughed. 'Is that an apology? You don't apologise to anyone. Why start now?'

I lowered my eyes again. 'Maybe not, but perhaps I should admit when I'm wrong. For starters, I owe Callie an apology.'

'Really? What did you do to her?' His voice sounded strained.

'We had this huge argument last Friday night. I told her what I thought of Jamie and said some other things I had no right to say. She started it, but it's all my fault – I'm always telling her what to do. I'm always telling everyone what to do, and I'm totally shit at taking my own advice. I deserved what she threw back at me the other night, but she didn't deserve what I said to her.'

'Oh? Is she okay?' He didn't look at me as he asked the question.

'I don't believe it! Alice wasn't exaggerating – you really have fallen for Cal.'

I watched him closely as he tried to stop the thoughts that would give him away from flickering across his face.

With a sigh he seemed to give up any pretence. 'Not that it will do me any good. She's with Jamie – but I'm hoping I've done enough to change her mind about that.'

'But how?'

'How have I tried to change her mind?'

'Not that, you idiot. I know you well enough to

know you would have completely bombarded her. Besides, Alice told me that the minute you saw her you launched a full-on assault. I want to know why all of a sudden Callie?'

'They never told you?'

'Told me what?'

'About the night Callie and I had together before she started uni.'

I shook my head. Callie hadn't told me – nor had Alice. I'd known that Callie had a crush on Matt all those years ago – we used to tease her mercilessly about it – but if I'd known that it had gone further I wouldn't have … Actually yes, I admitted to myself. I probably still would have slept with him without any thought of how she might have felt about it. It wouldn't have even occurred to me that she might have been upset. And if I had thought about it, I would have rationalised that what had happened with her and Matt was too many years ago to be relevant now. As long as I'd gotten what I wanted, nothing else mattered. Inwardly I cringed at the picture; I really was no different to Ainsley.

'Nothing happened that night,' Matt said. 'Well, other than a lot of kissing, but I'd always wondered, you know?' He didn't wait for me to answer. 'And then at the party she was dancing to some daggy pop song, whirling around in a dress that looked like it had been once owned by a Hollywood star. Some sort of pink colour.' As he spoke I knew he was picturing that moment in his head. He shifted slightly in his seat. 'She looked so beautiful, as if she'd burst out of a million stars and come to earth out of a mural to make me fall in love with her. Like in that bad movie.'

'What bad movie?'

'*Xanadu*.'

He said it so seriously, I choked on the olive I'd been nibbling on. 'Really?'

He smiled and punched me lightly on the arm. 'I know how corny it sounds, but in that split second I just knew she was the one for me. Do you know what I mean?'

'Yes,' I said softly, 'I know.'

Jake had said the same to me – that he'd fallen for me in an instant. Just as, I suddenly realised, I had for him. He'd smiled at me, and it had felt as though the sun had come out from behind a cloud.

'It all happened so quickly,' Matt continued. 'And I know I overwhelmed her, but it felt so right. Nothing has ever felt so right, and I knew that if I missed the chance that was there in front of me I'd never get it back again. I know she's with Jamie, but I have to hope that the weekend meant as much to her as it did to me. I'll see her again at Mum's sixtieth, and I promised her I wouldn't ring or try and influence her in the meantime – but I don't know if I can keep that promise.'

While his eyes were on me as he spoke, I could tell that his mind was back on the dance floor with Callie.

'I can't stop thinking about her, and I'm terrified that once she's had time to overthink everything she'll stay with Jamie and I'll lose her. Not that she was ever mine to lose, I suppose.' He paused and took a mouthful of his beer. 'At least I'll know that I gave it my best shot and I won't spend the rest of my life wishing I'd told her how I feel about her.'

After a short silence he realised I'd said nothing. 'Hey, you're okay about this, aren't you? I mean you and me and all that?' He laughed, but it sounded forced, as if he was hoping I'd laugh with him.

'God, yes!' I said. 'I never had any illusions that you and I would be anything other than what we were – we're way too similar to be together. You and Callie though? It makes a weird sort of sense. But as you said, there's Jamie – not that he deserves her, but she seems to love him. They're flying out to Phuket on Sunday, you know?'

His face fell. 'Yes, I heard. Alice told me yesterday. She also said that he'd bullied Callie into going and she really wasn't sure about it. I think Alice is hoping I'll do something to stop her from going.' He took a deep breath. 'The thought of her with him is doing my head in, but I have to let her make her mind up.'

'Do you? That's not like you at all. Normally when you want something – or someone – you'd march in, throw them over your shoulder and take them back to your cave.'

'Not this time. Callie means too much. I have to

know she's come to me because she wants to be with me.'

'I see.' What he was saying sounded scarily like what Jake had said to me. 'And if she doesn't?'

'I can't think about that – as soon as I even consider that possibility I'll be done for. No, I have to believe that she won't get on that plane on Sunday, and that she'll be at Mum's sixtieth – and she'll be there for me.'

I wondered whether that was what Jake was hoping – that he'd walk into the hotel bar on Monday night and I'd be there.

'Now.' Matt drained his beer and signalled for another round of drinks. 'Enough about me, what about my sister and Tommy? She seems happy enough with him, although he's not who I'd have thought she'd pair up with. A nice guy, and perfect for her on paper, but I don't know that he –'

'Sets her alight?' I finished.

'Maybe. Can I even say things like that about my sister? Anyway, Alice has Tommy, Callie has Jamie back, and you've made it onto Masters. All of you seem to be getting what you wanted.'

'I guess.' I popped the last olive from my martini into my mouth. 'They mix the best martinis here. Just the right amount of vermouth – almost wafted over the gin. Perfect.'

'Who is he?' Matt said.

'Who?'

'The guy who has you rethinking what you want?'

I sighed and, as he'd done earlier, gave up any thought of pretending. 'A travel writer. I met him on that bus tour Alice booked me on. His name is –'

I didn't get the chance to finish my sentence because Matt laughed and choked on his beer – all at the same time.

'What's so funny?' I demanded.

'You are. A travel writer? Really? What about that famous checklist of yours?'

'Oh, ha ha ha.' I scowled into the martini.

'I'm sorry, babe, but you've got to admit – it is pretty funny, but also not entirely unexpected.'

'What do you mean by that?'

'I always thought that when you fell hard it would be for someone who ticks none of your boxes.'

'Who says I've fallen hard?'

'You, my sweet. And not just because even if I hadn't been so into Callie and asked you very very nicely to come home with me tonight, you'd make an excuse. I can also see the fear in your eyes – you're scared this is too big for you. Am I right?'

I nodded my head miserably.

'Next you'll be telling me that the sex is even better than it was with us.'

'Sorry,' I said with the beginning of a smile. 'There's no comparison.'

Matt clutched at his chest dramatically. 'Don't

bother trying to protect my feelings. Seriously though, the guy's a travel writer. Where's he based?'

'He lives in this warehouse conversion in Richmond. He's not in Australia that often though, so it's mostly somewhere to keep his things –'

I stopped when I saw how Matt was trying to control his laughter.

'It's not funny,' I told him.

'No, not at all,' he sputtered. 'I shouldn't laugh, but this just keeps getting better. You really couldn't have gotten further from your checklist if you'd tried. What does he drive? No, wait,' he held up a hand, 'let me guess – a motorbike?'

'Actually no. Jake says he can't justify having a vehicle, so when he's in Melbourne he either takes public transport or cycles.'

By now Matt wasn't even trying to hide his laughter. I felt my face fall and I drained the rest of my martini, moving straight to the fresh one that had miraculously arrived.

'I know, it's hopeless,' I said. 'He meets none of my criteria, none. But –'

'But you're in love with him anyway,' Matt said quietly, the laughter all gone.

'Yes – no! I can't be in love with him. I refuse to be in love with him. But there's something about him – I can't describe what it is, but we fit. When I'm with him the time flies, and when I'm not I'm wishing I was.

When I'm with him things feel fresh and new and I see it all – I mean, *really* see things. He keeps me warm and I feel safe with him and none of that is supposed to happen. This is going to sound ridiculous, but I can feel him in my blood – and don't you dare tell anyone I said that.'

'It's in the vault, babe, as long as you don't mention the *Xanadu* thing to anyone.'

'It's a deal. Oh god, what if I am in love with him? I am, aren't I?'

Matt was nodding slowly. 'It's not ridiculous to say that. I feel the same way about Cal and it scares the living daylights out of me. Does he make you laugh?'

'All the time – even when I shouldn't.' I smiled as an image of Jake's grinning face came to mind. 'When I'm with him I feel like I'm more me and as though all of this,' I swept my hand down my expensive suit and shoes, 'is just a costume for a part I'm playing and that none of it matters. But how can I feel like that when I'm *this* close to getting everything I've always wanted?' I sipped at my drink. 'I know it's hopeless – the man only plans as far as the next six months, and even that's determined by destinations. He pitches enough stories to pay for the trip, then makes the rest up as he goes along and hopes he can sell them somewhere – which he apparently usually does. Other than that, he's completely spontaneous. And to make things worse, he's collecting travel stories for a book.'

'He sounds perfect for you,' Matt said, and I scowled at him. 'I mean it, Tiff. He really does sound right for you – so wrong, yet so right.'

I stirred my martini with the toothpicked olives. 'He told me he loves me.'

'That's nice,' said Matt. 'That would have taken some balls to say to you.'

'And he wants me to leave my job and travel with him,' I added quietly.

'To where?'

'Taiwan and Vietnam first, and then …' I shrugged. 'Who knows? Wherever the next job takes us. He wants me to do the photos for his stories. He says we'd make the perfect partnership.'

Matt was silent for too long.

'What do you think?' I asked him. 'No, don't say it – it's a stupid idea, I know.'

He shook his head slowly. 'Actually I think it sounds pretty perfect. You should seriously consider it.'

'But why? I'm so close to beating Ainsley.'

'Beating Ainsley? It's not just about her, is it? I thought the goal was to get to general manager and then beyond.'

I shrugged again.

'But in answer to your question of why quit now,' he went on. 'Possibly because you're close to getting what you always thought you wanted and you're realising that it isn't really what you want.'

'But –'

'No, Tiff,' he said gently. 'Hear me out.' He waited for me to nod before continuing. 'When was the last time you enjoyed a day at work? Hell, when was the last time you did anything at work that you felt good about? And I don't mean getting one-up on Ainsley; I mean doing something that made you feel good?'

I opened my mouth to argue with him, then thought about what he'd said. 'You're right,' I admitted. 'I hate my job and I hate my boss – and not necessarily in that order.'

'Yeah, I thought so. So take a risk. What have you got to lose?'

'Ummm, everything?'

'And what have you got to gain?' He watched as I moved the toothpick around my glass. 'You know I'm right.'

'Maybe,' I conceded. 'The thing is …' I hesitated and took another sip of my drink. 'The thing is, I'm worried that it's history repeating itself – like when my parents split. My mother's like me – driven and ambitious – and Dad is a creative. He was never enough for her and when she left it devastated him. I sometimes think I was the only thing that kept him going.'

'But he's happy now, isn't he?'

'Yes. He's remarried, and his art is really sought after. He's making a fortune.'

'But?' Matt prompted.

'What if once the sex settles down there's nothing else? What if I give it all up and find out that –' I stopped.

'That he's not enough for you?' Matt asked softly.

'No.' I took a deep breath and said it. 'I'm scared that I'm not enough for him.'

'Aaah.' Matt sat back in his chair. 'And there we have it.'

'I'm serious, Matt. What if he's right about what I do – how I don't believe in it, how I'm compromising myself, how all of this isn't really me? What if when I get rid of it all there's nothing left and what he thinks is underneath isn't there? What if I really am just a well-dressed bitch?'

He started to laugh.

'It's not funny!'

'I know it isn't, sweetheart. Is that why you gave up photography all those years ago? So you wouldn't get hurt like your father was?'

I nodded miserably. 'I vowed that no one was ever going to make me feel the way she made him feel. I love my mother, but she reduced him to nothing, and no one should have to feel like that. I thought that if I was more like her that would never happen. And look at me – I've got there. I'm financially secure, I'm on top of my game. My mother should be proud of me. I'm doing what she always wanted me to do.' I drained the last of my martini and Matt signalled for another round.

'I'm supposed to be the one with all the strength and the financial plans,' I went on. 'And yet when Jake said what he said to me, I felt like none of it mattered. Everything I've worked for and towards – all of it's fake. I'm fake, and he's so real and so honest. He told me how he felt, and I couldn't open my mouth to tell him how I felt. Not that I really knew how I felt then, or, rather, had admitted to myself how I felt – but I couldn't even tell him that. I let him open himself right up to me the way he has done since the day we met, and I gave him nothing back.'

'Have you ever spoken to your parents about why they split?' Matt asked.

I shook my head. 'I haven't needed to. I know what happened – Mum got offered a job in Perth, and Dad didn't want to go so she left. That's it. She wanted her career more than she wanted Dad and me. We weren't enough for her.' I felt my chin come out defiantly as if I expected Matt to challenge me. 'Don't get me wrong – I don't blame her for that. But Dad was inconsolable, and I was left to pick up the pieces. He should have stood up to her, but he didn't.'

'And done what? Held her back?' Matt thanked the waiter as fresh drinks were placed in front of us. 'That wasn't the solution.'

'Maybe not. But it taught me a lesson – to live a creative life you have to let your emotion into your work or it doesn't mean anything. You have to make yourself vulnerable, and I don't think I can do that. Jake does though. He's not afraid to take a chance and say and do what he feels – or he feels the fear and does it anyway. He's got more integrity than I can ever hope to have.' I shrugged one shoulder. 'When Mum left, I decided it would be strictly business for me from then on. And that's why I can't be with Jake – because he makes me feel everything I vowed never to feel. I should have made him leave that first night – that's where I went wrong.'

'But you didn't.'

'No, I didn't.'

There was a pause as we both sipped at our drinks.

'Now that you've experienced this with Jake, do you think you can live without it again?' Matt asked.

'What – love? Or whatever this is.'

'Yes. Love.'

'I have to try. What about you?'

He shook his head and smiled sadly. 'Somehow I think everything will feel shallow and meaningless after Callie. I want the whole she-bang with her: the big wedding, the kids, sports on a Saturday morning, a house in the suburbs. I'm ready to go home, Tiff.'

She waved her arm around the bar. 'And give all of this up?'

'Why not? It doesn't mean anything – not really. I'd give it all up for Callie in a heartbeat.'

'I didn't know that,' I said, 'that you want kids some day. I just always assumed ...' I trailed off.

'That I didn't?' he said, and I nodded. 'You never asked me.'

'We didn't have that sort of relationship,' I said. 'I thought you had the same ambitions as me. I think I even told Cal that you didn't want children.'

'When did you tell her that?'

'Weeks ago – before you guys hooked up.'

He nodded. 'That explains a few things she said to me that weekend. The truth is, I didn't know that I did want them, but when I saw Cal with Laura's youngest, I could suddenly see her with ours. The thought of her doing that with someone else kills me.'

'Why aren't you over there now then?' I said. 'Stopping her from getting on that plane with Jamie?'

Matt smiled as he recognised me going on the defensive. 'Because Alice told me how Cal has always drifted in and out of things. This time I want her to actively make a decision about us. I know that I overwhelmed her the other week, but I only had a couple of days to show her how I feel. Now I have to wait and hope she comes to her senses about Jamie. And when she does, I'm not going to let something like my job stand in my way. Can you say the same?'

I didn't know the answer to that.

'Has Jake given you a time limit?' he asked.

I shrugged again. 'His next job is in Taiwan and he'll be leaving from here early next week. He said if I'm not here on Monday night he'll know that I've made my decision. But I have to fly out to Masters on Monday – Fiji, five stars and all the trimmings.'

'Everything except Jake.'

'Yes, everything except Jake.' I put my head into my hands and looked up at him bleakly. 'Oh god, Matt, what am I going to do?'

'I can't tell you that, Tiff. Call your mother, talk to her. Who knows? You might be wrong about what went on between your parents all those years ago.'

I opened my mouth to argue with him, but his next words had me closing it.

'You've only ever had your own impression of that situation, and there might have been much more to it than you've assumed. Just like there's more to me than you assumed, and much more to Jake than your first impressions. Then talk to the girls, really talk to them. But the final decision has to be yours; and it has to come from your heart, not your head.'

I nodded miserably. 'It's laughable, isn't it? All these years I've trained myself to think things through before I act, to not let emotions get in the way of my decisions. I thought that Project Yes would be a way of finally getting Cal to think with her head and not her heart, and for Alice to stop bending her own rules and make sensible decisions. Instead it's me who has to change the habit of a lifetime.' I laughed ruefully. 'Why couldn't I have fallen for you? It would have been so much easier than what I'm going through now.'

He grinned. 'There have been times, my dear, over the last couple of weeks when I've asked myself the same question – why couldn't I have fallen for you? But it wasn't to be.'

'No, it wasn't.' I managed a grin in return. 'Even if you did tick every single box on my list.'

'And you on mine. It just goes to show that we're the last people to know what we really want.'

'I thought I knew,' I said.

'I know you did. But you don't, so deal with that. What did Mick Jagger say? Something about how you can't always get what you want.'

'But you get what you need,' I finished.

'Yes. And perhaps Jake is exactly what you need. I know that Callie's exactly what I need.'

I raised my glass. 'Here's to us both not getting what we want.'

'I'll drink to that.'

CHAPTER TWENTY-THREE

I let myself in and looked around my apartment. Everything was exactly as I'd left it less than a week ago. The kitchen bench was clean, with bills awaiting payment sitting in a little white pile at the end. How could everything look the same when everything was so obviously completely different?

It had been the same on the drive from the airport – the road as it always had been, the traffic as expected, nothing new or startling along the way. The missed calls from Ainsley that I'd come to expect as I got off an overnight flight were the same, although this time rather than call her back I ignored them. Even the rain was the same. It felt right that it was raining – the wipers in the taxi making that rhythmic swishing noise the way they should.

I wheeled my suitcase into my bedroom, where the bed was made – as it always was the minute I got out of it; where my clothes hung in an orderly fashion in my wardrobe – as they always did; and the empty laundry basket stood waiting to be filled by the contents of the bag I was yet to unpack. I thought briefly about leaving the unpacking until tomorrow, as if by that simple act I could also delay my return to the real world for an extra day. Yet that's what I had to do – find a way of returning to my real world.

Despite what Jake had said, this *was* my real world; and the office I had to return to after Masters was my real job. What we'd had together was an interlude – a pleasant one, but not one that could translate into the every day. Jake was a dream. These weeks with him had been a dream. The very idea that I could rekindle a teenage fantasy of being a photographer was a dream.

I closed my eyes and saw Jake's face swimming in front of me, the look in his eyes when he'd raised his head from kissing me that last time. It was a kiss that had very nearly changed my mind on the spot. Even now in my apartment in South Yarra, the memory of that kiss made me wish that I had changed my mind. If I had we'd be together now.

Jake had said it would be our last kiss, my last chance. If I walked away from his offer, the goodbye we'd said would be a forever goodbye.

A sob rose from somewhere deep within me and came out of my mouth in a gasp that sounded as if the sob was as surprised as I was. I steadied myself against the back of the lounge, my hand pressed to my chest.

'Oh, I want to see him again,' I whispered.

I knew that Jake had meant what he'd said. If I

walked away this time there'd be no going back. No more adventures, no more banter, no more mind-altering, bone-dissolving, explosive kisses. No more anything. I either met him in Hong Kong on Monday or I'd never see him again. Not in the flesh anyway. He'd be there in my Instagram feed and the Sunday travel lift-outs and on the cover of his book – when he finished it, which I knew he would. Seeing him like that would be worse than never seeing him again. Every Sunday morning I'd be reminded that once upon a time there had been another option for me on the table.

But at what cost? I'd be throwing my whole life away, everything I'd worked for. It was a ridiculous idea.

But it's not fun any more, whispered that annoying voice in my head. Then came another: *It hasn't been fun for a long time.* Yet another: *When was the last time you felt good about what you do? Nothing you've achieved at work makes you feel the way you felt when you saw your pictures and photo credits beside Jake's by-line.*

I put my hands over my ears to block them out. Only a few short months ago, I'd been content with my life. I had my apartment, my designer clothes, the money to do and buy almost anything I wanted. I ate at the best restaurants, had regular appointments with my hairdresser, beautician and manicurist. I did power yoga and hot yoga and ran. I didn't eat carbs. Everything, including my body, was as perfect as it could be. I was in control of every part of my life and that suited me just fine. I'd even thought that love was something I could control, and when the time was right I'd find somebody just like Matt to settle down with and complete the picture.

I'd thought I'd be happy ticking the boxes and climbing the ladder, but Jake had shown me love and another way to live, and it had thrown everything else wide open. He made me see and feel like I'd never done before. Even if I did nothing, even if I went to Masters, came back and returned to work, nothing would ever be the same again. The problem was that I now knew there was a different life in a different place.

Before Jake, the only colour in my life had been my father's paintings on these walls. Everything else was neutral. My clothes, my accessories, this apartment – all neutral, tasteful, stylish. In photographic terms, eighteen per cent grey was the ultimate neutral against which everything else could be exposed perfectly. Jake was that perfect eighteen per cent point for me against which everything was as it should be. He had shown me a world that was colourful and textured and made my oh-so-stylish life appear cold, dull and under-exposed. He'd helped me see below the surface of things, and for the first time in years I'd been inspired to capture not just the image of what I was seeing, but the feeling I was experiencing.

Now I'd done that, I didn't think I could ever be happy in my shiny, yet narrow world. But I couldn't just walk away from my job. What if I failed? What if Jake and I didn't last?

All the voices in my head replied together: *But what if you do?*

My eyes were drawn to Dad's paintings, so full of colour, life and joy. Mary had given him that, and I knew that Jake could give me the same if I let him – but at what cost?

My phone pinged with a message, this time from Shannon:

Just letting you know Ainsley has taken the day off so no need to come in – everything is under control. Enjoy Fiji and we'll see you when you're back.

It was typical of Ainsley to leave a pile of messages on my phone and then go off-line. She was probably out getting her hair and nails done, and buying a whole new wardrobe to impress the executive at Masters. Although I knew that I should be taking the opportunity to do the same, impressing the executive was, right now, the last thing on my mind.

I might not be able to make a decision about Jake just yet, but one thing I could do was apologise to Callie.

As I went to call her number my phone rang. For one heart-stopping second I thought it might be Jake, but it was Cal.

'I'm sorry,' I said as soon as I answered. 'I'm glad you rang. I was about to call you.'

The silence that followed made me briefly ashamed. It was no wonder she was surprised – as Matt had said, I wasn't in the habit of apologising.

'I'm the one that went off. I've got no idea what got into me,' she finally said. 'I shouldn't have said what I did.'

'Actually, you should have. It was long overdue and you were absolutely right – I have no idea how to mind my own business, but have no problem at all minding everyone else's. If Jamie makes you happy, who am I to deny you that. I'm your friend and I don't want to see you hurt, but that doesn't give me the right to stand in your way. It means I need to be here to pick you up if necessary. If the last few weeks have taught me anything, it's that I'm not right about everything after all. But we can talk about that later. What's happening with you? How's Jamie?'

I forced myself to sound interested. I mightn't like Jamie, but Callie was in love with him and I should have given her more support than I had done, even though it made me feel disloyal to Matt. If Cal had seen Matt's face the other night, the way he looked when he spoke about her, she wouldn't even be contemplating choosing Jamie over him.

'He's fine, but busy,' she said. 'I haven't seen much of him lately.'

'Aren't you flying out on Sunday? And Alice is leaving tomorrow too, right?'

'Yes, Alice leaves tomorrow morning and my flight's Sunday morning. And you're off to Fiji for Masters on Monday.'

The way she said it, it sounded like we'd all gotten what we wanted. Matt had said the same thing. It didn't feel like it though.

'Are you looking forward to it?' Callie went on. 'After all, you won. You got there.'

'I know. And yes, I'm sure it'll be fabulous.' I knew I didn't sound convincing. 'How's the packing going?'

'I haven't started yet.'

'Seriously? That's not like you. Last time you went to Phuket with Jamie, you were so excited it was all we heard about for days. You were packed and ready to go with all your outfits planned.' I paused. 'Actually, didn't we throw out your bathers in the great Jamie purge? That means you have a beach to go to and a pool to lounge beside but nothing to wear.'

'I hadn't thought about it.'

'Well,' I said, forcing some enthusiasm into my voice, 'it's lucky I've thought about it. I have absolutely no plans for this weekend, so we're going shopping for bathers tomorrow morning.'

'Are you sure?' she asked. 'You've just got back from Hong Kong, and you must have heaps to catch up on before you fly out on Monday.'

'I'm absolutely sure. By tomorrow afternoon you'll be beach ready.'

That gave me a few hours to try and change her mind about going. I might not be able to make a decision about my life, but I could help Callie make the right one for hers. There was no way I was letting her get on that plane with Jamie on Sunday.

While I had the phone in my hand, and before I could change my mind, I phoned my mother. Matt was right: I needed to know.

'Tiffany?' Mum answered at the second ring and sounded surprised to hear from me. I didn't blame her. Although we weren't estranged or anything, I rarely called, and she was the same. I certainly never called in the middle of a work day. 'Is everything okay? Is it your father?'

'No, everything's fine and Dad's good. In fact I saw him and Mary last week. It's ... it's just ... have I caught you at a bad time?'

'No, absolutely not.'

I smiled ruefully as I heard the muffled sounds of her shooing people out of her office. 'I can call back if it is.'

'It's fine, Tiffany. How are you?'

'I'm good. It's just ...' I hesitated briefly again before blurting it out. 'Why did you and Dad separate?'

There was silence on the other end of the phone.

'Mum?' I prompted. 'Was it because Dad was an artist and had no ambition?'

'Is that what you thought?' she asked softly.

'Yes. I knew that work was important to you and you'd been offered a role that you couldn't say no to. I understand that.'

'Do you? Yes, work was important to me, and for a time I thought it was more important than anything.'

'Even me?'

'No, darling, never you. Although given that I left you in Brisbane and went to the other side of Australia I can't blame you for thinking that. No, your father and I had reached a point in our relationship where things were stale. I had an opportunity to do something for myself that I wanted to take. I wanted you both to come with me, but he wouldn't budge. I honestly thought that because he worked for himself he'd follow, and when he didn't there was no way I was going to give in either.'

'So you were both hurt,' I said.

'Yes. Your father was devastated, and I know that it damaged his art for a time. But I had work to throw myself into, and I used that as my excuse why I couldn't come back home.'

'I see,' I said, even though I understood less than I had at the beginning of the conversation. 'Do you regret it?'

'Truthfully? I don't know. Your father is happier than he would have been if I'd stayed and his work is so much better. We weren't good for each other.'

'And you?'

'I've achieved everything that I set out to and more.'

'Are you happy?'

There was another pause before she said, 'You're the first person who's asked me that in a very long time. No, I don't think I am. I have everything that I ever wanted materially, but I'm not happy. To be honest, I'm facing a possible redundancy or, at best, retirement – I've reached that age, you see – and I have no idea what's next. I've invested so much of my life into climbing the ladder that I've forgotten how to live.'

'I'm sorry, Mum.'

I heard her sigh. 'I'm not. I made these choices. When it was clear that your father wasn't going to join me, I decided to put work first always so I wouldn't have time to be hurt again. That's why you're really asking, isn't it? You've finally found someone who's cracked that outer shell of yours and you're wondering if it's worth it.'

'Yes.'

'It is.' Two simple words that she obviously hadn't needed to think about.

'Even if I give up everything I've worked for to follow him halfway around the world or wherever he is?'

'Especially then. As long as you're doing it on your terms. Someone told me once that you have to lose yourself in order to find yourself, and I think he was right.'

'Was that Dad?'

'No, darling, someone after your father who wanted me to do what you're contemplating now. I didn't, and if we're talking regrets, that's the biggest one that I have.'

'I don't understand,' I said. 'You always taught me to be financially independent, you said my security could only come from myself. You told me that I didn't need a man's permission for anything, that I could do whatever I wanted – like you have.'

'That's true – all of it's true. You have to be responsible for your own outcomes, but that doesn't mean you can't make choices for love. As long as you're not being coerced into doing something you don't want to do, that is. That's not how it is, is it?'

'No,' I said quickly. 'Nothing like that. This is my choice to make – he's made that clear. He's a travel writer, you see, and he wants us to work together – with me doing the photographs.'

'You've picked up the camera again? I'm so glad. You had such a talent that I was disappointed when you chose not to go in that direction.'

'Really?' I was genuinely surprised. 'You wouldn't be disappointed if I decided I didn't want to follow in your shoes? You tried to talk me out of pursuing photography back then.'

'Only because I knew how much your father had

struggled to make a success of his art. I didn't want that for you.'

'It wasn't because you didn't want me to do it?'

'Heavens, no. I was so proud that day you won the major art prize at school. I was just worried that the joy you found behind the lens would be replaced by bitterness if you weren't successful as quickly as you assumed you would be. That's what happened to your father – and it's what destroyed us. I should have known that although you got your creativity from him, you inherited a practical business mind from me. I should have known you'd make a success of whatever field you went into.'

'Why did you never tell me about that before?' I said. 'About what went wrong between you and Dad?'

'Partly because you never asked, but mostly because what goes on inside a marriage is always more complex than it appears to be. I knew you had your ideas about what had happened, but I also knew that your father needed you.'

'But you didn't correct my impressions.'

'No, darling, I didn't. I've wondered over the last few years whether I should have. You were going in leaps and bounds in your career, but relationships seemed to pass you by, and I began to wonder whether you'd thrown yourself into work so you wouldn't have to risk your heart. Am I right?'

'I hadn't thought so, but maybe,' I conceded.

She sighed. 'You've grown up very like me. And before you bristle, that's neither a good nor a bad thing – it just is. I haven't told you enough just how proud I am of you; and how proud I would still have been if you'd gone in a different direction. In fact, I'll only be disappointed if you don't live the life that you really want to live.'

Mum's voice sounded suspiciously husky – as would have mine if I'd managed to get any words past the lump in my throat.

'You have people to catch you if you fall,' she went on. 'You have Callie and Alice, and I know I'm on the other side of the country and we don't talk nearly as often as we should, but you also have me.'

'I'm afraid to fall,' I admitted. Falling and failing – they were the same to me.

'So was I.'

It felt as though the words were stretched in the air between us. Even though we were thousands of miles apart, in that moment I'd never felt closer to my mother.

'I pulled back from the edge so I'd be safe,' she said. 'To fall for him was to risk failing at everything else I'd made a success of.'

What Mum was saying sounded dangerously close to how I was feeling about Jake. I pressed my wrist against my thigh to try and soothe the itch.

'Who was he?' I asked.

'Someone I'd met through work. He worked for the marketing company we use and we just clicked. It was one of those whirlwind relationships that sneaks up on you and blindsides you just when you think you've got it all figured out. Of course, I didn't have it all figured out or I would have gone with him when he left to work in London. I had all my arguments down pat – I'd worked hard to get where I was, the next promotion was just around the corner, I'd left you and your father to do this job so how could I leave it for him? What if we hadn't worked out and I had to come slinking back to Australia with two failed relationships and a failed career? He tried to get me to change my mind, but by the time I realised I was in love with him it was too late. Not that I blamed him – he'd told me how long he was prepared to wait for me and I thought he was bluffing. The promotion I'd been waiting for came through soon after and that led to my current role.'

'So you got what you wanted after all?'

'No, I got what I thought I wanted. What I needed was in London. And I've regretted it every day since. All I've done since he left is protect myself against everyone climbing up behind me who wants my job – or who I think wants my job. And one day very soon the career I gave it all up for will be gone – and I don't have any idea what I'll do with myself then.' She paused before adding, 'Don't hold me up as your role model, Tiffany, I'm not a good one. As stubborn as he could be, your father was more honest with his emotions than I've ever allowed myself to be. If the only thing holding you back from this man is fear of the unknown or concern that you'll lose whatever identity you have wrapped up in your job title, then put those thoughts out of your mind. If you think I'll be disappointed in you, forget that too. Your father would be thrilled to hear that you've thrown it all over for love and a creative life, but if he's still on the longest honeymoon in modern history I don't think he's in a position to influence you this time round.'

'I'm scared,' I said. 'What if it doesn't work?'

'Don't even allow those thoughts in. What you need to be asking is "what happens when it does work?" And if that brings a smile to your face you have your answer.'

For a few seconds I allowed myself the liberty of imagining life with Jake, and couldn't help the smile.

'You're smiling, aren't you?'

'I am. Thanks, Mum, you've helped a lot.'

'You're very welcome. Call more often, hey?'

'I will,' I promised.

'And come out and see me sometime.'

'If you retire maybe it's you who can come and see me.'

'Or join you wherever in the world you happen to be.'

'Now, there's an idea. Maybe you could even plan a trip to London?'

'Maybe I could.'

As soon as Mum and I finished talking, I typed out a message to Jake: *How long do I have?*

His reply was quick: *The flight to Taipei is Tuesday. I'll be waiting for you in the usual spot on Monday evening. Jx*

I held my phone to my chest, as if I could transfer the kiss in his response to my heart. Then I typed: *I don't know.*

His reply came flying back. *I think you do.*

My heart knew what it wanted, but my head knew better. It always had done – and I'd always listened to it. How did you start to listen to your heart when you'd never given it a voice before?

I itched absently at the inside of my arm. What if it wasn't Jake that was making me feel trapped, but my life?

CHAPTER TWENTY-FOUR

There was no way we could go shopping without coffee, so Cal and I stopped at a place in Abbotsford that she loved. It was in a converted factory or mill – something like that – and obviously a popular choice for the cycling crowd. Three months ago I would have turned my nose up at its quirkiness. Today, I had to stop myself from taking some pictures on my phone to send to Jake. He'd love it here, even though he would have laughed at the lycra.

'Cycling is the new golf,' he told me once. When I looked at him blankly he'd continued. 'Like golf it's got a high entrance fee – some of those bikes cost a fortune – and the sport comes with heaps of accessories you can show off. Like golf, businessmen use it for networking – it's not about what you know, darling,' he added with a wink. 'But it has an advantage over golf in that you don't lose an entire day to go for a ride. Although the clothes can look just as silly – especially on some people.'

I'd noticed a lot of the guys at work getting into

cycling but hadn't thought about it in that way. 'That's a pretty cynical attitude,' I'd said. 'What about the ones who genuinely like cycling as a form of exercise?'

He'd nodded. 'Sure, there are some who do – but they tend to cycle on their own or in smaller groups. They're the people cycling into work, not the ones doing the mass invasion of coffee shops on a weekend morning where they catch up on business talk and who has the most expensive wheels.'

Looking now at the large lycra-clad group sitting at one of the outside tables I wondered if there would ever be anything that didn't remind me of Jake.

'Just what I need – middle-aged men in lycra before I've had coffee,' I grumbled to Cal.

She laughed but it sounded forced. She didn't look like a woman about to get on a flight to paradise with the man of her dreams.

'I don't want to go away with him,' she said when I asked her about it. 'There, I said it. I know,' she added. 'If this had happened three months ago, I would have been beside myself with excitement. After all, not only is Jamie back – he says he loves me and he's doing everything he can to make up for what happened. I guess I'm just being ridiculous. Hormonal maybe. You know, I even –'

She stopped, her gaze focused on two women sitting at a table near the door.

'Earth to Cal,' I said, grinning.

'Sorry,' she said, her gaze still on their table.

'Do you know them?'

'No, but I suspect Jamie does.' Her tone was rueful as she explained that she'd seen one of the women watching her and Jamie one night, and was sure that the other one was responsible for a suspicious text he'd received another time.

'God, I'm so sorry, Cal.' I reached over to hold her hand. I didn't need to see her start to know she was surprised by the gesture.

'It's okay,' she said, 'you can say you told me so. You knew what he was like – everyone knew. I was the only one who didn't.'

'Even so, you love him. You can't help that.' I knew only too well now how love could remove all commonsense.

'Are you okay?' she asked.

'Absolutely. Why wouldn't I be? I'm off to Fiji on Monday – sun, sea, cocktails, rubbing Ainsley's face in the fact that I've won. I can't wait.'

I forced a smile and hoped it was convincing. The look on Cal's face was, however, sceptical.

She'd changed over the last couple of months, I thought. She seemed stronger, more confident. It wasn't just how she'd stood up to me the other night, it was the way she was carrying herself. Even now, when she was obviously putting two and two together in relation to the women at that table and coming up with something that added up to a lot more than four, she wasn't reacting as she would have before. Instead, her chin had firmed and she sat straighter in her chair than she would have done only weeks ago.

'Your nails,' she announced. 'This is the first time in years I've seen you without your nails done.' Her grin was almost gleeful.

I curled my fingers into my palms, then placed my hands in my lap, out of sight. 'I just haven't had time to get a manicure done. I'll make sure I get one tomorrow morning so it's fresh for Fiji. I'm thinking bright pink, or coral?'

Across the room, the two women were parting. We watched them.

'Maybe it's not what you think,' I said softly. 'Perhaps you need to give Jamie a chance to explain – you might have got the wrong end of this particular stick.'

I couldn't believe I was defending him, and Cal's raised eyebrows said the same.

'Do you really believe that?' she asked.

I hesitated, then shook my head. 'No, I don't. But I do think you need to give him the chance to explain himself. After all,' I added a short laugh, 'you are supposed to be getting on a plane together tomorrow morning for a romantic holiday.' I covered her hand with mine again. I was getting a little too comfortable with this touchy-feely thing. 'You said you'd do anything to get him back; and that once you had him, you'd do anything to keep him.'

'Yes, I remember. The truth is, it doesn't feel the same – being with him. It hasn't felt right almost from the start. There's something different – and I don't think it's him. Maybe I've changed.'

'Maybe he's not what you want any more?' I said it so quietly that she leaned forward slightly to hear me better. 'Maybe what you thought you wanted and what you really need are different? But don't listen to me. I'm the last person you should listen to right now.'

'You're right – I don't want him any more,' she said. She paused and laughed. 'What do they say? Be careful what you wish for – you might just get it. Now I've got it, I don't want it.'

'Ain't that the truth,' I said ruefully.

'What do you mean?'

'I've worked so hard all year to prove Ainsley wrong and get onto Masters, and now the idea of spending a week pretending to be nice to her and kissing up to the executive so they'll give me her job is the last thing I want to be doing.'

'What would you rather be doing?'

I almost told her then. I almost said that I wanted to be on a plane heading to Hong Kong to meet the man who made me feel really alive for the first time in my life, but I didn't.

'You know what – it's a long story. You wouldn't want to know.'

'I do want to know,' she protested. 'Please talk to me, Tiff.'

My eyes suddenly felt hot and my vision blurred. I fanned my face as if it would force the unwanted tears back inside. Now wasn't the time to talk to her – she had her own issues to sort through.

'No, sweetie, I will talk to you, I promise, just not yet. Right now you have bathers to buy, an excuse to listen to, and a holiday to pack for. And I need to get my nails done, take a deep breath and harden back up.'

'You know,' she said slowly, 'we all got what we wanted, but of the three of us, Alice is the only one who seems happy. Tommy fits the bill perfectly, and he adores the ground she walks on.'

'Perhaps,' I mused, forcing some enthusiasm into my voice. 'Come on – we need to buy you some bathers. And then you can decide whether you'll be wearing them on a beach in Thailand, or in the swimming pool in Matt's apartment complex in Hong Kong when you go to visit.' I grinned when I saw her pick up the packet of sugar that had been lying on the table. 'And don't you dare throw that sugar at me.'

Cal was silent on the subject of both Matt and Jamie as we shopped, and surprised me by buying the first pair of bathers that fitted her.

When I suggested that we stop for a bite of lunch, she declined. 'Sorry, Tiff, I've got heaps to do this afternoon.'

I didn't like to ask if she was going to be busy packing or busy with Jamie. Instead I smiled and wished her a good holiday. I even pretended to mean it.

'I will,' she said. 'And you enjoy Fiji. You've worked so hard to get there.'

'Thanks,' I said. 'I will.'

We both knew that the other was lying.

Before I went home, I called Matt. I might not be any closer to making the decision I needed to make, but I could certainly help Callie along with hers.

Matt picked up at the first ring. 'Tiff, is everything okay? Is there something up with Cal?'

'Everything is fine,' I assured him. 'I've just left Cal – and, oh Matt, you need to stop her from getting on that plane tomorrow.'

I heard his sigh. 'And how do you suggest I do that? I promised her I wouldn't ring, that I'd leave her to make up her own mind.'

'I understand that, but I think this is one of those times where she might welcome the call. She's starting to second-guess your intentions. Just let her know that you're thinking about her.'

He groaned. 'I can't, Tiff. If I could I'd catch the first flight over, but I can't. I have to respect her space.'

'For christ's sake, Matt! Fuck whatever promise you made her. You can't let her go with Jamie – it will be the biggest mistake of her life. I think she already knows that, but I also think it's worth reminding her what she's throwing away if she does.'

When he didn't answer me immediately, I knew he was wavering.

'Just let her know that you're thinking of her,' I said softly. 'That's all.'

'I'll think about it.'

'Thank you. Just don't think for too long. That flight leaves at around midday tomorrow and she had better not be on it.' He was silent. 'Matt? Are you still there?'

'Yes, I'm just thinking that I need to say the same to you. Please don't get on that plane to Fiji on Monday, Tiff. If you do, you'll be making the same mistake as Callie.'

I struggled to swallow as I heard the emotion in his words.

'You still there?' he asked.

'Yes,' I choked. 'I haven't decided … I don't know.'

'Yes you have, and yes you do,' he said softly before ringing off.

After another sleepless night where I'd succumbed to taking half a sleeping tablet, I started my Sunday as I always did – with sourdough toast, the Sunday lift-outs and a coffee in bed. I opened the curtains to let the weak winter sun stream into the bedroom.

Although I tried not to, I turned straight to Jake's

weekly column. This week's headline was *Traveller or Tourist – What's With The Label, People?* As I read the article I smiled, the words taking me back to the conversation Jake and I had overheard over dumplings on the night after we met. They were at the table beside us – two Australian couples who looked to be in their late forties or maybe even early fifties. One of the men was loud and opinionated and declared how restaurants like the one we were in was what travelling was really about.

'It's about getting off the beaten track, mate. None of the touristy stuff for me. I'm a traveller, not a tourist.'

At his words I'd seen a grin break across Jake's face.

'I've done South East Asia, mate, and I can tell you where to go,' boomed our neighbour.

'If I was travelling with him, I think I'd like to tell him where he could go,' I muttered.

'What's the difference between a traveller and a tourist?' asked the woman sitting opposite him. The loud man's wife turned to suppress a smile and in doing so caught my eye.

'I'm glad you asked,' her husband said. 'It's about living like the locals and doing what the locals do versus organised tours. Who wants to do one of those bus tours when you can get there under your own steam?'

'But you're seeing the same places, aren't you?' the

woman said. 'You're just not catching a bus there with other people – which, quite frankly, is sometimes the easiest way to see things when you're on limited time, which most of us are. Besides, most locals wouldn't go to those spots anyway – they're too busy working and doing the things you do when you live in a place. You're a Sydney man – when was the last time you visited the Opera House?'

Across from me Jake coughed to hide the laugh that had almost snuck out.

The woman hadn't finished. 'I'd like to bet that if you have visitors staying with you they'll want to spend their time doing things other than watching the football on the weekend or sitting in traffic to getting to the local shops for groceries, or enjoying the comfort of the commuter bus into the CBD during the week. They'll stay in the city, check out the sights and go home and tell everyone what a fabulous city Sydney is.' She leaned back in her chair. 'The last thing they really want to do is live the way the locals do.'

Jake had picked up his phone and was busy typing notes.

'What are you doing?' I'd asked.

'This is the perfect subject for a column. Traveller or tourist – what's your style? Something like that.'

'What are you?'

'I don't think I'm either. Besides, I can't stand labels. If you stay off the tourist path you miss out on some fabulous sights, and if you stay away from bus tours you could miss meeting your future wife and having a great story to tell your kids about.' The look in his eyes had sent a thrill rushing through me.

'Oh, ha ha.'

He'd put his phone back on the table. 'What about you? No, let me guess. You look to me like you're a woman who likes a good checklist – all the places that need to be ticked off.' His gaze narrowed. 'Although you probably turn your nose up at the idea of tourist spots. You prefer to travel to relax by a pool and shop somewhere air-conditioned and glitzy. Am I right?'

I'd bristled. 'What's wrong with that?' Was I really that transparent?

'Absolutely nothing. It's just that as soon as you put yourself into any specific box you're missing out on other experiences. Take our friend over there. If he has limited time in a city, he'll miss out on a lot if he doesn't take a tour that covers the main attractions; but on the upside, you get to feel the soul of a place by wandering or riding public transport. In your case, when you always stay in expensive resorts and visit the sparkling malls, you miss out on both the sights and the food on the streets. You could be anywhere in the world.'

'Okay, so what conclusion will you be reaching in this column of yours?' I'd asked.

He'd shrugged, that grin spreading across his face again. 'None. Just that it's not the travel style that's the problem, but the labels and snobbery – or reverse snobbery – that go along with it.'

As I read the finished article, I was taken back to that conversation and my naive idea that Jake was someone I could shag and forget. I'd known I was in trouble that first time I'd looked into his eyes. I should have walked away then. I certainly should never have contacted him afterwards. But if I hadn't gone on that tour, looked into his eyes, let him stay over, and given into my temptation to text him that night in Sydney, I would have missed so much wonderful.

I turned my attention back to the newspaper and the final paragraph in Jake's story:

What's the answer? That's simple – remove the labels and leave yourself open to saying yes to new experiences. Who knows – on that bus tour you could end up sitting next to the woman of your dreams. Now, that would be a story to tell the kids one day.

'Oh Jake,' I said aloud. 'You're not making this easy for me.'

On the table beside me, a text came through. My heart raced as I hoped it might be Jake – then dipped again when I saw it was Matt.

She's not going. I'm still in with a chance.

I smiled as I typed my reply. *Am glad to hear it.*

His response came through quickly. *Thanks. Now it's your turn. Say yes, Tiff. Don't get on that Fiji flight tomorrow.*

My eyes welled and I couldn't reply.

Instead I got out of bed and opened the suitcase

I'd wheeled back into my apartment only a couple of days before and began filling it again – although this time there'd be no business suits. Whether these clothes saw Fiji or Hong Kong and Taiwan I wasn't yet ready to say.

CHAPTER TWENTY-FIVE

The door buzzer sounded just as I was contemplating a glass of wine. On the intercom screen I could see Cal – and she was holding a bottle of tequila.

'Tequila, Cal? This can't be good.' I buzzed her in.

'Aren't you supposed to be in Phuket?' I asked as I found two shot glasses. I wasn't letting on that I'd already spoken to Matt.

Cal was chopping the lime and pouring some salt into a saucer. 'I didn't go.'

'I can see that.'

'I changed my mind.'

I poured shots for each of us. We clinked glasses and downed the spirit in one go.

'Just like that?' I said.

She nodded. 'Yep, just like that. Alice said it the other night – that it's okay to change your mind from what you thought you wanted. That sometimes we don't really know what's best for us. I thought I wanted Jamie back, but when I got him – well, I told you yesterday that things didn't feel the same.'

I looked for signs of tears – there were none. The Cal standing before me was a very different woman to the one who only two months ago had declared that Jamie was all she wanted.

'It's okay, I'm okay. It's done. This,' she indicated the bottle, 'isn't to drown my sorrows – it's to toast my decision.' She looked hard at me. 'But you look like you need to drown some sorrows. Why the face? It's five flipping degrees outside and you're off to Fiji tomorrow. You should be happy.'

She poured us each another shot. 'I should have flown out to Phuket this morning with Jamie, and instead I'm doing tequila shots with you. If anyone has a right to be miserable, it's me.'

We clinked glasses again and drank, grimacing as the raw alcohol hit the back of our throats.

I wiped my mouth with the back of my hand. 'This isn't going to end well.'

'Tequila rarely does,' Cal agreed. 'I wish Alice was here.'

'Yeah, me too.' I took a photo of the shot glasses and the bottle and texted it to Alice.

My phone pinged with a new message: *Tequila? Without me? That isn't going to end well. These days I'm the responsible one, so who's going to tell you when to stop? What's the occasion?*

Callie didn't go to Phuket, I told her.

'She's typing …' Cal said. 'I can see her typing …'

Wow, that's big. I'm on free wifi so let's FaceTime?

'Why didn't I think of that?' I said.

And then she was there. 'Sorry, girls, there's no tequila in the minibar, but Tommy's found me some Bintang. I'll do beer shots instead.'

'Isn't that against the rules?' Callie said.

'We'll make an exception.'

In the background we could hear Tommy moving about the room.

'Hi, Tommy,' I called.

'Hi, girls.' He leaned in and kissed Alice on the forehead. 'You could be a while so I'll go do some work in the bar. Bye, girls.'

Once we heard the door shut, Cal said, 'He's such a good man, Alice.'

'Yeah, I know. He's lovely. I keep waiting for something to go wrong. So, Cal – talk. What happened? Why aren't you in Phuket with Jamie? Not that I'm sorry you didn't go.'

Callie shrugged and updated her. 'On the upside,' she finished, 'now that I'm completely over him, there's room for someone great – and I'll be able to recognise him as such. You girls were right – you never end up with your Mr Big. That's not how it works.'

'Oh, I'm not so sure any more,' said Alice. 'I'm beginning to think that sometimes it can work – that Mr Big can also be Aiden. The wrong man can be the right one. Like Matt – he was your Mr Big, but he could also be your Aiden.'

At this point I was cringing at every opinion I'd ever voiced on the subject of relationships.

'Why is it that all your rules suddenly become flexible when alcohol makes an appearance?' Callie said.

Alice grinned. 'I know, right? That's what got me into trouble in the first place!'

'Let's drink to that!'

I tuned out for the next few minutes as the girls talked. It was only the mention of my name that brought me out of my reverie.

'Why is Tiff so glum?' Alice was saying. 'What gives, Tiff?'

I forced a smile and poured another shot. 'It's Jake – and that ridiculous offer of his. I know I shouldn't be considering it – and I'm absolutely not considering it – but I'm really going to miss him.' Cal reached over to pat my knee, but I waved it away. 'Why did he have to ruin everything? Our deal in the beginning was sex. Great sex. Now he has to go and make it all complicated and turn it into something more than that. I told him he didn't need to ask me to go with him – that things could continue as they were – but he says that's not enough for him. He wants the whole forever thing. God, I don't even know if he's got adequate superannuation.'

Alice sprayed beer out her nose onto the screen.

'Really? That's the story you're telling yourself? For fuck's sake, Tiffany, forget your ridiculous checklist and follow your heart. You love him, he loves you. He's even taken all the guesswork out of it by telling you how he feels. Just fucking do it.'

I could tell Alice was serious – she'd broken her no-swearing rule again.

'It's easy for you to say,' I countered. 'You had a redundancy and an inheritance to fall back on when you left the corporate world behind. I don't have that luxury.'

'I did, but I've also had to work to build up the structures I've got now,' she said. 'You can do the same. Anyway, since when have you needed a hero to rescue you? Throw the rule book away!'

I attempted to deflect her statement. 'Really? Is that the old Alice speaking?'

'Maybe. I still need the rules – god knows I can't be trusted without them – but you, my dear, do not.'

'What if none of it works?' I said. 'What if we don't get on? What if his editors hate my photos? What if it is just sex after all?'

'You can keep asking the what-if questions forever and a day,' Alice said. 'Can't you, Cal?'

Callie nodded. 'You sure can. I've spent the last two weeks asking myself why I want to lose someone I've spent so many tears on and so much effort in getting back. Then I wondered whether it meant I'd be always alone. Then I realised that the answer to my what-ifs was "so what".' She put her arm around me. The comfort was almost enough to bring me to tears – or maybe it was the tequila. 'Maybe that's the answer you need to give yourself,' she said.

I shrugged away from her and downed my drink. 'I can't. It's all too late. Jake leaves on Tuesday and I have the Masters conference. It's too late.'

'It's never too late,' argued Alice.

'It is this time.'

Cal topped our glasses up again, and miles away in Bali Alice ripped the top off another beer and thankfully brought the subject back to Callie and Matt.

As they talked, I watched Alice on the screen. I envied her self-awareness. Even though she messed up from time to time – although much less these days – she was able to laugh at herself and freely admit what she'd done and accept the consequences. Luke had hurt her badly, but she'd dusted herself off and started over again down here in Melbourne. She would be the first person to admit that at some point she was going to break away from the rules she'd surrounded herself with, but I knew that when that happened she'd accept those consequences too.

I realised just how lucky I was to have these two women in my life. Mum had been right – I didn't need to avoid love in order to stay safe. If I jumped with Jake and fell, Alice and Callie would be there to catch me, without judgment. Just as they would be if I did the same thing again and again.

When I returned to their conversation it was in time to hear Alice ask Callie if she loved Matt.

There was no hesitation in Cal's answer. 'Yes. I think I've always loved him. I think everyone since has been me rebounding from him.'

The part of me that envied Alice's self-awareness now felt the same about Callie's courage. I'd thought that I was completely fearless, but in many ways Cal was a much braver woman. I'd been so quick to tell myself and anyone who asked that I didn't believe in love, when the truth was I'd been too afraid to let myself go there. Somehow Jake had known that and had chipped away at my protective shell until there was nothing left of it. After having known him, I could never find my way back – and that thought terrified me in a way that nothing else ever had. Losing him forever, never seeing him again, touching him again, lying with him, laughing with him, feeling him moving inside me – that was unimaginable.

'Matt loves you too,' I said to Callie. 'He told me so. He said he knew it again as soon as he saw you. He could even describe your dress.'

Cal reached for the tequila, but not before I saw the moisture in her eyes. 'He lives in Hong Kong,' she said, a stubborn tilt to her chin. 'Anyway, Tiff, I think you were right when you said that no man should come before my career. I'm going to that interview at Helium, and if I get the job, I'm going to throw myself into it. Then I'll allow myself to think about Matt.'

'That's the problem though, Callie – I'm not sure I was right about that.'

I didn't say it, but I wasn't sure about anything any more – about any of the opinions I'd been so ready to give to anyone and everyone.

In her beautiful hotel room, Alice opened another beer. 'Perhaps none of us were right,' she said. 'I'm beginning to think that we have no idea what we really need until we get what we thought we wanted.'

'Be careful what you wish for,' Cal said.

'Because you might just get it,' I added.

Cal looked at me with concern. 'Talk to us, Tiff.'

'Yes,' said Alice. 'It's time. Talk to us.'

I looked at the concern on the faces of the two people I'd known for most of my life and for the very first time in all of those years I told them the absolute truth.

'I'm in love with Jake and I hate my job.'

'Oh, Tiff,' said Callie, reaching out to hold my hand. 'We know.'

Alice was nodding at the screen. 'Yes, darling, we know. What we don't know is what you're going to do about it.'

I shrugged miserably and didn't attempt to stop the tears as they began to flow. 'Bloody tequila. What did I tell you? It never ends well and someone always ends up in tears.'

'And that's what you're scared of?' Callie guessed.

I nodded.

'And there won't be any tears if you don't meet Jake on Monday night?' she went on. 'Can you really tell us that if you don't see him again you'll be fine with that?'

I shook my head and wiped ineffectually at the water streaming from my eyes, tasting the saltiness on my lips as the tears mixed with lime and tequila. 'No. I can't tell you that.'

Alice grinned. 'It would seem that you're screwed either way. If you don't see him again you'll be heartbroken because you'll know that you've let the love of your life go, and you'll still be in a job you've finally admitted you detest, dealing with Ainsley and whoever comes after her.' She paused for a second and took a contemplative mouthful of beer. 'Or you go with him, risk your financial security for a mountain of fabulous stuff that you can't put a price on, doing the job that you dreamed about doing since you were a child, but knowing that one day, possibly, maybe, you might be heartbroken.'

Cal joined in. 'And what if ... Alice, go with me on this ... what if, just maybe, possibly, it works?'

'Perish the thought,' said Alice. 'Think of the sights you'll see and the pictures you'll take.'

'And the love you'll make,' added Callie.

'Or you could say no to all of that and stay and deal with Ainsley.' Alice nodded slowly, a thoughtful look on her face. 'Yes, I can absolutely see why you're torn.'

Cal nodded too, the same serious look on her face. 'You're right, Alice. Why go with Jake when you can have a lifetime of Ainsley. There's no contest really, is there?'

I looked at the pair of them, trying – and failing – to keep a straight face. 'Okay, I get your point.'

'Good,' said Alice. 'That's our job done. Cal's got rid of Jamie, and if you can get rid of Ainsley that is to me a good couple of days work – and well worth the hangover.'

'What about you?' I asked. 'What have you learnt?'

'Oh, you know me – I'm a slow learner. But I think I'll wait and see how this thing with Tommy pans out. It's definitely showing promise.'

'Is he who you want though?' Cal asked.

'I have no idea. Not yet anyway. But we're having fun, I'm in no danger of having my heart broken, and I like him a lot – so who knows? Things are going well – business is okay, I'm having a great time with Tommy, and you two are finally sorting yourselves out. This whole rule-following thing is working for me, so why would I even think about upsetting that particular applecart?'

'Why indeed? I'll drink to that.' I raised a fresh glass of tequila to her image.

I lay awake most of the night, listening to Callie on the sofa snoring the snores of the heavily tequila-ed. and woke – if woke was the right word to use after a sleep like that – with a heavy head and a heavy heart. And no closer to knowing what I was going to do.

On the one hand was my job, the spot I'd won at the Masters conference, and a regular and extremely healthy income. I had money to buy the expensive designer bags and shoes that were the uniform de rigueur for the upwardly mobile female banker. If I left without notice it would cause hell, but, as Alice had half-joked last night, they'd forget about me soon enough and find someone else to sharpen their claws on.

'Besides,' she'd said, 'I'm sure Luke would be quick to step into your shoes – he was quick enough to step into mine. Oh my god, Luke in Melbourne – now wouldn't that be a dream come true … not.'

On the other hand was Jake. Dear, gorgeous, addictive Jake. Jake with a freelance income, eyes I could drown in and a kiss that could change my mind – and my life – in an instant. Jake who made me laugh as no one else ever had, and who could make me come like no one else ever had. Jake who was completely wrong on paper, yet so completely right.

To go to Fiji would mean giving up on a chance of a lifetime's happiness. To go to Hong Kong would be to throw away a career, financial security and everything I'd worked towards.

Cal passed me a coffee and a paracetamol, then rubbed at her forehead. 'I might not be waking up in Phuket, but I'm glad I don't have to go into the office today. What happened to Alice being the responsible one and telling us when to stop?' She glanced ruefully at the empty tequila bottle on the sink.

'Tell me about it,' I said. 'Haven't you noticed how Alice's sense of responsibility – and her rules –become very flexible as soon as alcohol is involved?'

'Sad but true,' Cal agreed. She tilted her head to one side and grimaced as if the action caused her pain. 'What about you? Did you get any sleep?'

I shook my head gingerly. Bloody tequila. 'No, not much.' I forced a smile. 'So, you and Matt, hey?'

'I know. I can't believe it either, but we'll see what happens.'

'I know you've arranged to meet up on the Sunshine Coast, but that's weeks away. Are you going to see him before that?'

'I want to so very much,' Cal lowered her eyes as if that meant I wouldn't see her blush, 'but I'm sticking with the plan. I have an interview to go to, and I really want to take my time with Matt. I've always rushed in and this time I want it to be different. You know,' she mused as she poured herself another coffee, 'I'm beginning to think that I ran away down here in the first place because he was due home from overseas and I didn't want to face that. I haven't stopped running from man to man since, convincing myself each time that it was love.'

'And Matt's the real thing?'

'Oh yes. He certainly is.' She smiled, grimacing again at the effort. 'Do you know what you're going to do?'

'I'm going to the airport,' I said decisively. 'Let's just say that I'm glad I packed my bag before you arrived.'

'But which departure gate will you be heading to?'

'I don't know,' I admitted. 'Every time I think I've decided, I get scared. I don't think I've ever been this scared before.'

'What scares you the most?' Cal asked, her eyes holding mine. 'The possibility of losing him, or of missing out on him?'

'Both. Equally. What if I give up everything and it doesn't work?'

'I understand that,' she said softly. 'But here's a question for you – what if it does? And if you don't really want what you're giving up, what does it matter if you lose it?' She paused and smiled. 'It makes a weird sort of sense, doesn't it?'

'I guess. I think I'm going to stop thinking about it

and leave it up to what Alice would probably call Fate, or the Universe or Karma or something. If I can get a ticket on a plane to Hong Kong, that's what I'll do. If there are no seats available, then I'll have my answer and get on the flight to Fiji.'

Callie watched me as I picked up my camera bag and passport and wheeled my suitcase to the front door.

'You're right to let yourself out?' I asked, trying hard not to let my voice break.

She smiled. 'I will, after I've had another little lie-down on this very comfortable couch. But just so you know, before I do that I'm going to hug you really hard. I'm telling you about it so you can be prepared, but it'll be an extra hard hug because it's from Alice as well.'

I hugged her back and swallowed the lump that was suddenly in my throat.

CHAPTER TWENTY-SIX

Ainsley was already holding court in the airline lounge when I arrived. Her idea of appropriate travel wear was a white halterneck jumpsuit that she'd thrown a camel trenchcoat over. Her hair was in its usual sleek up-do, and her tan sandals were almost as high as her hair. She looked me up and down when I strolled into the lounge, taking in my unstraightened hair, barely made-up face, casual clothes and leather sandals.

'Tiffany, just to be clear —' she started.

'Crystal clear?' I concentrated on mixing myself a bloody mary, stirring the recuperative mix with a celery stick.

'Isn't it too early for that?' Ainsley's look was disapproving.

'Oh, I don't know, it's 5pm somewhere.' I loaded a plate with pastries, smiling as I saw the look of horror on Ainsley's face. 'Don't worry, the carbs aren't catching.' I took a sip of my drink and closed my eyes briefly. 'That's better. Now, what did you want to be crystal clear about this time, Ainsley?'

Ainsley narrowed her gaze, but my smile was innocent. 'I think you should know that I didn't approve your place on this trip.'

I stirred my drink. 'Really? Haven't we been through this? I earned my place by achieving the results required.' My eyes met Ainsley's and held her stare.

'Perhaps,' she conceded. 'But if I'd had my way, those goalposts would have been narrower and higher.'

'It's fortunate then that you didn't set the targets last year.'

Ainsley pursed her lips, sucking the air in with a little hiss. 'You'll be sorry you said that. I won't be making it quite so easy for you this year.'

'I don't think I will be sorry.' I smiled. 'In fact, I'm positive that I won't.' I downed my drink. 'That's my flight being called.'

'I don't think so,' she said, attempting a frown.

The announcement was made again. '*Ladies and gentlemen, QF029 to Hong Kong is now boarding at gate eight. Please make your way to the gate in readiness for an on-time departure.*'

'Yes,' I said. 'It absolutely is. Here,' I handed her the plate of pastries, 'get these into you. You need a little sweetening.'

Then I picked up my camera bag and left. When I looked back she was still standing there, pastries in hand, mouth slightly open.

•

The reality of what I'd done hit me soon after take-off and the what-ifs that had been playing through my mind all night came back. Last night I'd tried drowning them out with tequila, but they were stubborn little buggers and wouldn't stay quiet for long. They had almost ten long hours of flying time to play with my head.

What if Jake and I didn't work?

What if Jake's editor didn't like my photos?

What if the work dried up?

What if all we were was great sex?

What if he wasn't at the hotel tonight?

What if I'd made a dramatic exit from my job and burned the biggest bridge of my life and he wasn't even there?

Between all the questions I had a few moments of glee when I remembered the look on Ainsley's face. I wondered how she'd explain my absence to the powers that be in Fiji.

I supposed I should write a formal letter of resignation, and wondered how far I was prepared to go to throw Ainsley under the bus. I knew I could bring her down with even a hint of an allegation of bullying. But as Alice had said: if you knock people like Ainsley down, there'll be another waiting to take her place – just like her, or worse. It was the culture that was the problem – it allowed the Ainsleys of the world to survive and thrive. As tempted as I was, I knew the revenge would be hollow.

Alice would say something like how karma's a bitch and would sort Ainsley out sooner or later. I smiled to myself as I pictured her face. 'Why bother?' she'd say. 'You're off to be happy – that's better than any revenge.'

I remembered when I'd first told Alice that I suspected Ainsley had played a part in her departure from Chartered Pacific. 'I don't care any more,' Alice had said. 'Between her and Luke they've done me a favour. Let's face it, darling, I should never have gotten engaged to Hayden – that disaster was all on me. Can you imagine if we'd actually got married? Luke and I were never going to make it either, and as for the job, I'm much happier here with Stella and you and Callie. I wouldn't have made that move if I hadn't lost my job – I'd still be fighting Ainsley for space on the ladder.' She'd paused and smiled. 'When you think about it I should be grateful to her. In fact, maybe I should send her a thank-you letter.'

'God no,' I'd said. 'She'd love that.'

'Well then, it can be our little secret.'

I'd been sceptical at the time, but now I understood what Alice had meant. If I'd been happy in my job, if I'd believed in what I was doing, I'd be in Fiji now. But I hadn't been happy. The incident over the branch closure had shown me just how far out of touch with the real world I'd become. Jake had known; he'd connected with the people I'd dismissed. Jake was worth a million Ainsleys.

No, I decided, I'd say nothing in my resignation letter. Leaving in the way I had would be message enough to the executive. And despite all the what-ifs going around in my head, I had to believe that in a few months from now if I saw Ainsley I'd be able to thank her for showing me what I didn't want to become.

Given that I was now effectively unemployed I took the train rather than a taxi into the city, and then a taxi from the station at Central to my hotel. The heat hit me like a wall when I exited the train, and again as I paid my driver at the hotel. The downpour that Hong Kong frequently gets during midsummer hadn't long ended and steam was rising up from the street. The taxis flew by, many with their boots open to dry the clothes and towels hanging inside.

I checked in, and wheeled my bag into the bar. Jake was sitting in the corner, tapping away on his laptop, a beer in front of him. It was the same seat he'd sat in only a couple of months ago while he'd waited for me to shed the skin of my business day. If someone had told me back then that your whole life could change in just over two months I would have laughed at them. Now I knew that your whole life could change with just one smile.

He was wearing the same clothes as when we'd

first met – a surf T-shirt, shorts, and a pair of old trainers. The only thing missing was the cap.

He looked up from his laptop, saw me and smiled that same smile that had made my tummy flip-flop that first day on the bridge. The smile that made me feel warm and alive and happy.

'I'm glad you could join me,' he said.

Then he was beside me and hugging me so tightly that I felt as though I was a part of him. I supposed in a way that I was – he was certainly already in my bones.

'I brought my camera kit and left my job,' I said into his chest.

'I hoped you would,' he murmured into my hair.

And then I said it for the first time in my life. 'I love you.'

He pulled back and looked into my eyes, his smile wide. 'I know you do and I love you back.'

'How could you know that when I didn't know?' I protested.

'That's easy, you didn't want to know. But now that you do, can you tell me again so I'm sure that I heard you right the first time?'

'You know, that first day you looked into my eyes the way you're doing now and when you smiled it felt like the sun had come out from behind a cloud,' I told him.

'Awww, listen to you. Leaving your job has made you go all romantic.'

'It's because I took off my business suit.'
'And those ridiculous glasses.'
'I love you, Jake.' I stroked the side of his face.
'I love you too.'
And then, finally, he kissed me.

BEFORE YOU GO

If you enjoyed *Careful What You Wish For* I'd love it if you left a review in the usual places. If you'd like to stay up to date with my next happy ending, you can sign up for my newsletter at my website: https://joannetracey.com

You can also drop by and see me – virtually speaking, of course – at any of these places:

Facebook: https://facebook.com/joannetraceywriter
Instagram: https://instagram.com/jotracey

ACKNOWLEDGEMENTS

I've been wanting to write about Hong Kong ever since I was fortunate enough to be project managing a couple of office relocations up there a number of years ago.

During my downtime I wandered streets and lanes discovering markets, and gems such as Sik Sik Yuen Wong Tai Sin Temple – where Tiff and Jake made their wishes. I bought my own set of chim sticks, had my fortune told, and ate my own body weight (and more) in dumplings. Early one Sunday morning after a long-delayed flight I even did the tour to see the bridge, the beach and the Buddha. It was on that tour that Tiff and Jake first came into my head.

The city has, of course, changed since then, so any errors (or embellishments) in Tiff's story are mine. Also, in the year since I finished writing this book the COVID-19 pandemic has hit, taking travel off the radar – for now, at least. It feels surreal releasing a book into the wild that has a travel writer as a protagonist, but there you go.

That aside, the usual thank you has to go to my

fabulous editor, Nicola O'Shea. I know that I've said it before, but indie publishing is a team event and I'm so glad that Nicola is on my team.

Thanks also to my sister-in-law Pieta for reading a few drafts of this one, and a massive thank you to everyone who has bought or, indeed, read, one of my books.

Finally, to Grant, Sarah and Kali – my love, always.

ABOUT THE AUTHOR

Joanne Tracey lives on the Sunshine Coast in Queensland Australia with her husband, daughter and a cocker spaniel who takes her role as resident flop-dog and guardian of Jo's office very seriously. She has, however, been known to sleep a tad too much on the job – the dog, that is, not Jo.

An unapologetic daydreamer, eternal optimist, and confirmed morning person, Jo writes contemporary romance, romantic comedy, women's fiction and what she likes to call foodie-lit – which is the perfect excuse to indulge her baking habit in the name of research. Her characters cook whatever it is she wants to be cooking – or learning to cook. Then there are their occupations; through her characters Jo can try out occupations she'd never conceivably do or the business ideas that her husband says, "maybe that needs a little more thought darling." It's the daydreaming thing again.

Even though she lives in paradise, it's Jo's travels that inspire her stories. From Melbourne to Queenstown, Bali, Hong Kong and The Cotswolds, you never quite know where you'll end up, but it will be somewhere that takes you away from your every day.

When she isn't writing or day jobbing, Jo loves baking, reading, long walks along the beach, posting way too many photos of sunrises on Instagram and dreaming of the next destination and the next story.

Jo's life goals (apart from being a world-famous author) are to be an extra on *Midsomer Murders* (perhaps a dog walker in Badger's Drift), to appear on *Desert Island Discs*, and to cook her way through Nigella's books – yes, all of them.